YES! I'm skinny with no breasts but I'm mostly EMBRACING it.

Name: H
(That's what my family call me.)

Address: Derby. That's it! I don't want to be stalked. Who actually writes their address anywhere?! Weirdo Jen told me 1 in 7 people are capable of murder. I don't want them to know where I live. (Weirdo Jen also thinks trees can attack you with their branches if you abuse their trunks with graffiti. She might be slightly paranoid. I'm not risking it though.)

Phone: See above!

Email: OMG! Like I would?! No, thanks, spammers. I do not want half-price pharmaceuticals. I had to explain what Viagra was to Dimple. It was OFFICIAL near death from embarrassment.

Date of birth: Who wrote this diary information bit?! Gran?! Obviously someone who has never heard of Internet security.

In fact definitely Gran — all her passwords are "password" or "Gran". She thinks no one will ever think of that.

Best day of the year: 14/2 ~~Birthday!~~ NO, Valentine's.

Best day of the week: Thursday. No Matfield — the EVIL teacher who has killed art and craft for a generation of innocent children and teenagers.

Best month: August. No Matfield! Weirdo Jen says she has slaughtered creativity. Actually Weirdo Jen's MUM said that. If adults know that we are getting tortured with glue and tissue paper why don't they do anything about it?!

Best time of the day: 4p.m. No Matfield and it's usually before Mum gets home. DOUBLE FREEDOM from the forces of darkness.

Best movie: NOT *Spiderman*. Goose has seen it 27 times but a man who spins webs from his wrists and probably eats fly-and-small-insect sandwiches in private just makes me want to VOM. Why do men never grow out of YUCK stuff? I was OVER worms at 4 – if things in the garden can't even be bothered to grow a face I'm not interested.

Best band: Nothing with fit boys singing stupid songs about how much they love me when actually they only snog models, TV presenters who accidentally but totally on purpose flash their nice pants or Miss "I'm so pretty my face may explode" Gorgeous Knickers (MGK).

Best author: Not Jane Austen. She can wind her neck RIGHT IN. Sorry, Dimple, I know you think she's great but Mr Darcy does not exist, has never existed and grumpy men are not sexy. They just get fat and old and want their dinner at the same time every day. I remember my grandad. He hated Christmas and didn't wear sexy britches, just green cord trousers with stains on them for weeks. AND they always smell weird. If Mr Darcy *does* exist I bet he talks to the vegetables in his allotment and smells of eggs.

Best book: *Vogue*. I'm not being shallow. I LOVE FASH. Especially when it goes totally mental and people wear lobsters on their heads. Gran says it's "ridiculous" and "things with claws should be in a cream sauce not on a hat". Gran is not fashion forward. She is fashion hopelessly-lost-in-a-foul-dress-desert-and-the-search-party-has-been-called-off.

Best website: YouTube. I'm a bit off Facebook. MGK just uses it to spread stuff about me on Messenger, like "Hattie Moore only has a shower when her mum forces her to"(I am totally clean and use Impulse), "Hattie Moore couldn't tie shoelaces till she was 11" (so what if it's true?) and "Hattie Moore's gran has a Scottish lorry driver toyboy who brings her boxes of broken biscuits from his truck". This might be true — Gran always has manky custard creams in her house and the packets look GROSS. It could just be her cupboards though. She daren't clear them out as Princess the dog tries to eat EVERYTHING. And I mean the actual tins too. She punctured a can of spaghetti once, ate half of it and played with the rest of it on Gran's pure-wool rug. Even after a bottle of Vanish you can still see the stringy orange stains.

Best place: My room. As long as my mum and brother aren't in it. My mum stands there asking me why I've got a funny look in my eye — she watches too many crime programmes — and my brother actually tries to give me a funny look in my eye by poking something IN my eye. Like the time he put vinegar in a water pistol and went STRAIGHT for my face. No, Mum – not "just high spirits" and "considerable aiming talent" – TOTALLY MENTAL.

Best person: My gran. ← But don't tell her!

Worst person: Miss Gorgeous Knickers and Matfield. They get the gold medal for total cow faces.

← Especially now we are totally related.

Gran says I HAVE to fill the next bit in "just in case". She also says wear nice underwear "just in case" you get run over. I'm pretty sure that if I ever get hit by a bus I'm not going to be too worried about my diary OR my pants but ANYWAY...

In case of accident or emergency call:

MUM – She IS my mum BUT she might be too busy making fry-ups for builders in her cafe or moaning about the state of the house to actually listen to you telling her I'm seriously injured. Though, after last year, I now realize she's actually amazeballs lovely inside and didn't tell me about my real dad because he is medically useless.

ROB (stepdad) – Driving instructor. He's on hands-free for most of the day but won't answer if his pupil is trying to parallel park as he says that "85% of people can't do it and never will be able to". He's in a car so he can get to a hospital quickly but won't go over the speed limit because if he loses his licence – he'll lose his job. Also he's precious about his leather interior, so if I'm bleeding put carrier bags over the seat first. He's LOVELY though. COMPLETELY TOTALLY LOVELY. He's been around since I was born. He's black so we know he didn't "do the Hattie deed" (that's what my brother Nathan calls it).

GRAN — DON'T call Gran if I'm in trouble. She's mental already and she will panic. She can barely use a mobile phone as it is and if she's at bingo there's no point. She will NOT answer. Also if her dog Princess wants anything or is "trying to talk to her" other humans are NOT important.

DIMPLE — My BEST friend. She is REALLY annoyingly AMAZING — totally sensible and smart AND her dad is a surgeon. She is aces to ring BUT never risk it after 7 p.m. Her dad works funny hours and if he's on call and you ring the home phone he goes mad. He will shout at you for "talking about gossip when somebody's head could be exploding".

Actually now I'm writing this he HAS got a point. In an emergency he could be saving MY brain. That IS slightly more important than the fact Dibbo Hannah's new boyfriend tried to pierce his nose with a stapler.

There's no point calling Dimple's mob. She loses it every 5 minutes.

WEIRDO JEN — I love her but because of her white witch beliefs she thinks that you can cure flu with herbs, oats and chanting. If my leg is dropping off I need more than a nice song and a mint-and-turmeric-paste blend.

NATHAN – My brother. DO NOT CALL. He has caused me more injury than any other person ON EARTH. When I was little he used to pull me down the stairs one by one till my bum was RED. He also tried to sellotape me to the wall every Christmas as a human angel "decoration". He managed it till I was 9 and could fight back. If he hears I'm in hospital he will probably come and put me entirely in plaster "for a laugh".

GOOSE – Actually he would be fantastic to call. We've lived next door to each other for ever and he's UNBELIEVABLE in a crisis, like when Gran ran over the shed last year. He could also probably sing me out of a coma – as long as he doesn't do anything from *Joseph*. He starred in it last month at school and I am OVER hearing him doing the entire musical. I'd decide to stay unconscious if I had to listen to "Close Every Door to Me" again!

It's complicated though because I don't know HOW I FEEL ABOUT HIM. He's been my friend for so long but then I get these weird thoughts in my head and sort of tingles. I know he's just my friend but ... when other girls are near him I feel sort of jealous. I feel like shouting, "Get your paws off him, woman! He's..."

I think I do know what I feel but I'm scared of just admitting it.

In fact don't call him. I need to get physically better not more emotionally confused. Hormone-mess could stop my recovery.

KEITH – My REAL dad, the one I'm about to meet. Don't call. He lives in Australia. He didn't care at all for the first 14 years of my life. Plus in an emergency what can you do from Australia?! Not even send a card. Keith has never managed that.

PRINCESS THE DOG – Don't call her. She's a dog. LOL! And she's not a kind, useful rescue sort of animal either. She'd let any human die for a pork chop.

MGK – OH, COME ON, HATTIE MOORE – BE SENSIBLE! I know you are meant to list everyone EVER here JUST IN CASE, BUT NO. I may have found out she is my TOTAL half-sister but she is also my TOTAL ENEMY. Even though she is now my relative it means NOTHING. DO NOT contact her. She's like my brother. She'd turn up in casualty and take a video of me for YouTube – especially if my injuries were embarrassing – like a broken nose. DEFINITELY DO NOT call her if I have a face accident or even a bad zit. Let me suffer alone. It's better that way.

Is this like EastEnders or what?! No – THIS is actually MY life. Thanks, Mum and Keith.

IN FACT – in case of accident or emergency just call 999 and don't tell anyone I know. Thank you.

Also by Rae Earl:

OMG! IS THIS ACTUALLY MY LIFE?

First published in Great Britain 2014 by Walker Books Ltd
87 Vauxhall Walk, London SE11 5HJ

2 4 6 8 10 9 7 5 3 1

Text © 2014 Rae Earl
Cover artwork © 2014 Sarah Jane Coleman
Interior illustrations © 2014 Walker Books Ltd

The right of Rae Earl to be identified as author of this work has been asserted by her in accordance with the Copyright, Designs and Patents Act 1988

This book has been typeset in GFY Brutus
Printed and bound in Great Britain by Clays Ltd, St Ives plc

British Library Cataloguing in Publication Data:
a catalogue record for this book is available from the British Library

ISBN 978-1-4063-4002-0

www.walker.co.uk

OMG! I'M IN *Love* WITH A GEEK!

★ Rae Earl ★

WALKER BOOKS

MONDAY 21ST DECEMBER

9.45 p.m.

So much has happened, I need to get it down! Dimple says in times like this it's important to assess WHERE you actually are and WHO you are.

Goose wants to see me urgently. Face to face. Could this be it? The moment that we get all this weird stuff sorted? We NEED to sort it out. I NEED to sort it out. Weirdo Jen calls it "the friction between 2 souls that may have been entwined since the time of the pharaohs". Dimple calls it "Hot Lust Tension". I think I prefer Dimple's theory. The thought of being a mummy and covered in bandages freaks me out. It reminds me of what my brother would do to me given half a chance.

9.54 p.m.

I've just hidden the first-aid kit to be on the safe side. There were only some Mr Men plasters, 1 bandage and an antiseptic wipe in there but Nathan could ruin my life with that. He's got a mind that is dedicated to causing me massive brain pain.

Now Goose.

I think I just need to admit that ... I LOVE GOOSE. WHY DENY IT?! IT'S TAKEN OVER MY ENTIRE BRAIN! OMG! I'M IN LOVE WITH A GEEK. HOW DID THIS HAPPEN?! THIS WAS NOT MEANT TO HAPPEN!

I feel sick. I think he likes me too. Well, I THINK he likes me in the snog way. That MUST be why he wants me to come round. Because he is BURSTING with it like a massive love balloon.

OMG!

I really feel sick now. Need to brush my teeth. And tongue.

10.35 p.m.

MEN!

OMG - UNBELIEVABLE!

When I got to Goose's bedroom his mum AND ROB were there. How can you have a decent snog when your parents are around? Goose just looked at me for ages. There was a massive pause and then he said, "I've got a new gecko — I wanted the most special people in my life to be here to see him first!"

I've got a new gecko?!

A GECKO.

Goose did not want to see me about our eternal love destiny spanning back thousands of years or our mahoosive hidden PASH feelings. He wanted to see me about a little lizardy thing WITH OTHER PEOPLE THERE!

Random or WHAT?! It was the last thing I was expecting. I know I rushed round to tell him about my guinea pig "Sergeant Nibbles" when I was 7 but we are slightly older now!

I said, "Great, Goose – enjoy your new pet." It has a big tongue, legs that stick to anything and looks like something Rob my stepdad tries to bang on the head with his shoe when we are abroad. Rob, though, was saying things like, "He's lovely!" (LIAR!) Goose's mum kept saying stuff like, "You'd better look after him!" ER? IS THIS *DOCTOR WHO*? HAVE WE GONE BACK IN TIME TO PRIMARY SCHOOL OR WHAT?

I felt like such an idiot. TOTAL IDIOT. And ANGRY. I didn't say anything. Then Goose's mum had to do something and Rob had to do something else (it was a bit weird that they went out together) and I was left with THE GEEK WHO DOESN'T ACTUALLY FANCY ME AND HIS CRAPTACULAR FROGGY THING.

Goose said, "Hattie – you can name him if you like!" "OK," I shouted, "call him Freak. Freak the gecko." Goose didn't like that. He said reptiles should be given decent names as they are very intelligent. I told him I didn't think a gecko would mind what he was called as they can't actually speak English or they'd be running branches of Sainsbury's. Goose reminded me I've always hated being called Hattie (actress who played a fat matron woman). YES, Goose, but I have a brain bigger than a small pea and actual sophisticated womanly feelings (AND HOPES AND DREAMS ← I didn't say THAT YOU HAVE JUST SMASHED TO that but I PIECES). Whereas the gecko only cares about thought it. food and climbing on ceilings with his big gluey Pritt Stick fingers. Then I said, "Call him Major Freak Geek the Gecko!" Goose looked really cross and yelled, "Thanks for your lack of interest. I thought you would ... that YOU ... and me might be able to sort out some stuff. That's why Rob and Mum but... Look, I've got to get his vivarium ready. I'll see you tomorrow, OK?"

Why do I expect it to go all *Dirty Dancing* with Goose the geek when it's always going to end up with lizards?!

I feel like such an idiot. I thought he REALLY liked me in a totally erotic way. Instead it was all DORK-MONGERING and ... STUFF! What STUFF? NOTHING HOT. I was going to tell him I wanted to snog him. That's a lesson learnt AGAIN. NEVER tell a boy you like him. Check whether he's got a gecko first.

Oh, Goose. Goose. Goose.

I'm gutted.

10.55 p.m.
No, Rob — the gecko is not cool. Please let's not have a conversation when I feel like a doughnut and my heart is in pieces.

What's a vivarium?

10.59 p.m.
A vivarium is what a gecko lives in. It's a hot, sweaty tank. Sort of like a sauna only you can't fit in it so it's TOTALLY pointless.

Pets are getting luxury spas. I'm having to make my own facial masks with Weetabix. You're meant to use porridge oats but it's basically the same thing. It's all bits of cereal.

I might suggest Gran gets a mini hot tub for Princess. Why not? Pets clearly matter more than actual people.

11.03 p.m.
No point. Last time Princess heard the word "bath" she tried to run away on Gran's friend Tony's mobility scooter.

11.14 p.m.
Geckos are the most useless pets ever.

Apart from Weirdo Jen's stick insect Malcolm. He spent his life trying to be a twig.

I'm trying to cheer myself up. It's working. At least I didn't make a dork of myself. In fact I was a bit of a cow. GOOD.

11.23 p.m.
Geckos lack eyelids.

Hope MGK comes back in the next life as a gecko. No eyelids?! She would collapse without black mascara and Boots No. 7 eyeshadow in khaki-shine.

I HAVE TO REMEMBER: she is my sister.

11.29 p.m.
Apparently geckos eat live crickets. Bet MGK can catch LIVE insects with her tongue — she's had enough practise!

11.46 p.m.

HAVE TO REMEMBER: she's my HALF-sister. Not the real thing.

I'm googling gecko stuff. Need to stop. That gecko is a total symbol of a complete LOVE FAIL.

OH, GOOSE. And the worst thing is ... I STILL like him. I could honestly kick him but I could still snog him too.

TUESDAY 22ND DECEMBER

9.10 a.m.

RIGHT.

Next year, Goose, you can concentrate on your gecko and I will concentrate on finding a REAL NON-GEEK MAN who puts ME before his pet and isn't afraid to show his FEELINGS.

Goose and me can still be friends. JUST TOTALLY PLATONIC.

The gecko and me can never be friends.

10.23 a.m.

I can't believe I have wasted hours on animals when my real dad turns up in 2 days. Am I actually a loon? I can't think about LOVE or PETS! Goose should have realized I am going through something MAHOOSIVE. I am about to meet the man who is my Jeremy Kyle DNA-revealed-in-an-envelope moment. This is LIFE-CHANGING. NOTHING will be the same again. This is my DAD. The man I've been wondering about for years. The one I just KNOW will GET parts of me that Mum doesn't and who will be there for me when things get rough. Like when you get ignored for a gecko. Or dumped. Or when Matfield at school is a cow about something. Just a hug, that's all I need. A hug from my real dad will just make things better. I know he sounds a bit rubbish but people can change... He can change. And he's coming all this way.

Please let it be OK. I've already had one MASSIVE REJECTION FAIL from someone I love.

This whole situation with Keith feels like it's happened a bit too fast though. I can't keep up with my own head. I don't even really know how I feel. Dimple says, "Just go with it, Hattie," but the past few weeks have been TOTALLY MENTAL. I have a new dad called Keith, MGK is my new half-sister and I find out my grandad was a Mafia Godfather!

10.46 a.m.

Actually my grandad was a thieving postman who stole letters and parcels — not a crime legend mastermind. If he had been we'd live in a house like MGK's with a conservatory and a power shower — instead of a "bloody dribble" as Rob calls it!

11.34 a.m.

I've decided I can't call MGK "Ruby" yet. Ruby. I KNOW that's her name but a real name makes her a REAL person with REAL feelings. We all know she hasn't got any. She's had complete nice-emotion liposuction.

1.10 p.m.

I can hear Mum stomping about downstairs. She is not happy at ALL at Keith coming. I have caused this and I KNOW she's TOTALLY cross at me about it. She's not actually saying it but my bacon sandwiches are not crispy any more. I heard her tell Gran that it's the "crappest Christmas since there was a power cut on Christmas Day and you gave me a novelty squirrel nutcracker." Gran said it was cute and practical. Mum yelled, "Rob can't look at a cashew without swelling up to twice his size!" Gran told her that nut allergies are all in the mind and that she could prove it.

This is the most outrageous thing she has ever said.

1.23 p.m.

Apart from the time when she told everyone at her local pensioners' club that you can cure the common cold with 2 boxes of Maltesers and an entire bottle of brandy. "The brandy is a natural disinfectant," she said, "and the honeycomb chocolate just gives you a lift." She ended up in bed at 2 a.m. with a "men at work" sign under her duvet. It was in her spare room for ages!

1.42 p.m.

AND the time that she said the ACTUAL men at work could come in for a "hot toddy" post-work so they could collect their stolen sign. Gran says you have to look after the workers – especially the young fit ones. She was right. They fixed her guttering for free and gave her a hard hat as a souvenir. She uses it in the shower when she wants to keep her perm dry. Most people have a plastic cap. Not something with "Fairways and Son – We build it better and bigger!" written on it.

7.25 p.m.

TOTAL DRAMA! Gran hid a peanut in Rob's dinner! When he hadn't had a reaction half an hour later Gran started jumping up and down in the middle of *Coronation Street*, saying, "Told you! Told you! I've cured you. It's all in that overactive imagination of yours, Rob. Now you can look at an almond with kindly eyes."

8.43 p.m.

Rob started being violently ill about 8.15 p.m. He started swelling up. He's had to go to hospital. Gran think he's "worked himself up into an inflatable frenzy". Mum says she's tempted to call the police!

10.35 p.m.

Rob's been given a thing called an EpiPen. It's like a biro with magic medicine stuff in it. You have to stab yourself with it if you eat a nut or something that's been hanging around nuts. Rob has to carry it round with him EVERYWHERE. Mum thinks Gran should be prosecuted for murder. Gran thinks it was a genuine mistake. She was just trying to prove that Rob's problem is "in his brain not his immune system". Mum told Gran that watching *Doctors* every afternoon does not make you actually medically trained.

I personally think Gran might be one of the potentially murdering maniacs who Weirdo Jen warned me about.

It's what happens when you fill your life with programmes about posh people getting murdered in the countryside. Gran always acts odd after *Silent Witness*. She always says that had she been born in a different generation she would have been a pathologist — one of those people who examines murder victims and gets clues. "It's got everything I need from a career, Hattie — good money, justice and gorgeous young policemen asking me for guidance. Don't you think a white coat and a surgical hacksaw would suit me?" When I asked her if she wouldn't be a bit creeped out by dead people Gran started cackling and said, "Hattie, I'd love to go to work every day with people who can't answer back. It's my idea of heaven!"

Gran is a teensy bit psycho-mental. I'm glad she does come from a time when women left school at 14, got married and had babies!

11.07 p.m.

No, I'm not — that's awful! OMG — whoever thought THAT was a good idea?!

11.12 p.m.

It was probably men frightened of young girls nicking their jobs. Especially pathologists.

11.25 p.m.

And policemen frightened of flirting grannies with scalpels!

I have had NOTHING from Goose today. He is obviously too busy with his gecko to think about my life changing for ever. Talked to Dimple earlier about it. She said perhaps I was too "dismissive". When I asked her WHAT THE HELL THAT MEANT she said, "Perhaps Goose was trying to get you involved in something he really cares about. It sounds like you were a bit ... mean, Hattie!"

ME MEAN?! It's OBVIOUS I LIKE HIM! What more do I have to do? Be happy about THE MOST GEEK THING IN THE WORLD?!

I don't know why I ask Dimple about men – it's not like she's had loads of boyfriends.

11.32 p.m.

That DID sound mean. Dimple is lovely.

The truth is, I am officially jealous of a gecko. This is a not good situation. I don't want to be evil. I want Keith to like me – not to think I'm this horrible spoilt thing that doesn't like people or creatures. He's already got that with MGK! LOL!

All this and Christmas shopping looming...

WEDNESDAY 23RD DECEMBER

12.04 p.m.

Christmas shopping on a ~~low~~ NO budget was difficult but I think I've got it sorted. I've got Gran a pair of nail clippers (that's all the technology she can handle, apart from her Nintendo DS), a tartan weatherproof mini coat for Princess, some Britney Spears perfume for Mum (it was MASSIVELY reduced), some furry dice for Rob's car (Weirdo Jen says it's an ironic take on the boy racer culture and he'll appreciate it?) and NOTHING for my brother. It's tradition!

4.55 p.m.

I went to see Gran this afternoon. She called me into the bathroom. She'd been to the Christmas dinner at her pensioners' club and "got a bit too much in the festive spirit". She'd only put diamante vajazzles of Father Christmas's face on her bum AND used superglue! She kept shouting, "I can't get it off, Hattie!" I was telling her to go to hospital but Gran thought she couldn't because Rob went yesterday! She didn't want the doctors and nurses thinking we were "a family of nutters". We ARE a family of nutters! Why deny it?! Then Gran said, "I'll end up on the Internet or on 24 Hours in A&E – even if they blur my face people will know my voice and my bum!"

5.36 p.m.

How will people know Gran's bum?!

6.05 p.m.

Gran just rang my mob. The Father Christmas beard has partly come off. Gran is wearing rough cotton pants as punishment.

Does she even realize what vajazzles are and where they SHOULD go? I'm not telling her!

6.55 p.m.

Vajazzles. Geckos. Nut allergies. What on Earth is Keith coming into?! I'm confused about everything. Mum is angry with me and Gran is FURIOUS — partly at her itchy body art but mainly at Keith. Rob's not said a lot but I know he's worried. He's spending a lot of time in his shed. I want to tell him he'll always be THE BEST SORT OF NOT REAL DAD EVER ... but that sounds craptacular.

7.37 p.m.

I can tell you what Keith is coming into — he's definitely coming into the most uncomfortable accommodation in history. I saw it earlier. It's totally obvious that Gran really, REALLY hates Keith. The bed in the spare room has disappeared. She said the mattress had lost too many of its springs. She's put the ancient fold-out camp thing out with the itchy blanket. Gran's got a deluxe queen-size airbed! When I asked her where it was she snapped, "It's got a puncture — Princess thought it was a cat." Beds do not look like cats. I think she told Princess to attack it. I'm not arguing though. I'm NEVER going to argue with an OAP who's had a vajazzle disaster.

8.14 p.m.

OFFICIAL SERIOUS AND MAX AWFUL CONVERSATION WITH MY BROTHER.

I asked Nathan how he felt about Keith. It's because he keeps acting like nothing is happening and IT IS: OUR BIOLOGICAL ACTUAL REAL DAD is turning up TOMORROW. So I said, "Nath — how do you feel about it all?" And he said, "Hattie, I don't know how I feel. I just wish that things were the way they used to be. They were fine. Rob's the best dad ever. Who cares about anything else?" I said, "But don't you want to know THE TRUTH? Like where we come from and who he is and why he's never bothered?" Nathan just shrugged and grunted. Then he said, "And think what it's like for Mum — she has to have all those bad memories back in her life again. AT CHRISTMAS. But you know what, Hattie? I'm over it."

SO IT'S ALL HATTIE'S FAULT AGAIN! FANTASTIC! All I wanted was what I actually deserve!

I don't get it. Why is THAT so bad and why isn't Nathan even a tiny bit interested? HOW can he be all cool about it when I'm having a massive emotional earthquake that's causing major structural damage?!

8.55 p.m.
That last bit made no sense but I know what I mean. I'm in a mess.

And now I feel like I'm letting Mum down and, even though I hate him, I'm letting Nathan down too. I actually don't want to do that. I REALLY, REALLY don't want to hurt anyone. I just want to meet Keith.

9.12 p.m.
Just rang Dimple about Nathan. She said men are often "resistant to change". When her mum swapped her dad's shower gel he went really moody for about a week until

he admitted that "a lack of lather" was making him grumpy. Dimple's mum put washing-up liquid in the bottle to teach him a lesson but he LOVED it. He doesn't know but he's been using it ever since! Dimple thinks men just see what they want to see. "If there's lots of foam, Hattie, then they're fine. Even if they smell lemony fresh and have skin like a dinner plate."

Can you compare a family crisis to a bottle of Fairy liquid?

10.01 p.m.
Just asked Mum what I should call Keith. I don't want to call him "Dad" but "Keith" seems weird too. Mum said, "Call him what you like, Hattie! Up to you!" I told her I was thinking of a mixture of Keith and Dad — something like "Kad". She started laughing in a weird way and said, "Yeah — that suits!"

I don't get it.

10.21 p.m.
Texted Weirdo Jen. She says "cad" is an old word for a bloke who is a lying scumbag. Jen thinks my mum "really needs to get over her bitterness or she will end up with stomach ulcers". She is going to bring a Native American dreamcatcher round to help ease her subconscious negative feelings.

I don't think a big wind chime can really solve this problem but it's a nice thought.

10.45 p.m.

Just told Mum about Jen. She says she needs a dreamcatcher the size of Wales for all her bitterness. Then she told me to "get some sleep as it's a big day tomorrow".

It IS a big day. It's bigger than big. It's mahoosive. There needs to be a new word.

10.56 p.m.

Lord Megamahoosive of Enormoushire.

I'm quite proud of that.

11.02 p.m.

I always make up craptacular things when I'm nervous and can't sleep.

11.16 p.m.

I think I can hear Goose talking to his gecko. He should be comforting me, not chatting to him!

I thought Goose REALLY liked me. If I can get THAT wrong, what else can I get wrong? What else have I GOT wrong? Have I actually just created the biggest disaster ever?

I wish humans hatched from eggs. It would save a lot of trouble.

THURSDAY 24TH DECEMBER

Christmas Eve

2.12 a.m.

I am completely nervous about Keith turning up. He's on the plane now. I can't sleep for worrying about it. What have I started?! I was so desperate to meet him that I hardly thought about anything or anyone else. That was WRONG and MGK-style horrible. I didn't even think that I now have another person to buy for at Christmas!

2.32 a.m.

OMG – I'm naturally starting to think of others. This is what maturing feels like.

2.45 a.m.

I'll go to Boots on Boxing Day. They always have half-price smellies gift sets. I'll tell Keith I wanted to meet him first before I bought him anything. You have to actually meet a man before you can buy him aftershave.

2.50 a.m.

When I say aftershave I'm not talking anything by Dior or Gucci. I mean Lynx.

2.52 a.m.

Bet MGK buys him something posh. She says she can smell how much money someone earns by their fragrance and she can sniff out a man's ENTIRE personality! She was preaching to us all in Maths once like some kind of stinky love goddess. She reckons any guy who wears Beckham Intimately for Men is the opposite of Beckham. They are usually poor and look dreadful in tight underpants.

Gran has that advert of Becks in his knickers hung in her kitchen. She says she nearly dropped her scrambled eggs when she saw it first but now it gives her "a natural lift" every time she boils her kettle.

How would David Beckham feel about being near a Berwick-upon-Tweed tea towel that has a beetroot stain on it?

2.55 a.m.

I could use any Christmas money I get to buy Keith something really impressive and designer.

2.57 a.m.

No. It's the thought that counts.

6.47 a.m.

Keith just landed. I checked online. He is IN THE COUNTRY. HE IS HERE!

I don't feel any different yet. I thought I would feel excited. I just feel...

I feel nothing really.

Except for a weird feeling in my lip.

6.57 a.m.

I'M GETTING A COLD SORE. THANK YOU, UNIVERSE. My dad is going to meet the world's scabbiest, most contagious daughter.

I know things like that aren't meant to matter but they do.

7.06 a.m.

Time is going very slowly.

7.12 a.m.

No, Mum — strangely enough I don't fancy Coco Pops at this present moment.

7.33 a.m.

Why do adults try to make you eat? Like food solves anything. How can 2 bits of toast and Marmite calm you down? I am going to puke.

7.44 a.m.

Just had 2 bits of toast and Marmite — feel less sick.

7.50 a.m.

Text from Goose:

> Thinking of ya Hats. Luv from
> me & Freak

Goose has called his gecko "Freak". That's sweet.

That's really sweet.

Goose does just like me as a person. Just life, lizards and, I think, my lack of actual breasts get in the way. Why can't things just WORK OUT?!

8.09 a.m.

What if Keith hates me? What if it's a total disaster? What if Gran makes him one of her "left-over pastry fun flans" and he decides that this is all not worth it. People have felt very extreme things after being exposed

31

to Gran's flans. For all I know some people have left the country because of them. He could be one of them.

8.46 a.m.

Gran has just called my mob for the weirdest conversation ever.

GRAN: Hattie – we need to talk.

ME: Is it your vajazzles?

GRAN: NO! You haven't told anyone about
        them have you?   *I've only texted Jen –*
ME: NO!   ←   *she doesn't count.*

GRAN: I want to talk to you about YOU
        and Keith.

ME: Look, I know you don't—

GRAN: NO! You listen to me, lady. This
        is important. Sometimes in life
        we don't get what we want and it
        isn't our fault. It's other people.
        They don't appreciate us for what
        we are and what we deserve.   *I was actually*
ME: Gran, I KNOW we don't get ← *thinking of Goose*
        what we want or deserve.   *but I didn't say it.*
        Look at the state of my mobile.

GRAN: I don't mean crap like that. I
        mean THE REAL STUFF THAT MATTERS!
        Like the people who should love
        you. From what I hear from Rob
        you're not so good at picking up
        on signals, so let me tell you
        now – you're an amazing young
        woman with an amazing brain,
        you're funny and you've got a
        figure I would have died for at

	your age. You need to wake up to what you really are!
ME:	Have you accidentally put whisky in your porridge again?
GRAN:	NO! I mean it, Hattie. WAKE UP! And don't expect your father to breeze into your life and solve all your problems. He isn't Superman. Life is not that easy. It's NEVER that easy.
ME:	I don't expect him to make everything better.
GRAN:	Good. He's just a man, Hattie.
ME:	RIGHT! OK – MESSAGE RECEIVED!!!
GRAN:	Good. See you later.

← *Part of me does. A bit.*

That was helpful in no way whatsoever.

And what's all this about not picking up on signals? I can totally tell everyone is cross with me! I've already written it here. It's fairly OBVIOUS. Nathan is currently going through his entire "Angry" playlist on his iPod. He has "Happy", "Sad" and "Angry" playlists only. They are the only emotions he feels apart from "hungry" and "sleepy".

9.15 a.m.
Keith is getting the train here and doesn't have a mobile. He could arrive at Gran's at ANY TIME.

9.40 a.m.
Just rung Gran. He is not there yet.

10.12 a.m.
He is still not at Gran's yet.

10.14 a.m.

Gran has just rung me to ask me to stop calling her. She promises she will call me the moment he arrives.

10.55 a.m.

I think I might have left an important Science textbook at Gran's. I might go over there.

11.01 a.m.

Rang Gran again to tell her I was coming over to get my book. OMG! OVERREACTION!

She shouted, "You've never shown an interest in Science before. Why now?" I told her I had a sudden need to find out about biological things. Gran said, "You have a sudden need to be there first when someone might need a rest." Then Mum piped up in my ear behind me with, "Harsh but fair." Thanks, everyone, for their sensitivity in this issue of MY REAL DAD ACTUALLY TURNING UP. Mum is just punishing me for making her terrible past her present. I've read her diary – I know it was bad.

I've READ HER DIARY! HER TERRIBLE PAST!!! What the HELL AM I DOING?!

If I were her I'd give me RAW bacon sandwiches.

Got to think of something else – when are your feelings just not as important as other people's?! I don't want to be a pushover sappy-fest but I don't want to cause anyone actual head-mess pain! HOW CAN YOU TELL? Where do you learn this? I need to learn how to get what I want and not upset people at the same time.

I can't think.

I actually WANT to do schoolwork now.

11.27 a.m.

I had a quick look at the Science exam syllabus on the Net just to take my mind off things. It's full of stuff like natural selection, how your genes affect you and how the fennec fox has evolved to its desert environment. Actually these ARE things I DO need to know about NOW.

11.39 a.m.

The fennec fox can probably wait. He can't help me understand my dad. He just has a big brush and eats other people's cold chips.

11.47 a.m.

Rob just explained that after a long flight you need to freshen up and have a little rest. Only Rob ever talks sense. He's from Guyana and understands long-haul travel. It's not a small bottle of Chardonnay and a mini tube of Pringles on easyJet for 2 hours, Mum!

Nathan has a point. Rob is perfect. What am I doing?!

Too late now.

And I need to know.

11.54 a.m.

Gran yelled down the phone that she is doing some final checks. Mum said, "I bet she's hiding her valuables." I WENT MENTAL. I shouted down the phone, "Give him a chance, will you? It's been 14 years — he might have changed!"

Gran said, "I'm sorry, Hattie, but I can guarantee he hasn't. Men like that don't! You can't go from Keith Richards to Cliff Richard in one lifetime."

When I asked, "Men like what?" Gran said, "Your dad could fit an antique nest of tables in his suitcase!"

Antiques?! Gran has no antiques. Her furniture is called stuff like "Knutstropper" and comes flat-packed!

Gran sighed and start muttering stuff like, "Oh, I can't argue with you, Hattie. I've tried to protect you from it all but you had to know. Sometimes ignorance is bliss, you know! You need more life experience before you start doing things like this!"

So I shouted, "Yes, I'm glad you finally agree! That's why I'm going to leave school and go travelling!"

Everyone went mad then. Rob told Mum to calm down.

I'd only go travelling to Norfolk but I just wanted to scare them all.

At least an argument passed some time.

1.31 p.m.

Keith still isn't here. Gran says trains are a nightmare on Christmas Eve. People have to stand FOR HOURS and the buffet car runs out of stuff at Luton (that's miles away from anywhere northern!). Apparently, Brian from the pensioners' club went to stay with his family in Glasgow last Christmas and ended up having to share his fruit cake with a starving nun, 2 soldiers and a woman who cried all the way from Doncaster because her boyfriend had dumped her and she had to spend Christmas with her parents. Gran always says, "Trains are like living through a war, Hattie — you're never the same after. You carry the scars of public transport with you."

This from the woman who seems to think I'm making too much of a fuss about my real dad turning up!

2.06 p.m.
Keith is still not here. I'm watching *Toy Story 2* to pass the time.

5.12 p.m.
OMG — that was just the weirdest experience ever.

How do I even write what I feel when it's such a ... I don't even know.

That was a TOTAL mistake. WHY DID I WATCH *TOY STORY 2*?! Jessie the cowgirl being dumped at the side of the road always makes me cry.

TYPICAL! Gran didn't ring to warn me and Keith just arrived at the house! I was a mess about abandoned toys but he thought I was crying over him! He gave me this crap half-hearted limp hug and said, "I understand, Hattie — it's a lot for a girl of your age to take in!" I couldn't tell him I was sobbing because I was having flashbacks to when my brother squashed "Mr Fluffyton", my teddy, in a milk bottle and sent him down the river on what he called an "epic pirate voyage" (TEDDY TORTURE). I must have looked and sounded about 5 years old. Keith probably now thinks I'm the most immature girl ON EARTH. Then I did start to sob properly because it was just all too much in my head. I couldn't even stop. Then Mum said, "You know what, Hattie, this is a lot for you to handle. How about Keith goes to Gran's for a nice long rest and he comes back tomorrow after he's had a good night's sleep and you've had a chance to just ... calm down a bit?"

This made me mad because it was mainly *Toy Story 2* I was crying over, I think, but when I tried to speak I just did that totally embarrassing crying-snorting thing and Rob said, "Yes – I think that's a really good idea, Hats. It would be a lot for anyone. You're not being silly."

Keith sort of looked confused and nodded and Rob drove him back. Mum came over, started hugging me and said, "I did try to tell you, Hattie." I was so angry I pulled away and shouted, "This isn't about you – it's about ME and *Toy Story 2.*"

She looked puzzled. I don't blame her. I DON'T KNOW HOW I FEEL BUT IT WASN'T MEANT TO BE LIKE THIS.

So apparently me and Keith will talk tomorrow. I've only waited for 14 years. What's another 24 hours?!

I'LL TELL YOU WHAT IT IS! It's another day of nerves and feeling sick.

I think I might write to Disney and complain. They should NOT make films that make people cry.

It was all just such an anticlimax. I thought I'd feel this big rush of ... love but it just felt like ... bad PMT.

6.46 p.m.
Honestly, right now I feel sadder about Mr Fluffyton than I do about Keith. Mr Fluffyton was a teddy pioneer of the high seas. Well, of the Derwent river. I don't feel anything for Keith. What was I expecting? Perhaps Gran was right.

6.58 p.m.
I do feel something! I feel a bit...

7.22 p.m.
Patronized. Thank you, Dimple, for the EXACT word. BY EVERYONE.

Rob has just been up. Am I OK, PUMPKIN? He only uses "Pumpkin" when he's really worried.

I love Rob. That makes things harder now – not easier.

Dimple says give it a chance. Dads can be difficult. She should know.

7.41 p.m.
Dimple's dad totally loves her though and he tells her ALL THE TIME. He even laughs at *Mrs Brown's Boys* when no one is looking.

8.52 p.m.

I just told Weirdo Jen what happened today. She is bringing round another dreamcatcher to make sure Mr Fluffyton the teddy can be at peace. Jen understands priorities.

(Christmas Day) FRIDAY 25TH DECEMBER

8.01 a.m.

Rang Gran. Keith is still asleep. It's jet lag. Gran has apparently been playing her special festive album very loudly since 6.17 a.m. She's done "White Christmas" twice.

8.50 a.m.

It's not working. Keith is still sleeping on the world's most uncomfortable bed and yet he still will not wake up.

Gran says she's going to sort it.

9.21 a.m.

Gran has sorted it. She said, "I got to the end of the Slade song 'Merry Christmas Everybody' and shouted 'It's Christmas!!!' at the same time as Noddy Holder. That soon got the bugger up, Hattie."

Thank you, Noddy Holder, whoever you are.

9.34 a.m.

Fancy calling your kid Noddy? Sometimes I think I got off fine with my name.

9.45 a.m.

Gran came round WITHOUT Keith! Apparently he's just doing some "New Age meditating nonsense" near Gran's airing cupboard. Doesn't he realize how much I have to ask him?!

Perhaps he has to get his head together. Perhaps I NEED to get mine together FIRST!

11.04 a.m.

We have just opened our presents. I got mainly money. Boring but good.

THEN it happened.

If I haven't got enough to cope with, I NOW have a MAJOR responsibility! Gran has bought HERSELF an iPad! AN IPAD!!! She said she was sick of getting "soap and rubbish" for Christmas and wanted "to go 21st century". She got interest-free credit over 48 months! She can't work out how to connect it though. Good. As long as she sticks with Angry Birds everything will be fine. I can't deal with apps that connect her to the rest of the world and actual people!

Mum pretended to like the smell of the Britney Spears perfume I bought her but obviously didn't. I saw her put it under the sink with the Ajax and her rubber gloves! Rob also said he would keep the furry dice in his glove box as it "doesn't look professional to hang them up". I wanted to say, "Nor does using the drive-through as part of a driving lesson to pick up an Egg McMuffin but that's not stopped you before!" Rob says it teaches people to manoeuvre into small spaces. In fact all it does is teach people to drive to window 2 to collect Rob's secret brunch!

Mum would go mad if she knew he did that. It's only because I love him so much that I don't tell her!

12.34 p.m.

Apparently Princess doesn't like her present either. There's a Scottish guy at Gran's pensioners' club who doesn't like dogs. Princess associates tartan with "hostility and men who smell of smoke and pickled onions". I said she could change it but Gran says the shop probably "wouldn't like a half-eaten coat — besides she's only a young dog and checks are very ageing!"

Princess has better fashion choices than me! She has about 5 coats. All picked to complement her fur.

I'm telling you all this because Keith still isn't here. I'm nervous as hell and I'm worried that me having a total emotional breakdown has totally put him off me for life.

5.09 p.m.

Keith finally turned up for dinner at 2.10 p.m.

Mum and Rob were polite. In the way you're polite to someone who has a VERY obvious spotty skin rash you don't want to catch. Gran was openly rude. She kept saying waking Keith up was like getting a "bloody tortoise out of hibernation — but they have a more varied diet and better conversation".

She's got a point. Keith doesn't say a lot. He also wouldn't wear a paper hat because it was a "mass-produced novelty hat". He also didn't eat turkey, only vegetables. He had 2 parsnips and a sprout for Christmas lunch. He won't even eat Roses chocolates because of excessive packaging. Gran said, "Can I have your Country Fudge then? More fool you."

He seems to be very green. I'm not against green but he's a bit ... too green, I think. I know the polar ice caps might be melting but don't ruin Christmas dinner over it.

THEN MAX UNCOMFORTABLE HORRID MOMENT.

After the queen's speech Nathan suddenly left his pudding and went upstairs. He listened to his ANGRY playlist for TOO LONG and WENT MENTAL. He said to Keith, "Listen, mate – I'm not interested in you. I've thought about it and ... well, I've got a father figure in my life – Rob. You've never bothered before so why now? So just stay out of my way." Rob went to interrupt him and Nathan said, "No, Rob, mate – I've made up my mind. He's not going to be part of my life. That's just the way it is."

Keith said, "I'm sorry about that, Nathan. Sorry that you won't let me into your life and the lightness of forgiveness into your heart."

Nathan shouted, "No, mate. I won't let a pillock into my life!"

OMG – am I being horrible to Rob by letting Keith into my life?! This is just a non-stop brain crash.

Then Gran said REALLY SARCASTICALLY, "When did this new Keith start then and how long will this version last?"

Keith just looked sad and said, "I've been an idiot, I realize that. It was all about women and drinking. I took, took and took but now – I try to live better. I just try to do my bit and there are some things I believe in that might not sit well with you. And when I found out one of my kids wanted to meet me I had to see them, didn't I? And I want to make things up to all of you and thank Rob for doing such a good job. I just won't eat animals."

Gran snorted and said, "With all the spaghetti bolognese you used to eat you've killed more than your fair share of the world's cows already. Don't ever think you'll take the place of Rob. You won't!"

Keith said, "I'm not trying to. I just want to meet my kids. Believe me I'd rather not be pulling crackers with you, Violet." Then he winked and EVEN MUM LAUGHED.

Gran went beetroot-angry – she HATES being called by her REAL name as she says it's a weak, useless flower that can't stand a mild frost. She even tells people at the pensioners' club she's called Rose ("It's got thorns, Hattie – that's what you need in life").

Keith may be green but he managed to shut Gran up.

I love her but it was a bit magnificent to see!

Rob looked sad though. I think he's worried about Nathan.

Me and Keith had a bit of a chat.

```
ME:      Why did you NEVER get in touch?
KEITH:   Because I'd made such a mess I
         just wanted to run and get away.
         I was a pillock like Nathan says.
         But Hattie I'm not that person
         any more - I was just a kid. I
         thought about you all the time.
         And Nathan. And Ruby.
ME:      Oh. Good.          ←——— WHAT COULD
                                  I SAY?!
```

I've noticed a lot of adults blame a lot of stupid things on being a kid or a teenager or being "young" – yet when YOU do something they don't like they go MAD.

6.49 p.m.

I asked Rob if I had ruined his life by bringing Keith into his actual house. He said, "Of course not, Hats. I understand that you want to know your dad. We all understand that!"

He did look upset though. I knew I should have bought him a deluxe car-washing kit with antifreeze. That would have at least softened the blow.

I don't think we'll all be playing Wii Sports this evening as I thought we would be.

I might have to play tennis by myself. Again.

7.44 p.m.

Gran has had 3 sherries and is currently doing ski-jumping on the Wii. She can barely lean forward so she is doing 2-metre jumps. She seems happy though. No one else is. Mum and Rob have been washing up for about 6 hours. I know there was a lot but no roasting dish needs that amount of scrubbing. Nathan is in his bedroom listening to Mumford & Sons. Keith is asleep in the chair. I want him to stay asleep, I think. It's not his fault but he's like an emotion bomb.

8.34 p.m.

Keith has woken up to say he wants to meet MGK! BOOM! And NOT in the good way. I have warned him she is from the Planet Cow with udders of pure evil. He says it's his duty.

This whole day really has turned out to be the Christmas pudding that caught fire, got horribly out of control and burnt down the entire house, Santa's sleigh, Rudolph and all the other reindeers whose names I can't remember. Even the elves are crying. I have sort of killed Christmas by introducing Keith the Greenish Grinch.

9.41 p.m.

Gran and Keith are going back to Gran's house. I am surprised she is letting him in after what has happened today but she has to – Gran needs help. She has hurt her hip doing the ski-slalom on the Wii. Princess tried to join in and knocked her over. Before Keith shoved her in the taxi Gran was trying to argue that dogs could do winter sports and that they should probably be introduced as an event at Crufts.

Princess wouldn't be allowed anywhere near a pedigree dog show. Certainly not on skis.

10.12 p.m.
Before Keith went he shouted, "Bye, Nathan." He's trying. Nathan had been listening on the landing for ages but he pretended not to hear.

Gran's tomorrow. It's a Boxing Day tradition. It usually means trifle and Monopoly and lots of telly. This year it means Keith-based TENSION.

What have I done?

SATURDAY 26TH DECEMBER

Boxing Day

7.23 a.m.
Goose just texted:

How did it go Hats?

What I really want to say is IT'S AWFUL, Goose. Keith doesn't care. Princess won't be competing in the Winter Olympics any time soon and I have made an OMG! TERRIBLE mistake. PLEASE let me come and hide at your house, Goose, and live with Freak. I want to be Freak. I want to live with you. In a nice tank. PLEASE LOVE ME THE WAY I WANT YOU TO.

But I just replied:

Good. C U soon. X

Hopefully from that Goose will realize something is wrong.

8.12 a.m.

Goose said:

```
Glad it's good :-) Luv GX
```

I don't think he does realize something is wrong.

Perhaps I'm rubbish at giving out signals too.

9.23 a.m.

Keith got up and apparently didn't wash or have a shower. He said that "water is as precious as diamonds" and "too much washing can damage your pheromones". He explained that "pheromones help you invisibly communicate with others and attract a mate". Gran said, "You need to wash them off for a start! All the trouble they've caused! You're a man not a skunk."

Keith didn't say anything to that but Gran said he "laughed like a madman". I think he quite likes her in a way. Perhaps "like" is the wrong word. Something. I don't know.

1.35 p.m.

Gran has bought Keith 3 bottles of deodorant for Boxing Day. This is her not at all subtly telling him he stinks!

Keith doesn't like aerosols. Gran snapped, "I'll get you some roll-ons then." He doesn't like those either. Glad I don't have to waste my money at Boots on a present – LOL!

3.57 p.m.

Gran keeps spraying Keith with a combination of Febreze and air freshener behind his back. She's trying to do it secretly but he keeps asking her what she's doing. When she says, "Cleansing the air!" he tells her she's ruining the ozone layer. Gran says environmental damage to something she doesn't actually believe in is a small price to pay not to have her nose assaulted every time he walks by.

Who IS this man? He isn't the "Carlo" everyone talked about! He is even more of a stranger than the stranger he is. He doesn't seem like someone who would leave his kids. He thinks about everything. He washes jars out before recycling them. No one actually does that!

4.32 p.m.

Hang on, Gran — how can you not believe in the ozone layer?

5.15 p.m.

Gran says she's never seen it — it might as well be the tooth fairy.

The whole house now smells of Vanilla and Jasmine Glade Plug-in. It's making Rob sneeze. Gran thinks Rob needs to toughen up. She said, "Nuts?! Air fresheners?! You'll be allergic to water next."

6.23 p.m.

Keith thinks that British tap water IS poisoned. It's the fluoride apparently (that's in toothpaste — how can it be bad?!). Keith hopes that one day the environment will be so clean we will be able to drink from streams without worry. Gran said, "You can do that now if you'd like your water served with oil slicks and empty energy-drink cans."

That was the sort of conversation we had till Mum said she had a migraine and we had to go. It was a migraine she treated with 2 glasses of Pinot Noir when we got home and she had a miraculous recovery. I honestly don't blame her. Keith is...

Keith is a bit DULL. How can I have a dull dad?! I was expecting this guy who would be a bit wild and perhaps even let me have a glass of wine in a pub. With these genes will I grow up dull and end up growing my own tomatoes? What's the point? You can get them TODAY at Asda!

6.49 p.m.
Perhaps there's been a mistake! Perhaps Rob IS my REAL dad and I'm sort of an albino! There's a really cool albino in Year 11 called Charlie Swain. His parents are actually black! Perhaps I do need a DNA test!

6.52 p.m.
Just googled albino. I'd have red eyes and be really pale.

I'm not Rob's. I belong to Keith.

7.14 p.m.
Perhaps I should make more of an effort. I should talk about things that Keith likes. I might look up British wildlife and see if I can learn something and start a conversation about that.

7.48 p.m.
OMG – if female ferrets don't have sex they die! Better stick to stoats.

8.12 p.m.

Stoats are boring.

Keith has decided he is going to come round every day till he goes back. This shows he wants to make an effort.

I want to talk to Goose about this. Have to KILL my lust and just concentrate on BEING FRIENDS. I'm too tired now though. I've spent the last hour in virtual forests, looking at virtual wildlife. I might go round tomorrow.

11.38 p.m.

Just had a dream that I invited a giant robin into my house. It seemed really friendly at first and then it tried to peck me to death!

I don't need to ask Jen what that dream REALLY means. I know.

It means birds are actually evil.

11.51 p.m.

Or it might be something to do with Keith anxiety.

SUNDAY 27TH DECEMBER

10.12 a.m.

I was just about to go next door when I saw Jen walk up to Goose's front door. I bet she's come to see his gecko. She is a total reptile expert and a "great fan of the cold-blooded mind". Apparently reptiles give you a "unique affection". Just thinking about Goose and her laughing and chatting makes me so jealous I might explode.

I have definitely matured. I know when I'm jealous these days almost immediately and can totally admit it.

10.43 a.m.

I need something to love. I might get a python. Something that could eat both of their stupid pets in one go!

11.11 a.m.

Perhaps I have not matured. Jen and Goose are both totally lovely and yet I'm currently enjoying the thought of "Devil" – my imaginary snake – gulping them ALL down as a brilliant snack.

5.32 p.m.

Keith spent all day negotiating with MGK's mum. MGK doesn't want to see him – especially now she has found out he is not loaded and lives in a massive shed.

6.35 p.m.

Keith spent ages staring into space tonight and then said to me, "I'm not doing very well Hattie, am I? You're the only one speaking to me. Nathan has told me exactly what he thinks of me and Ruby won't even meet me. Can you help?"

I explained to him that Nathan had been torturing me since I was a baby and that MGK hated me because I was not cool at school and did not wear Versace on a regular basis.

Keith said, "I can tell you now, Nathan loves you. And Ruby – well – indifference is the opposite of love. Ever thought Ruby might be jealous of you in some way? And that's why she's nasty?"

Dear Keith – seriously you are talking TOTAL crap now. I just laughed at this. I said, "Trust me – she is not jealous. She thinks I'm Dork Central."

Keith said, "Sorry to hear that. School is cruel."

OMG! At least Keith GETS THAT!

BUT WHY IS my actual real dad more interested in MGK than me? WHY? WHY? WHY?

7.59 p.m.
Gran told me it's like that with all men: "Treat them mean – keep them keen." Apparently, I've got to be less nice (?), ask less questions and demand less time.

Gran also told me she looked in the mirror and Santa's vajazzle hat is still on her buttock. She thinks the glue marks will fade. So MGK is Number 1 in my dad's eyes but my gran's arse decoration is gradually improving.

Hurrah. That's great news.

8.21 p.m.
Perhaps I AM a bit too sarcastic sometimes like Weirdo Jen says.

I'm going sales shopping tomorrow with Mum and Gran. It might be hell but at least it isn't Keith and MGK worry.

MONDAY 28TH DECEMBER

7.32 p.m.

Keith and MGK would NEVER get on. He has spent most of the day lecturing us on our sales shopping. Do I really need another top? Does Mum really need another saucepan? Does Gran really need a plush bulldog wearing a Union Jack that plays "God Save the Queen"? Do we realize about landfill and how mass production is polluting our world?! YES, KEITH!

ALL I DID WAS BUY A NICE TOP!

Keith! Here's a tip! Stop saving the world and save me!

8.16 p.m.

I have to make an effort. I have to make this work. This is OFFICIALLY my mission – GET A REALLY DECENT RELATIONSHIP WITH KEITH – MY ACTUAL DAD – BEFORE HE LEAVES! There are totally lovely bits to him.

TUESDAY 29TH DECEMBER

7.46 p.m.

Keith took me out today! It took ages to find a cafe that he "approved" of (fair-trade coffee, vegan food – those are just the requirements I remember!). This took about 2 and a half hours. He then started reminiscing about drawing his name in concrete in an old toilet block and insisted on going to see it. It was still there. His nickname, "Carlo", in big letters. Keith looked really happy and said, "That's history there." I didn't have the heart to tell him it's just a bit of graffiti and very unlikely to end up a tourist attraction. Oh, and carrot, hummus and gherkin filling on gluten-free bread is CAPTAIN VILE! He's OK but I have to really try to keep the conversation going. When we get to silence it's really uncomfortable. We are just not ... how I thought we would be. I have a funny dad, then a dull dad, THEN a dad that gets some things and is TOTALLY clueless on others.

When I got home Mum said, "How did it go?" I shouted at her. "I don't want to talk about it — and have you got any ham?"

The truth is, I don't want to talk to anyone. I thought knowing Keith would give me a parent that GOT me! Instead it's got me totally confused, loads of time away from my friends and probably malnutrition from rubbish sandwiches.

My Keith mission may be a *Mission Impossible* film without Tom Cruise to save it.

10.01 p.m.
OMG — Nathan just came into my room and asked me how it went?! When I told him he said, "Keith sounds like most of us, Hattie. A little bit good. A little bit rubbish."

This is a BREAKTHROUGH for Nathan, who previously was describing Keith as that "Total b****** that ******* left my ****** mum and me and didn't give a s***".

Perhaps THEY will end up as friends and it will be just me that is TOTALLY messed up by the thing I MOST WANTED. HOW DOES THAT EVEN WORK?!

WEDNESDAY 30TH DECEMBER

11.01 a.m.

Mum and me had a MAJOR conversation this morning:

MUM: Hattie, I think you expected too much — but don't take it personally. We are all a bit … confused by it. He's different. He's not even the man I knew. I don't know what to think… But I know it must be so, so tough for you, Hats.

ME: It is tough, Mum — because he's MY DAD! He's meant to GET ME naturally!

OMG, she is being so nice!

MUM: You're wonderful, Hattie! He's just the man who sowed the seed. I'm so sorry you aren't getting what you want. Or what you deserve.

URGH — TMI, MUM!

I don't know whether to agree with her or argue with her so I've gone on the Internet to look at videos of people falling off things

3.12 p.m.

Gran has just rung me. Princess and her have overstretched themselves doing winter sports and are sitting on the sofa with hot-water bottles and menthol muscle rub. The muscle rub is not for dogs but Princess loves it. According to Gran she's been licking her own leg for over an hour.

The only things that are having a good time this Christmas are dogs and reptiles.

5.24 p.m.

I've just read the greeny blog that Keith writes. IT IS UNBELIEVABLE!

Greetings from the UK. I am finding it tough here. It's all about shopping. WHAT you can buy. WHERE you can buy it. Nail varnish seems to be more important than pollution. My daughter is lovely – she's a special young woman – but she seems a bit obsessed with what she looks like and what so-called celebrities are wearing. I wonder how many teenagers in Britain have walked barefoot in a wood, camped under the stars and cuddled a koala. They MUST be taught that bonding with the Earth is more important than what the latest *X Factor* winner is wearing. NATURE must win. Let's take photos of things that really matter – the sky, the moon, the stars. The REAL stars. Celebrities will pass. The forest is for ever. That said – this is turning out to be such a unique experience. A LIFE GROWTH lesson. I've made some horrible selfish mistakes that have hurt people. I regret them deeply and I am trying to make them better. My advice is: don't do what I did. Think about the people you love and do something about it. Pick up a phone, write a letter, email – it doesn't matter. Don't miss out like I have. My daughter and son have filled their lives with a wonderful father figure I can never replace. Don't end up with regrets like me. Peace out.

1. *You're* finding it tough, Keith?! Spare a thought for the rest of us. Sometimes it's like living with a massive TUT machine that disapproves of everything WE do.

2. Nail varnish isn't more important than pollution but I have no control over Chinese smog. I can, however, take control by painting my hands a positive shade of "Tangerine Daiquiri".

3. "My daughter is lovely." Thanks for that. DAUGHTER?! You've got 2, Keith. He'd better mean ME.

4. "Peace out"?! What does THAT mean?!

5. OMG, my dad cuddles koalas! How do they feel about that? I bet they just want trees and other bears. Or a nice It bag to stash their eucalyptus leaves in – LOL! I know koalas aren't really into Prada. I'm just feeling annoyed.

6. The last bit makes me ... want to cry. He DOES feel all these things. He is SORRY and he does think I'm lovely – WHY DOESN'T HE SAY IT TO MY ACTUAL FACE?!

7. I want to tell him it's not too late to make everything better – but perhaps it is. I don't know.

7.34 p.m.

Just rang Gran to tell her to read the blog on her iPad.

10.57 p.m.

Gran has just worked out how to read the blog on her iPad.

She sounded a bit choked up when she said, "Hattie – look at the bit at the end. Take it in. Don't miss things like you normally do."

YES, GRAN – I HAVE SEEN IT … AND WHAT ELSE AM I MISSING PLEASE?!

THINGS I KNOW:

1. Keith is sorry. I thought that would make me feel good but it just makes me … sad. Then angry. But mainly sad.
2. Mum, Gran and Rob LOVE me.
3. Dimple and Jen are my best friends.
4. Nathan probably loves me but still wants to cause me emotional and low-scale social humiliation.
5. Goose loves me but does not want to snog me. When you want to snog a girl you snog her. Not invite her round to a gecko-naming ceremony with others. He loves me LIKE A FRIEND. I need a boy that loves me LIKE A GIRLFRIEND.
6. Goose makes me sad, angry, happy, tingly, a bit mental – but mainly totally like my head has been put in a blender.

THURSDAY 31ST DECEMBER

3.12 p.m.

I hope New Year is better than last year when we were all in bed by 11 p.m. Gran is not going to her over-60s' '80s theme party. It got too messy last year. She wants a "quiet one".

5.37 p.m.

Keith is coming to our house for New Year but he's a bit (HERE IT COMES) funny about helium balloons as apparently they are leading to a shortage of helium in the medical world. He asked Gran how she would feel if she couldn't have keyhole surgery because somebody wanted a more colourful party. Gran said, "I wouldn't mind! A big scar wouldn't bother me. I haven't worn a bikini since 1979!" Keith just stared at her and said, "Are you sure about that, Violet? I've heard all sorts goes on when you have your OAP day trips to Hunstanton." Then he winked at me. Gran has met her match! LOL!

6.22 p.m.

Gran has suddenly decided to go to the '80s New Year party night at her over-60s' club. "I haven't got as much time as you left on this Earth, Hattie," she said. The party's fancy dress – with an '80s theme. She's borrowed some of Mum's old net curtains and is going as Madonna in her *Like a Virgin* bride stage.

6.44 p.m.

Just googled Madonna in 1984. PLEASE, Gran, DON'T WEAR a "Boy Toy" belt.

7.12 p.m.

Gran has just made herself a "Boy Toy" belt out of a cornflakes box and one of my old glittery Primark belts because she says she has to look authentic.

I'M SORRY. I'M SO OVER FAMILIES.

Goodnight, this year.

9.13 p.m.

Text from Goose:

> B4 it all goes mental just want
> to say HNY! Luv, me and Freak
> for ever XX

"For ever"? Only in a platonic way though.

Goooooseeeeeeeeeeeeeeeeeeeeeeeeeeeeeeee.

11.45 p.m.

I'm sure I can hear Keith sucking helium out of a balloon and pretending to be a Smurf!

CAN PEOPLE PLEASE MAKE THEIR MINDS UP ABOUT WHAT THEY ACTUALLY ARE AND WHAT THEY ACTUALLY FEEL?!

FRIDAY 1ST JANUARY

11.21 a.m.

HATTIE MOORE'S OFFICIAL LIST OF WHAT THIS NEW YEAR IS REALLY ABOUT:

Finding REAL FULL-ON love.

Last year I spent too much time LOOKING FOR MY DAD (a year of trouble that has just led to mass confusion and the weirdest time of my ENTIRE life!) AND I spent too much time on what Weirdo Jen calls fleeting relationships – AKA hot snogging.

1. <u>THIS year is about FULL-ON LONG-TERM</u>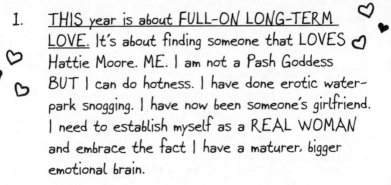
   <u>LOVE.</u> It's about finding someone that LOVES
   Hattie Moore. ME. I am not a Pash Goddess
   BUT I can do hotness. I have done erotic water-
   park snogging. I have now been someone's girlfriend.
   I need to establish myself as a REAL WOMAN
   and embrace the fact I have a maturer, bigger
   emotional brain.

Yes, I still have tiny tits — but I know now that a) I can't
do anything about that and b) larger boobs do NOT solve
all your problems. In fact, as Gran says, people often
forget she actually has a face. Plus buying big pretty bras
is a nightmare — "I don't want 2 marquees, Hattie! I want
gentle feminine support, preferably in cream with dainty
blue flowers." I told her not to worry as only Gran will
ever see her own underwear at her age! I felt her death-
staring me so I didn't look at her. Gran said, "People see
my undies on the line, Hattie. Everybody judges you on the
state of your whites — trust me."

Gran could have loads of secret boyfriends for all I know.
She always acts REALLY odd after bingo and often loses
her dabber.

1.12 p.m.
Weirdo Jen says all women are goddesses. I am apparently
not a hotness goddess but an Amazon goddess. I am
athletic and of the jungle. I am a natural hunter.

This is nonsense because I can never find the bacon in Tesco.

STILL I will find real love. A REAL LOVE that lasts longer than the bananas in the fruit bowl. I know that sounds mental but I deserve the sort of love that doesn't go black and mouldy after a week. And I want to be a banana on my own terms.

ALSO:

2. Be nicer to Mum. I may fail at this as she has a mutant totally annoying gene but I will try because I owe her for the Keith bomb.

3. Get to know Keith. I have to now I've started. It's a duty – like finding Gran's dentures when she puts them down somewhere safe she doesn't remember (always on the front windowsill – where everyone can see). AND I can tell he has good bits. Inside. When he's not going on about chimps in captivity. Or something.

4. Just make sure I don't lose Goose as a friend. I have to just forget the tingles and be more ... just how we used to be. I was expecting too much. You can't snog a boy that you used to play Postman Pat with. But ... GOOSE. It's hard. He is this massive geek problem I can't get out of my head.

5. Avoid MGK as much as possible. So what if she's my sister? She's still the enemy. Families hate each other all the time! It's what daytime TV is actually based on.

6. Help Gran with her iPad so she doesn't end up a global laughing stock.
7. Train Princess to do tricks so she can earn her own treats and her own money (I will take a percentage of the profits).
8. Go out of the house more to do ANYTHING that isn't staying at home!

3.15 p.m.

Told Mum I was going to get out of the house more. Mum says I need a job, or how else am I going to pay for the cinema, clothes, mags, pizza, make-up— Er ... CHRISTMAS MONEY OBVIOUSLY, MUM! And NO ONE can get a job. Adults are doing paper rounds!

5.23 p.m.

Gran rang. She came home last night dressed as George Michael. She doesn't know who ended up in her Madonna costume. She says it was all much of a muchness in the '80s.

SATURDAY 2ND JANUARY

5.25 p.m.

Weirdo Jen turned up to see me today BUT she spent all her time with Keith! They had the best conversation ever about angels. Then Keith looked at Jen's aura. Apparently we all have a colour around us that portrays our true nature. Only certain people can see them, "people with a third eye for the spiritual world" Keith says. Mum reckons it's "people who believe in any old crap".

Jen's aura is apparently golden and connected.

If mine was a colour, it would be green — in the bad, JEALOUS way. Jen and Keith just get each other in a way ... IN THE WAY KEITH AND ME SHOULD GET ON. It's all seems so easy for them.

6.13 p.m.

Gran told Keith that his aura was actually coming out of his arse. Keith laughed at this but not in a nasty way. In a way that he sort of knew he sounded like a bit of a doughnut. Then he said, "Violet. Your aura is black. It's as black as your roots used to be before they went white!" Gran death-stared him but didn't reply! This made me giggle. Gran called me a Judas for laughing. I told her that he was just joking. Gran said, "You don't joke about hair, Hattie. A woman's hairdo is the embodiment of her very soul."

6.53 p.m.

Gran went on eBay just to buy something in protest against Keith's anti-shopping thing. She's bidding on a Radley handbag.

Keith would actually probably approve — it's second-hand! LOL!

7.17 p.m.

Gran has withdrawn the bid. She didn't really want the bag. She just wanted to get at "that sanctimonious man".

7.37 p.m.

I just looked up "sanctimonious". It means a massive nagging bore-fest basically. That's what Keith can be. But he can be really funny too. I think I might be getting him ... a bit.

SUNDAY 3RD JANUARY

10.22 a.m.

OMG – MGK has FINALLY agreed to see Keith this afternoon. He will HATE her. She is Consumer Queen. Her aura actually lives in Topshop!

1.33 p.m.

He likes her.

Keith really likes her.

He says she has hidden depths.

What hidden depths?

1. She has FAKE Prada soap that Dimple (SUPER intelligent – knows everything) says is probably made by tiny children in sweatshops.
2. Her favourite programme is *The Vampire Diaries* NOT *Countryfile!*
3. She says real girls never fart and you can train your stomach to hold it in for days.

I can't even bear the thought of going back to school with MGK there.

Keith obviously sees the good in everyone. This is annoying.

4.55 p.m.

UNBELIEVABLY MGK wants to see Keith AGAIN.
WHY?! They have NOTHING in common. It's like the
queen going down the pub with the man who works in the
kebab shop.

5.16 p.m.

Not that MGK is the queen.

5.35 p.m.

Keith would also be anti-kebab. He would say it would
offend his inner lamb and probably his inner yoghurty
dressing and pitta bread too.

That's not fair. JEALOUS again. Am I actually the
world's most jealous person? Aquarians are not meant
to be jealous! WHAT AM I? This whole Keith thing has
made me wonder more about me than I ever have. It's
like everything I thought about me may be craptacular
rubbish. WHO IS HATTIE MOORE? I cannot answer this
question.

8.23 p.m.

Rob just came up and sat on the bed and said he's noticed
I'd been a bit "quiet". I told him that honestly I was so
confused that I actually couldn't even explain it. Rob then
started singing this bizarre song called "There Are More
Questions Than Answers" and gave me a massive hug.
He said, "Hattie – I can tell you who you are. You can't
cook, you can't hoover properly and you keep missing the
bit by the skirting boards ... BUT you are great company.

Why don't you stop driving yourself mad up here in your bedroom and come to KFC with me? All things come in time. Stop thinking, start doing and let's get a Bargain Bucket!"

So we did. Rob may be the best person ever from Guyana and maybe the world. And everything feels better after chips and gravy.

Tomorrow I START DOING.

MONDAY 4TH JANUARY

10.19 a.m.

Time to think about what Hattie Moore REALLY wants to do this year!

For SERIOUS LOVE you need to be full-on noticed. You need to be different yet true to yourself.

That's why I'm totally taking the hem up on my school skirt. New school year – new shorter-skirt Hattie. No one here will notice but boys will! LOL!

1.32 p.m.

I think it looks OK. It goes slightly wonk-wonk in places but you can only see if you massively stare at it.

4.36 p.m.

Mum noticed immediately. She says it's so uneven it looks like a flamenco dancer's dress. She was PEEING herself laughing. She's mended it.

I SWEAR she's made it longer. Yes, I feel like a doughnut but at least I have DONE!

5.13 p.m.
How come Mum notices a hem but I can be in a bad mood for weeks and she never says a word?!

7.12 p.m.
Mum has told Gran I took the hem up on my skirt. Gran rang up to give me a lecture about it. She ended up going on about visiting the baker's. Apparently, "The best cakes in the shop hide their filling. Only the cheap buns have their synthetic cream on show. Be a Victoria sponge, Hattie."

What has this got to do with me showing off more actual leg?!

TUESDAY 5TH JANUARY

First day back.

5.16 p.m.
TOTALLY annoying first day back at school.

MGK is talking about Keith (her "REAL dad") like he actually HAS saved the planet! She says he is one of the world's most important activists and has already played a "major part in saving lots of endangered species". In reality he really only writes a blog that is read by about 20 people worldwide, MGK! He's hardly on an actual Greenpeace boat saving things that need saving. PLUS Gran says that when he makes out he's doing meditation he's actually snoring. Gran said, "Hattie, I lived through the 1960s – there's a deep spiritual trance and then there's just being asleep."

6.01 p.m.
Looking around there seems to be more adult nutters than ever before. Perhaps it's a virus.

6.18 p.m.
Dimple told me that MGK is now officially telling people I'm her sister but "only vaguely". Apparently MGK keeps saying "accidents do happen!" and laughing. MGK, YOU WERE AN ACCIDENT TOO!

I'll never actually say that to her. I know what it's like to be a deliberately on-purpose accident. I actually don't want her to feel terrible.

OMG! I DO have Keith's nice gene.

6.36 p.m.
Dimple says I'm just lovely. And mainly I always have been and what am I getting worked up about?

How do you explain to someone who knows where they come from that meeting the person you come from can be like putting your entire actual self in a massive fry-up?

Thinking too much again.

6.55 p.m.
Weirdo Jen says all the vegetarian food I'm eating is reducing my "natural aggressiveness". Red meat makes you angry.

I might have a tin of ravioli to test that theory.

7.22 p.m.

I still don't want to hurt MGK.

I might have a Chinese-style pork mini riblet to see if that really pushes my temper over the edge.

7.45 p.m.

I still feel calm. This must be a permanent personality change NOT a meat-based one!

9.22 p.m.

Gran just had a MAHOOSIVE freak-out at Keith about MGK. Gran was yelling at him, saying, "You were always impressed by pretty, shiny things with money! For all this 'Save the world!' crap you haven't changed. You're still impressed by money and you're always out to get some without working!" Apparently Keith busks with a converted biscuit tin, does odd jobs and has a market stall when he "feels like" working. Gran started chanting, "Work-shy! Work-shy! Work-shy! Work-shy!"

Gran was doing ALL THIS after a cold beef-and-pickle sandwich! Jen is right! Meat does make you mental.

Keith was really calm and said Gran needed to keep up. He HAD changed. It was a shame that SHE was still the old judgemental woman of old who was worried what everybody else thought. Gran went loony and said, "You need not have flown to Australia! I would have kicked you up the arse there. Well – you're missing out on some wonderful children!"

CHILD, Gran. CHILD! Nathan is not interested and MGK is not wonderful!

I think Keith HAS made an effort though. In his way. It's a weird way.

God, I want to see Goose. I want to talk about all this with him.

WEDNESDAY 6TH JANUARY

4.56 p.m.

We had Personal and Social Education at school. We were talking about equal opportunities. It's always about "Men versus Women" or "Black versus White". What about "Fit versus Not Fit" or "Designer versus Primark"? That's what is REALLY happening! Feminism doesn't affect me! I want to be able to shave when I like!

6.39 p.m.

Gran just gave me the biggest lecture on women's rights. She said, "Your generation don't know they're born. Feminism isn't about having hairy legs! It's about getting what we deserve! Being paid the same as a man, having the same opportunities as a man! Do you think that always happened?" Keith AGREED with her! "Your gran is right, Hattie. Women had to throw themselves in front of racehorses just to be able to vote!"

Why did they involve horses? Were they on the men's side?

Gran told me not to be silly. "The point is YOUR generation has got to keep the fight up! Have respect for yourselves! Be independent. I protested for the likes of you!"

I asked Gran where she protested, when she protested and what about.

She really snapped back at me, "Well, I certainly felt strongly about it and shouted at the TV a lot!"

Gran is the sort of person who just presses the "like" button on Facebook and thinks that something magically changes. Her heart's in the right place but her legs are usually on the sofa! LOL!

At least Keith DOES stuff.

Perhaps I do need to be more feminist though.

7.21 p.m.
I just told Rob that it was his turn to wash up. It wasn't but he fell for it. I am an OFFICIAL feminist activist!

I'm still shaving though.

I've got to go round and see Goose. I can't keep putting it off. I can't not have him in my life — I just have to accept there are other boys who will fancy me and he is like a ... boy that's a girl. I'm just going to pretend he's gay in my head.

8.56 p.m.
I finally got to see Goose tonight. He seemed a bit off with me at first but then the more we chatted, the more he was

like my Goose again. He agrees with feminism. His mother,
Donna, doesn't – she says she doesn't want to be equal
with men. That would involve a step down. Donna ROCKS!

I'm seeing Goose after school on Friday to talk about
EVERYTHING EVER. Dads. Feminism. And lizards.

And, PLEASE, THE FACT THAT HE LOVES ME LIKE
A GIRLFRIEND!

No. No. No. He's not interested. He's my non-gay gay friend.

I can't raise it with him EVER – he HAS to. That's
feminism. It's not the man taking control. It's the woman
not doing the running as that's a man's job!

Thursday 7th January

10.15 p.m.

Or is that being pathetic?

What should girls actually do?!

I can't risk feeling like a total dork like I did after
"Gecko Night".

Friday 8th January

9.12 p.m.

Keith came over while me and Goose were having a Maccy
D's. He talked AT us for ages about fast food and how
it was bad for you, cows and Mother Earth. Goose said,
"I appreciate your views but I really like chicken nuggets –

---

and Keith, what about your leather boots?" Keith said they were a by-product ... of an already dead cow. Goose said chicken nuggets were a by-product too ... of an already dead chicken!

I could have kissed Goose.

Actually I really massively could have FULL-ON kissed him HARD AND FOR AGES.

But all we had was a hug when he left. He patted my back. That's not sexy. That's like when you have a trapped burp.

After Goose went Keith said, "He seems like a lovely boy. I like people who challenge me. They help my spiritual growth."

I said, "Yes – he's nice."

I was thinking, he's lovely, he's a geek, he's HOT as the actual SUN or something you have microwaved for ages and forgotten about and I LOVE him.

But instead I said he was nice.

CRAPTACULAR.

SATURDAY 9TH JANUARY

3.39 p.m.

Keith ended up being involved in a protest in a shopping centre today about terrible conditions in third-world factories. He got carried out by security guards. He said,

"What has happened to Britain? They used to allow peaceful protests." Gran said, "Bloody attention-seeking idiots were outlawed in 1998. Besides, instead of making a fool of yourself over third-world working conditions how about putting things right by getting closer to Nathan? What about getting a relationship with your son? Poor boy has been knocked sideways by all this. You ignored him as a baby and now you're ignoring him as an adult. DOUBLE REJECTION."

Keith said, "But he won't speak to me."

Gran yelled, "Try bloody harder."

Keith didn't say anything for ages and then said, "You're right, Violet... You're totally right."

Gran snapped, "Yes, I am. And stop calling me Violet."

Good luck with that one, Keith!

5.12 p.m.

OMG — I just found out that Weirdo Jen joined Keith on the protest. I have told her I don't want her hanging out with him. I have already asked Dimple to tell Jen how hard it was for me that JEN seemed to click with him more. Jen looked a bit embarrassed and said it was just really hard to find people around Derby that cared about the fate of penguins AND believed in ancient Mayan prophecies (???).

Did the ancient Mayans predict my dad could be a bit of a tit?!

SUNDAY 10TH JANUARY

11.22 a.m.

Got up this morning to find a note from my brother pinned to the kitchen wall:

> DON'T USE THE TOP OVEN AS A
> SAUSAGE IS STUCK DOWN THE BACK.

Only my brother could cause havoc with a sausage!

11.57 a.m.

KEITH HAS JUST SPENT 20 MINUTES SURGICALLY REMOVING THE SAUSAGE!

He said it was a "complicated job" but "quite easy" for a plumber. Keith said, "When you've removed an entire man's shirt from a bathroom system, Hattie, a sausage is a piece of cake."

Nathan just grunted something, made himself a full fry-up and took it to his bedroom.

OMG! RUDE! I know Keith deserted us but if he gets the oven to actually work again he AT LEAST deserves a "TA, MATE". I realize that would mean Nathan using a sentence of more than 1 word but COME ON!

12.35 p.m.

Nathan and me have just had the following ~~discussion~~ FULL-ON argument:

```
ME:       That was a really kind thing to do.
NATHAN:   What?
ME:       Rescuing the sausage!
NATHAN:   Hattie - removing a pork product
          from the back of an oven does not
          make up for leaving Mum, having
          nothing to do with us FOR ALL
          OUR LIVES and turning up only
          because YOU, MISS BLOODY MARPLE,
          go looking for him.
ME:       It's MEAT. He hates MEAT. He
          touched MEAT so you could eat MORE
          FRIED DEAD THINGS!
NATHAN:   So that means I should just
          forgive and forget everything?!
```

You can't argue with him. Keith overheard and said, "Thank you for trying, Hattie - that's really kind."

The weird thing is, I would LOVE Keith and Nathan to get on, but the thought of him getting on with MGK is just ... WRONG. But then, how could he? She is EVERYTHING that he should NOT like.

4.46 p.m.

Keith came back after 2 and a half hours this afternoon and announced he'd been on a "nature walk" with MGK. Apparently she loves deer. MGK loves deer?! Since when?!

I want massive antlers so I can BUTT MGK in her perfect bum.

MONDAY 11TH JANUARY

4.23 p.m.

In English today Dr Richards told us we had to write about a TV show that we hate. Dimple wrote about *EastEnders* as there is too much sex in it — apparently watching it with her parents is like "slowly dying of embarrassment". Her dad starts coughing and her mum has a sudden need to descale the kettle. Weirdo Jen said she hated most TV as it stopped her "experiencing the actual fabric of reality and feeling nature" — though she did like things with David Attenborough (Jen, are you 80?).

I said I hated the *Green Balloon Club* as children should be kept from arguments about the environment — it's totally boring and not all about being nice to badgers.

Keith has made me cross about badgers a bit. It's not their fault. I don't want them culled. I just want them to, in their stripy way, STOP MGK and Keith clicking!

7.57 p.m.

Shouldn't I feel closer to Keith by now? Shouldn't there be something DEEP and biological that just kicks in? Sometimes I just feel annoyed by him — he "embraces" the sun every morning. Jen does that and I LOVE her. Why don't I love Keith COMPLETELY AND TOTALLY like Mum and Rob?!

I love Rob more than my REAL dad. That's not right, is it?

TUESDAY 12TH JANUARY

4.32 p.m.

MAHOOSIVE downer.

Me and Jen have totally fallen out.

I'm gutted.

Jen said that ever since my dad arrived I've changed. Apparently I've been "deliberately argumentative" (she always uses too-long words) about "things that really matter now"!

I said, "Jen, I would actually put an ENTIRE whale in a sandwich RIGHT NOW. I am so sick of everything being GREEN." Jen said that was the most stupid thing she had EVER heard and it showed how little I knew because you would never find bread big enough to fit a whale in. Even a wafer-thin slice! Then she stormed off.

Jen's aura is not golden – it is very red and unreasonable and she puts sea mammals before her friends.

5.39 p.m.
This is partly Keith's fault – I was sympathetic to Jen's weirdoness before HE happened.

7.11 p.m.
I hate falling out with Jen – she's like my mad weird sister. More than MGK will EVER be. I was an idiot.

9.23 p.m.

Weirdo Jen and me gave each other a hug and we both said sorry. She said she just wanted me to be "open-minded". I promised I'd never eat an endangered-animal sandwich even if I found a roll big enough. I also told her I loved her and I'm open to her. I'm just closed to Keith. The truth is, he's hurt me. I thought he would LOVE me and be my friend. He's just a friend of the Earth. There's no room for the actual people who live on it in Keith's brain.

9.51 p.m.

The terrible truth is I think Keith would love me more and GET me more if I was a squid.

WEDNESDAY 13TH JANUARY

8.12 p.m.

It's the middle of January and I am nowhere near finding love. Inside my heart I thought me and Goose would be planning holidays by now.

9.34 p.m.

Just remembered! Something happened today that confirmed my belief that men never grow up. The boys all started playing "Spot the Penis" in a Chemistry for You textbook during break. Basically Nicky "bad boy" Bainton had drawn tiny men's bits in the illustrations and photos and the other boys had to find them. There was one in the photo of the man at the petrol station, one in the illustration of an atom and 2 in the periodic table. This was apparently HILARIOUS.

I'm definitely becoming a feminist — but a feminist with a love agenda.

9.54 p.m.

Dimple and Weirdo Jen agree feminism is the way to go. As long as you can still wax and snog.

Men are FOR EVER immature and totally unpredictable!

↓

THURSDAY 14TH JANUARY

6.24 p.m.

Out of the blue!

Keith has suggested that "we" go and see him in Australia over the summer holiday. "We" cannot mean Nathan after the sausage. That sausage SEALED it. IT MUST MEAN ME AND MGK.

1. WITH MGK?!!
2. That's MILES off anyway.
3. What if I'm in a relationship?
4. Does a feminist do what a man wants her to do?!

Dimple and Weirdo Jen think it's the chance of a lifetime. If I do go I will Skype them every day!

7.12 p.m.

OMG! Keith doesn't have the Internet! He goes to the library to write his blog! I can't go to that level of country-style backwardness!

7.39 p.m.

I can totally tell that Mum is secretly so THRILLED that me and Keith aren't best friends by now. I must make more effort with him.

8.27 p.m.

Goose (who likes everyone) admitted today that he doesn't exactly LOVE Keith either. He thinks he's a MASSIVE kid. "And if he upsets you at ALL, Hattie, I don't like him anyway." ENORMOUS DORKERY — but cute!

8.42 p.m.

Very cute.

TOTALLY cute. BUT he's not interested. He's like all men. Reptiles and mammals and trees come first.

Actually that's not fair. Rob puts me first.

8.58 p.m.

He does love his car though. He calls her Pat — after an ex-girlfriend who, he says "was wonderful to be with and easy to control". LOL!

9.52 p.m.

Actually that's not funny — that's SEXIST! Is Rob a secret anti-feminist person?!

10.22 p.m.

I just asked Rob if he believed in the power of women. He said totally. He believes in the power of women, except in 3-point turns. Apparently we can't do those as well as men.

10.49 p.m.

Mum heard Rob say that men are better at driving than women and went mental at him! They are now having a competition in the road. It's nearly 11 at night!

11.02 p.m.

Rob beat Mum but only because she said she had to do an emergency stop to avoid a cat. Now she is shouting at Rob that men have to win no matter what and that "preserving life is more important". Apparently this is why men start wars!

The thing is, as women, do we need to get tougher and squash pets to win the battle of the sexes?

11.32 p.m.

Goose just texted to say he saw my mum save the cat and he thought it was amazing. Goose is what my gran calls one of these "new men – they even do the hoovering if you ask them and hand-wash your tights"!

I wish he was my man. OH, GOOSE – WHY DIDN'T YOU SEE MY LUST STORM?!

FRIDAY 15TH JANUARY

4.47 p.m.

Dear MGK – STOP SMIRKING at me at the side of your actual face every day at school. You are getting totally on my nerves.

~~Love,~~ Whatever,

Hattie

7.23 p.m.

I just can't think of romance properly while Keith is around. I should be building my relationship with him but IT'S HARD. I look a bit like him but that's it. He's OK. Sometimes he's actually really sweet, but then he does mad stuff. Gran says she's even had to hide her broken biscuits because he doesn't like preservatives and E numbers.

7.55 p.m.

OMG – perhaps MGK is right. Perhaps Gran does have a lorry-driver boyfriend who brings her stolen goods off the back of his truck!

8.29 p.m.

I asked Gran about the biscuits. She looked a bit weird and said it was someone she knew with a "connection". Her pensioners' club is just full of old people doing illegal stuff because the police would never suspect them. Apparently no one thinks you're a criminal if you've got a Zimmer frame or if you buy seedless raspberry jam ("seeds play merry hell with your dentures").

9.14 p.m.

I wonder if I'm a stealing genius like my grandad the thieving postie. Perhaps it's genetic. I've realized a lot of things are. I think I do get my caring bit from Keith despite the fact that he totally left us.

9.35 p.m.

Gran says I'm not built for a life of crime. She can tell I'm lying just by the way my knee twitches. Apparently I'd crack easily under interrogation and torture.

9.59 p.m.

Keith wants to spend time with me tomorrow. I hope it doesn't involve deer.

SATURDAY 16TH JANUARY

4.55 p.m.

MENTAL DAY!

I went to see Keith and Gran. Gran irons shirts before she sends them to charity shops! She says, "Even really poor people and the homeless should have standards, Hattie — how else will they get a job?"

Keith was very impressed that Gran recycles clothes. When she heard this Gran threatened to just put clothes in the bin — and she didn't mean the recycling one!

Then Keith decided we should "upcycle" Gran's dreadful wardrobe into something "retro fabulous". It's apparently what he does on his "occasional" market stall. This is the wardrobe that no one speaks of. The BAD family secret that Mum warned me about. Gran's wardrobe — the wardrobe of PURE FASH HORROR! The wardrobe stacked full of BAD TASTE BARGAINS AND NEEDLEWORK GONE WRONG.

While we were sorting through Gran's stuff I asked Keith why he'd left and NEVER got in touch. I think I wanted some better answers.

KEITH: Hattie, I was a very different person back then. I couldn't cope with the chaos I'd created. Your gran said it was best for me to go, too. She was right. They needed plumbers in Australia and I – look – I just wasn't very nice. That's the truth.

ME: But didn't you ever think of me? Of us?

KEITH: Yes. Of course. ALL the time. BUT it's not simple. It seems like a different world down there. It's so far away. This place seemed like a different planet. I was changing too. I could start again. No one knew me. I ran away, I suppose. I thought if I got in touch it would…

ME: Would what?

KEITH: Complicate things. Rob has been an amazing dad to you.

ME: I know that! BUT YOU SHOULD HAVE GOT IN TOUCH.

KEITH: I know. I'm sorry. I just began to see that I wasn't anything special. Without all my lad friends egging me on I realized I had no friends and I'd messed up the real stuff. And Tasmania just made me realize the Earth matters. Beautiful mountains and streams and things hopping around in your garden. Look, please just spend tomorrow with me and let's try to have a good time upcycling some of your gran's stuff.

ME: What, you think that blouse has got potential?

KEITH: It's perfect for upcycling, I'd say. Shall we try it tomorrow? What do you reckon?

ME: I reckon customizing an old bit of clothing is bound to solve everything.

This made Keith laugh and he said, "Hattie – I don't think it will – BUT I like being with you. You're smart and funny and a little bit sarcastic."

He didn't add, "Not like MGK." BUT he's too kind to do that.

SUNDAY 17TH JANUARY

5.38 p.m.
It's retro craptacular!

Upcycling was a TOTAL LOL! NO ONE can rock crochet FRAYED brown waistcoats OR an over-the-knee skirt with a slit up the front that Keith made (badly – it just looks like a 4-centimetre rip!). You also cannot rock a grubby white handbag with a rainbow and stars doodled on it IN BIRO. The rainbow was in just 3 colours — black, blue and red. Keith said, "It's the message that counts." I told him that I would ring *Vogue* and report him! We ended up peeing ourselves.

Gran caught us giggling at her awful wardrobe and called me a traitor.

6.12 p.m.
Keith and me bonded over Gran being mental. I feel a bit guilty but also a bit relieved.

6.46 p.m.
I've just realized everyone in Australia must look dreadful.

7.13 p.m.
They don't wear a lot of clothes though because it's so hot. You can't really mess up a bikini!

MONDAY 18TH JANUARY

4.55 p.m.
Like I haven't got enough to deal with, EVIL teacher-torturer Matfield has decided we are doing a 3D ceramics project in Art. We have to make an animal that we love or have loved. Florence Morse — ultimate rebel — said she went on a seaside holiday once and fell in love with a group of plankton. She just rolled her clay into loads of little dots. Matfield went mad at her for "disrespecting artistic materials", so Florence went mad at her for "disrespecting a deeply held and fond childhood memory". Then Matfield asked her what her animal was called.

When Florence answered, "Plankton the plankton" Matfield went mad!

What can I do? I could make Hammy the hamster but his face would be too hard. It's the same with Sergeant Nibbles the guinea pig. Rodents have difficult faces to model!

Trust Mum to give me pets that are artistically challenging.

6.02 p.m.
I definitely can't do Princess. She doesn't stay still long enough for you to even see what she looks like. Perhaps if I buy her some nice food I can do a sketch.

6.48 p.m.
Gran says Princess likes M&S chicken slices. I can't stretch to that – she will have to have Lidl slices.

6.52 p.m.
Jen just texted. She says this is my karma for calling Freak "Freak".

I'm going to have to try to make Princess.

Wish I was spending more time with Freak. AND his owner.

TUESDAY 19TH JANUARY

7.28 a.m.
Just woke up feeling sick about clay.

6.49 p.m.

Went round to see Princess — she just ran off. Gran says she can sniff out low-price food. She won't touch anything cheap. She can recognize the label. Keith, though, managed to do me a quick sketch of her. KEITH IS MY HERO (for the minute).

Gran usually goes to zumba on a Tuesday but she's decided that it's actually just quick line dancing. That is at least the 202nd health fad she has given up. Princess uses her yoga mat to sleep on!

7.24 p.m.

Just remembered! Princess also buried Gran's juicer in the back garden! She hasn't missed it. She told us she cured her joint pain with a daily breakfast mix of carrot juice and wheatgrass! We know she really just has a cup of tea, a massive bowl of Frosties, 2 Nurofen and a nap in front of *Homes Under the Hammer*. She fancies Martin who hosts it! She says, "Lovely hair and he knows what to do with property. That ticks the boxes for me at my age, Hattie."

7.46 p.m.

OMG — Keith decided to attack Gran tonight for being closed-minded, unsupportive to her daughter and unusual domestic situations. He also said she was someone who gives up on things too easily, like zumba. He actually meant being closed-minded to HIM!

Now I think it's funny when Keith takes the mickey out of Gran but THAT is NOT ON, because a) although Gran is mental she has always been there for us, and b) Keith is not in a position to criticize anyone giving up zumba when he gave up 3 kids. Anyway it made me sad and MAD and that's when I said it:

"You do realize, Keith, that the latest research shows you have messed up my relationships with men for life by abandoning me."

Keith actually got angry and refused to believe it.

Then he just walked off in tears.

8.26 p.m.
Bet MGK didn't say anything like THAT.

MGK is officially more forgiving than me.

I think that's slightly depressing.

WEDNESDAY 20TH JANUARY

4.01 p.m.
My 3D ceramic sculpture of Princess has gone wrong. I may transform it into a gecko.

4.55 p.m.
How can I concentrate on recreating Freak out of basically mud when I've made Keith cry, Mum and Nathan seem to be sort of avoiding me, Gran is upset and even Rob is spending a lot of time in his shed?!

I AM THE QUEEN OF FEELINGS MESS-MAKING.

Thursday 21st January

7.01 p.m.

Today Mr Thomas, the new and young teacher, kept asking me questions. Why? MGK said he fancied me as he's a geek too. It wasn't that. He admitted it's because I'm the only name he can remember because it's unusual.

I stick out for all the wrong reasons — name, braces and BARKING family.

7.36 p.m.

Goose has just told me REALLY CASUALLY that he's been asked on a cinema date by ANNA SHARPLES on Friday! He stared at me for ages after. What was I meant to say? "CONGRATULATIONS!"?

Hattie BREAKING NEWS!

Goose:	Probably love of MY entire life ever — is going to the cinema with a girl called "The Tongue".
Keith:	I've upset him and he seems to enjoy recycling more than me.
Rest of family:	Confused, upset, avoiding me — I think TOTALLY mad with me for finding my real dad.
MGK:	Gone green.
Me:	Gone green in a different way and may melt with envy again.

I don't actually blame them.

5.15 p.m.

Matfield told me today that my ceramics project does not look like either a dog or a gecko. I need to emotionally connect with it to "make it work". I can't emotionally connect to humans successfully — let alone clay.

Nicky "bad boy" Bainton then spread it around that my ceramics project looked like "tits with a tail-y bit". I'd tried to capture the gecko's big eyes. He says I am making myself the boob job I have always wanted.

I am dying a slow social death with clay in front of everyone in the school ever.

6.30 p.m.

I've decided I am officially changing its shape and turning it into a penguin. I've never had an emotional connection to one but I'll lie.

6.42 p.m.

That's not true — I love Pingu.

11.12 a.m.

Goose came round. He went on a cinema date last night but he was more worried this morning about Freak the gecko. He apparently looked "off-colour" and wasn't eating much! I told Goose that perhaps Freak needed more company (IN OTHER

94

WORDS, TURN DOWN ANY DATES). I said, "Why don't you wear him like a brooch! You'll be fashion forward, Goose, and Freak will get to meet people!"

Then Keith interrupted and said, "Using live animals as clothing is not acceptable."

YES! Thank you, Keith, for not being able to take a joke!

When is Keith going home?!

11.34 a.m.
Just casually asked Keith — he says he has 2 passports and can stay as long as he wants.

12.19 p.m.
Gran has checked! Keith can stay as long as he wants but if he stays longer than 3 months he might have to start paying tax. She slipped this into a conversation with him. She tried to make it sound natural but it was totally obvious she was saying "get lost". Gran said, "He HAS to go. He's making my fridge vegetarian. I never thought I'd have tofu in my home. If people knew! The butcher wouldn't give me bones for Princes any more!"

6.38 p.m.
Keith told Goose tonight that Freak is unhappy because he has been ripped from his natural habitat. According to Keith the reason he's not eating is because he's depressed.

Goose is now going to avoid our house till Keith goes home. Great!

7.22 p.m.

EVERY adult in my life TOTALLY stops me from experiencing full-on PASH! It's like one of the conspiracies that Jen talks about!

Every adult except the US President and the big lizards disguised as humans that Jen thinks really run the world — they are NOT involved!

7.42 p.m.

OMG — unless Freak is in on it! He could be a gecko spy. Perhaps he is hunger-striking to stop me and Goose getting together!

SUNDAY 24TH JANUARY

8.39 a.m.

After 10 hours' sleep I can see that Freak is just a gecko.

4.29 p.m.

UNBELIEVABLE!

Keith has decided he is going home in a few days as HE HAS A LONG-TERM PARTNER. Er … WHY DID HE NOT MENTION THAT BEFORE?! I NOW SORT OF HAVE A STEPMOTHER TOO.

Then he started going on again about how he wants all his kids to go to Australia. It's the worst idea ever! 24 hours on a plane with MGK would be THE WORST! But then, I know she'll get upgraded anyway because she looks like a model.

A dad who was meant to make everything better has just made everything MORE COMPLICATED – and tomorrow it's ART. That means MY CLAY PROJECT. At the moment it really is a massive craptacular triangle display of poo macarons!

Or something.

9.25 p.m.

Mum has just been up and has been UNBELIEVABLE in an UNBELIEVABLY UNBELIEVABLE way.

```
MUM:      Hattie – I just want to say how
          proud I am of you.
ME:       If this is going to be you
          actually having a go at me, do it
          – because, you know, I probably
          deserve it and—
MUM:      NO! This has been hard for you.
          But you've thought of other people
          and that is a … well it's a lovely
          thing. I heard what you said to
          Nathan and … look, I don't like
          what Keith's done to the 2 most
          amazing and special people in my
          life BUT you've shown a lot of …
          thinking about us.
ME:       I didn't think of you. I was a cow
          bag.
```

MUM:	You were a bit selfish – BUT that was your right… We should have been more honest.
ME:	But Mum – Keith just doesn't get me like I thought he would. He—
MUM:	He DOES love you. He's learning to be a parent. Give him a chance. I CAN'T BELIEVE I'M SAYING THIS AFTER WHAT THAT BAST— MAN DID TO ME, BUT he's trying. And don't forget, me and Rob are so PROUD of you.
ME:	Have I really upset Rob?
MUM:	Rob is your dad, Hattie. He loves you. He gets you. Don't you worry about that.
ME:	Thanks, Mum.
MUM:	Now, do your homework.

I love my mum. Even though she ends every conversation NAGGING ABOUT HOMEWORK.

No – I love her.

MONDAY 25TH JANUARY

5.34 p.m.

At school I tried to turn my clay-model penguin into something else as I couldn't do a proper beak. According to Nicky "bad boy" Bainton it looked like something else.

Yes, Nicky – it DID look TOTALLY like a willy SO I changed it to a fish.

I've never bonded with a fish.

Jen says I probably bonded with them in another aquatic lifetime. I don't think that's true. I've basically made a lemon with a face.

TUESDAY 26TH JANUARY

5.26 p.m.

Goose has been sensationally dumped by text after 1 cinema date as Anna Sharples said he couldn't kiss properly! This is school romance reputation DEATH. Anna rates ALL the men she goes out with – and she understands full-on kissing more than ANYONE! The weird thing is, he's not even bothered that he is currently filed under "Slurper Snog". He's more scared that Freak the gecko is now not eating anything at all.

I love the way Goose doesn't care what other people think of him and is more worried about his gecko. I wish I could be like that.

I wish I could teach Goose how to kiss.

6.13 p.m.

I've googled it. Geckos can live for 30 years! Bet Goose hopes he stays on hunger strike. His LOVE LIFE is RUINED. He can't go out when he wants to in case Freak gets hungry. Basically he's a teenage father who can't even claim any government benefits.

Good. Don't want him to go out with anyone else.

WEDNESDAY 27TH JANUARY

3.58 p.m.

It's OFFICIAL! I can't even make a clay fish. Matfield said my gills had made it look more like "a loaf of bread".

So I just rolled it into a long tube and said it was a snake. Matfield wanted to know when I'd EVER had a specialist pet. I told her that I have a massive python who swallows anyone I don't like. This python only exists in my head but it's VERY REAL to ME!

At that point Matfield backed off. YES! DON'T MESS with a girl who has been through what I have been through. Weirdo Jen says I'm still in my emotional chrysalis. This is a nice way of saying I'm completely confused.

THURSDAY 28TH JANUARY

5.32 p.m.

Keith is leaving on Sunday!

WHAT HAVEN'T I SAID OR DONE YET?! What do I need to do? What should I do?

Dimple says I'm thinking too deeply and may be torturing myself.

FRIDAY 29TH JANUARY

7.24 p.m.

Keith took me aside tonight for a "quiet word".

He said, "Look, I know it hasn't been easy but I've realized being a parent takes so much more than I ever thought. You will soon learn, Hattie, that adults make

I know that, Keith – I've got MASSIVE METAL BRACES because of Mum!

mistakes and I'm going to try to make it up to both you and Ruby. And even Nathan if he'll let me."

SATURDAY 30TH JANUARY

8.12 p.m.
Keith went round to MGK's to say goodbye. He was gone for ages.

9.45 p.m.
OMG – I was bouncing a tennis ball against my wall and Nathan STORMED into my room and shouted, "Any chance you could STOP taking your mood out on the house?! I'm trying to watch *The Walking Dead* in my room. It's not the wall's fault you invited a New Age dork-head into the house."

I threw my ball at him. It missed.

Then Nathan started to tear up and shout, "It's OK for you, Hattie. You haven't seen Mum SOBBING and SOBBING night after night. Hiding in the bathroom. Don't YOU EVER EXPECT ME TO TALK TO THAT MAN!"

10.13 p.m.
I've just had a massive quiet cry. I don't think Goose is in his room but I think Freak must have heard me sniffing.

I miss everything and I WANT everyone to stop hiding the truth from me. I CAN HANDLE IT! I CAN COPE!

The only thing that did hear me cry was a gecko. They can't even pass you a tissue!

11.23 p.m.

Just gave Mum a big hug goodnight and told her I loved her. I hate the thought of her crying over this. I am now even going to eat one of her floppy bacon sandwiches to prove my love.

SUNDAY 31ST JANUARY

3.23 p.m.

Just said goodbye to Keith! We gave each other a big hug and he said, "I'll see you soon!" And then he was gone.

What do I feel?

I should feel emotional. But I feel slightly annoyed with him. He can be a dull preachaholic. He seems to love snails more than humans. He saw the postman tread on one and went mental. This is the postman that didn't sue a Dobermann when he tried to eat his ankle. Everyone knows when there's canine blame there's a claim! BUT though Keith's really annoyed me at times, he has been sweet at times and he HAS tried. BUT I don't want to upset the people I love any more. I even don't want to upset Nathan.

I'm letting Keith do all the work now. HE can contact ME. He can prove he cares. It's the right thing to do and it's also totally feminist.

8.42 p.m.

Freak the gecko is eating again! Perhaps he was bored to tears by Keith too!

MONDAY 1ST FEBRUARY

4.02 p.m.

MGK apparently cried for 3 hours as she felt such a deep personal connection with her "dad". This must be because she thinks he's a secret millionaire or something. Like Walter the tramp, who played the xylophone on the bench opposite the main post office every day and ended up leaving £3.2 million to the cats' home.

Anyway I had a full conversation with Dimple and Jen about my dad. It's all right for them. They've had dads they have always known.

Only Goose really gets it.

Anyway I am not going to think about THE WHOLE KEITH/DAD THING!

BTW – got my clay project back today after it had been fired (put in a big oven and cooked to Gran-pastry hardness standards). I hadn't made a Princess, a gecko or a snake. I'd made a pet wiggly line. I've given it to Mum.

She said she was going to use it to unblock the sink then she gave me a massive cuddle.

Mum gets it. She was crap at Art too.

I am still not thinking about KEITH.

TUESDAY 2ND FEBRUARY

6.13 p.m.
RIGHT – time for LOVE. Massive FULL-ON CONCENTRATE ON THIS LOVE. It's A MAN FOR HATTIE.

Sorry, Mum, I don't care about the failure of your savoury muffins. I have tuned out. Though it's obvious that Cheddar cheese and jalapeños won't work. We want double, double chocolate with double chocolate chips.

6.37 p.m.
Actually, Mum, I WILL try one of your savoury muffins.

6.56 p.m.
I've just eaten a bit of it and told her it was lovely. It wasn't. I've hidden the rest in the airing cupboard. It's difficult thinking about your mum's feelings. It's even more difficult on your taste buds.

Perhaps I should text Goose and see if geckos like savoury muffins as a side dish to complement their live crickets.

No, Hattie Moore – that's just an excuse and you know it is.

WEDNESDAY 3RD FEBRUARY

7.22 a.m.

Mum just tried to give me a savoury muffin for breakfast. She has about 30 of them. I predict they will die in the back of the freezer and we will only see them again when she defrosts it in about 3 years' time! Then she will bin them.

I took one though "for school". I am trying.

6.54 p.m.

OMG!

1. Gran has set up a "World According to Princess" Twitter account!
2. Dimple is acting really oddly. I know I've been spending a lot of time with my family and I've ignored her a bit but she's being really secretive. It's like something is going on in her life but she can't actually tell me. We've never had big secrets before. She can tell me anything.

7.12 p.m.

Except for, "Hattie, I've been asked out by the boy who you have fancied for AGES but I didn't tell you." BUT that was last year. We are at a totally different stage now. Our relationship has moved on.

8.13 p.m.

I asked Weirdo Jen about Dimple. She said she felt the same. Her vibes have felt off. I thought Dimple might have told Jen something but Jen promised on her life without

crossed toes that she hadn't. Jen means that.
She totally believes that if you lie on your life
something like a piano will fall on your head
the next day.

I don't want to tell her that I tell white lies
EVERY DAY and no musical instrument has
ever attacked me.

8.49 p.m.

That's not true. Nicky "bad boy" Bainton hit me on the
head with his recorder about 2 years ago. Perhaps he IS
actual karma.

9.16 p.m.

No, he's just an idiot. You don't expect a thump on the
head during a round of "London's Burning".

9.52 p.m.

I just checked Princess's Twitter account. She has
tweeted:

> I don't do leads. Give me a chicken leg and shut it.

It's been favourited by 28 people and retweeted by 7.

I give up.

Dimple hasn't updated her Facebook status ALL night.
She must be talking to someone.

<u>WHO?</u>

THURSDAY 4TH FEBRUARY

4.35 p.m.

I texted Dimple to see if she fancied coming over. She's doing extra Bollywood dance classes. Her parents are so strict – it's the only time she's allowed to get out.

There's more to it though.

Dimple, there is something you are not telling me and I WILL FIND OUT!

And if it's a boy I may be a little bit annoyed and worried.

OMG – please don't let it be Goose.

5.12 p.m.

No. I'm just being silly. Dimple hates creepy-crawlies. A money spider makes her scream, let alone an actual thing with a tail and a 10-metre tongue.

7.35 p.m.

Talking of things with tails and 10-metre tongues, MGK is following Princess on Twitter. And I mean MGK not Princess. LOL!

FRIDAY 5TH FEBRUARY

5.12 p.m.

Gran's Princess Twitter account now has 12,724 followers.

She thinks she's rich. I said, "Gran – how?" She said, "Hattie – it's the Internet. I'm going to make SERIOUS

MOOOOOO-LLLARRR." I said, "But HOW, Gran?" She couldn't tell me. She just thinks that someone will offer her millions for her idea.

Gran thinks she is Instagram.

She is not.

9.23 p.m.

OMG — I cannot even believe I am writing this!!!

DIMPLE HAS A SECRET BOYFRIEND. I am the only person who knows and I cannot tell a soul on Earth ever. Even in 50 years. Even when I'm dead! If a psychic contacts me on stage I can't even tell her.

Dimple met this boy called Bhavin at a wedding. Their eyes met over hundreds of people doing mad arms-in-the-air dancing. They had a Sprite together and talked about "deep stuff". Then they decided to meet up in secret! Dimple is meeting him in the park when she's meant to be at dance classes. DIMPLE IS HIDING IN ADVENTURE PLAYGROUNDS AND SNOGGING BHAVIN!

Or, as she calls him, "The Bavster".

BUT IT'S CIA Top Secret. I cannot even tell you the level of mentalness that Dimple's parents would reach if they knew. It would be SO over and Dimple would be grounded till she was at least 45.

She's TOTALLY in love. It HAD to happen – she's unbelievably pretty and she can't have her hormones removed. I'm sure her parents have looked into it. LOL!

10.03 p.m.

Just want to say that Dimple's mum and dad are lovely. They are just really strict. They are not evil or anything. She gets more than me at Christmas even though she's Hindu!

10.38 p.m.

YET AGAIN – have you noticed REAL love gets RUINED by families ALL of the time? They mess it all up. I think they should butt out!

Even when they DON'T know about the affair in the first place!

Family has ruined my love life.

No, I've ruined my love life AND my family life by being mental about Keith.

11.02 p.m.

Me and Dimple have created a secret code word for all of this. We are calling it "Operation Bhavin". It's SO obvious no one will guess. It's James Bond genius.

SATURDAY 6TH FEBRUARY

8.45 a.m.

I'm part of a massive secret. It makes things really exciting even when nothing is happening except cornflakes!

12.01 p.m.

Bit confused. I messaged Dimple this morning asking how Operation Bhavin was going. She replied:

```
Operation proceeding well.
Would you like to rendezvous in
the park tomorrow and meet the
subject?
```

Don't really get it.

2.12 p.m.

OMG – SHE MEANS MEET BHAVIN!!!

CANNOT WAIT!!!

3.33 p.m.

Princess (aka Gran) has been retweeted by Stephen Fry for the Tweet:

> Give me a bit of your breakfast or next door's pedigree cat gets it.

4.01 p.m.

Oh. It's not the actual Stephen Fry. It's a bloke from Cardiff who's into StarTrek and lighthouses. He's got 23 followers.

Gran's a bit disappointed but she still thinks she's "on to something".

7.04 p.m.

Mum just discovered the savoury muffin in the airing cupboard.

I told her I didn't want to upset her so I'd hidden it in some beach towels.

Then Mum said, "Hattie, I appreciate that but you should tell me the truth. I can take it."

I've noticed though that the truth can actually be a bit rubbish and if you can hide a craptacular ~~real dad~~ muffin somewhere you should.

SUNDAY 7TH FEBRUARY

10.02 a.m.

Operation Bhavin starts tonight at the park, under the slide at 5 p.m. Dimple has to go to the community centre, run out the back, meet Bhavin, have a laugh, snog Bhavin, run back to the community centre and find out what dance moves they were doing at Bollywood class from her friend Kelsey. I am going to the park to find them.

I hope Bhavin is worth it.

6.34 p.m.

HE IS WORTH IT!

Bhavin is gorgeous! It was amazing. When I turned up they were snogging under a tree near the public toilets. Even though they were under a massive orange street light it was TOTALLY romantic. He had bought her a Twix and then they pretended to have a sword fight with the bars. It's everything I've ever wanted. They stare at each other and eat chocolate. They don't even have to talk. It's BEAUTIFUL.

And Dimple got back in time.

I gave her some chewing gum so she didn't have Twix breath. Dimple's dad is the kind of man that would smell things like that and get suspicious.

8.16 p.m.
I am living my actual life through someone else's relationship. I don't care. It's like watching *Romeo and Juliet!*

9.02 p.m.
The romantic, middle part of *Romeo and Juliet* – not the horrible double poison death at the end.

9.16 p.m.
I do care. It's what I want. It's what I REALLY want.

OH, GOOSE! This could be US, you know. I'll take on your gecko like Rob took on me and Nathan. I think I could cope.

MONDAY 8TH FEBRUARY

5.35 p.m.
At school today Weirdo Jen started asking Dimple and me if she had offended us because we seemed a bit "distant". Poor Jen – she is max sensitive but we can't tell her because she might accidentally spread it. Dimple told her it was NOTHING but she is a terrible liar too. It was

really uncomfortable. I know Jen is going to ask her tarot cards what's going on.

8.45 p.m.

LOL! Just looked at Twitter! Gran has been hacked – Princess is suggesting ways you can lose weight with guava.

TUESDAY 9TH FEBRUARY

4.38 p.m.

Jen told us her tarot cards gave her "lots of wands and cups" – and told her that her friends were completely trustworthy.

I think she should stick to her runes. She has more of an affinity with them.

7.09 p.m.

Gran has disabled her Twitter account. Gran said, "It's gone to Princess's head. She wanted tucking in twice last night. I'm not doing divas."

She CREATED a diva.

I asked her about all the thousands she was going to make. Gran told me that there was, "No money in a fake pet Twitter account. It's a shame, Hattie, because I was going to use the profits to have a bit of a nip and tuck. I'll have to use my winter heating payment for Botox instead now."

Wednesday 10th February

7.01 p.m.

Dimple can't meet Bhavin tonight. Her dance class has been cancelled because practically the entire roof of the community centre has been stolen by people nicking building materials.

14 people saw them doing it but just assumed they were taking the roof off and putting it in the back of a white van for "maintenance".

I asked Dimple why she just didn't tell her dad about Bhavin. He's a lovely boy – completely sweet and polite. Mrs Rathod would LOVE him. Dimple said, "Hattie, last night Dad told me he was really, really worried about humanity and society. When I asked him what had caused this he said, *Come Dine with Me*. He can't handle me snogging!"

I hope the roof thieves realize the misery they have caused. I hope they all end up lonely with just plumbing pipes for company.

I have agreed to lie to Mum and Rob about meeting Dimple at the cinema tomorrow. Rob will ring Dimple's dad, tell him he's dropping us off and picking us up. Bhavin will meet us outside Screen 4.

THURSDAY 11TH FEBRUARY

9.37 p.m.

Went to the cinema. Bhavin and Dimple just snogged during the entire film. Then he took her to McDonald's and bought her a Beauty and the Beast happy meal. Then they snogged more and more till Rob arrived and Bhavin hid in Maccy D's toilets.

I got a milkshake.

Other people's love is lovely but it's getting on my nerves.

FRIDAY 12TH FEBRUARY

10.01 p.m.

I told Goose about Bhavin today. The truth is it's making me feel EVEN MORE lonely and GOOSE-needy. He said Dimple should tell her parents and that "true love shouldn't be hidden". I shouted back, "I think you fancy Dimple and you want it to be over so YOU can go after her!"

I have absolutely NO IDEA why I said that. NO IDEA. Goose looked at me like I was a total mental. At that moment I was.

I'm being driven mad by love. I always do the WRONG thing when I'm with him these days. I'm like a fire extinguisher that's completely putting out ANY Hattie love fire that's left in him.

11.39 p.m.

Think I might get a gecko. They keep you sane. And we'll have something in common.

SATURDAY 13TH FEBRUARY

8.08 a.m.

Mum says I can't have a gecko as they stink.

Why is my brother allowed to stay then?! LOL!

11.07 a.m.

Mum, JUST WEARING A BRA ON TOP, barged in whilst I was on Skype to Weirdo Jen and started telling me that if I shave my legs I need to clean the bath afterwards. Then she had a go AT ME for not telling her Jen was there and embarrassing HER! MUM!!! Jen now knows I am unhygienic AND hairy!

I could not have a secret ANYTHING.

5.40 p.m.

It's my birthday tomorrow. As far as I can see no baking has been done and there have been no suspicious trips to retail parks. I predict I will get money, which I will be forced to use on things that I should get as part of the whole deal — like my mobile.

BIRTHDAY AND VALENTINE'S!

SUNDAY 14TH FEBRUARY

8.29 p.m.

I am 15 today. The following happened:

---

1. I got £52.56. The odd amount is due to the fact that Gran had been collecting some of her winter fuel payment for my birthday as she realized Botox was pointless. This is actually a very sweet thing.

2. Keith left me a fake "I'm glad I'm not a plastic bag" cloth bag with a handmade card of a mouse holding some flowers. For a first birthday present EVER it was a tiny bit crap but it was a nice thought.

3. Mum revealed that Keith forgot her 21st birthday – "He thought I'd just put balloons on the gate to make it look pretty." BUT then she said things would be different now. SO she does admit HE HAS changed.

4. Bhavin sent Dimple's Valentine's flowers and balloons to me. Now everyone thinks I have a secret lover when all I actually have is a secret that belongs to someone else.

5. Dimple came round to collect her flowers and balloons so I had to give someone else a present on Valentine's Day.

6. Dimple said she thinks her parents might have found out about her and Bhavin because they seem a bit preoccupied and keep having "chats".

7. I looked REALLY guilty (what if me telling Goose has made it spread?!) but I hid it by turning round and saying how amazing her bunch of lilies were.

8. I went next door to see Goose. He assured me he hadn't rung Dimple's parents to tell them

about Bhavin and how could I EVER think that he would DO THAT?! Then he said, "JUST GO, HATTIE."

9. It's my birthday and Goose yelled at me. Great.

10. My birthday surprise meal was fajitas with Gran's special non-alcoholic tequila (aka watered-down lime juice).

11. It pays to go out with a slightly older 16-year-old who has a decent part-time job – Dimple's flowers cost £30!

12. The best present on my 15th birthday was someone else's Valentine's.

13. I have fallen out with someone I love.

14. I am going to bed. Goodnight. Sod off.

(HALF-TERM)   MONDAY 15TH FEBRUARY

1.10 p.m.

Goose came round to apologize. Then he gave me the nicest necklace. He said, "I was going to give it to you on your birthday but ... but I thought it might be ... I saw that massive bunch of flowers that got delivered to you and this looked a bit ... er... Anyway. I should go – I've got to help Mum hoover the stairs."

I didn't get the chance to say they weren't my actual flowers.

Oh, Goose, why can't it just happen?! Even your mum's Henry hoover comes before me.

Tuesday 16th February

10.12 a.m.

Just rang Gran for half-term LOVE advice. Gran said she was in the middle of watching *Colour Me Purple*.

10.37 a.m.

No! Gran just called back. She is watching *The Color Purple* and finding the best shade for her skin type on the "Colour Me Beautiful" app. Gran said, "It's all colours, Hattie – it's easy to get confused! The film is a bit too depressing for me so I thought we'd talk."

I asked Gran about men. Conversation as follows:

ME: I like Goose.

GRAN: Of course you like him. You used
         to play in his Wendy house.

ME: No. I think I really … like him.

GRAN: Does he like you in that way?

ME: I don't know. He never says so.
         And he's been kissing other girls.

GRAN: Then, Hattie, I hate to say it
         but you've messed it up – because
         he did. EVERYBODY could see it.
         Men can't hang around for ever.
         You need to spread your net a bit
         wider. There'll be other people
         who like you. Find out who!

ME: I messed up WHAT?! I haven't done
         anything.

GRAN: You should have said something!

ME: YOU tell me NOT to do that.

> GRAN: Hattie – I'm nearly in my 70s and I'm still confused about men. WE ALL ARE! Even men are confused about themselves!

Then I heard that Gran was sniffing. I asked her if the film was upsetting. She said, "Yes, Hattie, and I've just found out that I should only wear pastel shades and camel-beige. I'm a BRIGHTS person. What's wrong with orange?!"

Perhaps apps can tell the truth where humans can't.

I've messed up.

He's gone.

Goose is gone.

Got to get over it.

We can be friends. Now I need to find healing love.

WEDNESDAY 17TH FEBRUARY

11.03 a.m.

I have officially sent the word out via Dimple and Weirdo Jen that I'm available. There must be someone who fancies me. Even Dibbo Hannah has had more boyfriends than me!

11.16 a.m.

Is it feminist to just want a boyfriend?

11.37 a.m.

Weirdo Jen says just wanting any boyfriend could be seen as "a bit desperate".

A BIT DESPERATE?! Hattie Moore is NOT desperate! I am my OWN woman!

11.57 a.m.

I have just been into Nathan's room and ripped down his poster of some woman with massive mams wearing nearly nothing. That makes up for me being "a bit desperate", Jen! I told Jen that I'd destroyed something sexist. Jen said it's fine for a woman to feel comfortable in her own body. In fact there's "not enough of it".

I'm confused now. Are naked women wrong or not?

3.37 p.m.

Nathan wants to know where his poster is. I've hidden it in the recycling bin under 2 empty boxes of mango granola and Rob's big posh newspaper. Health foods and something clever – Nathan will never find it!

4.38 p.m.

Nathan has found it and gone mental. I told Mum I was offended by it as a woman and that it encouraged me to think I needed a boob job. SHE WENT ON MY SIDE!!! FANTASTIC!

Dear Mum,

Some other things that make me want a boob job are:

* Not having any money.
* Not having enough clothes.
* School.

LOL!

THURSDAY 18TH FEBRUARY

12.59 p.m.

OMG – apparently there is a rumour going round that Simon McKinnon fancies me! Simon McKinnon is vaguely uncraptacular but a bit of a mega-brain goth.

4.53 p.m.

Rang Dimple to find out more about Simon but she was out with Bhavin. She'd told her parents that she was doing homework with me! I said, "Dimple, you need to TELL me things like this. What if your parents check and ring my house?!" Dimple just giggled and said, "Oh yeah! Sorry Hats. Listen, got to go. The Bhavster and me don't have long. I told my parents I was asking you about a medicine through time project. See you soon."

Medicine through time?! Dimple's dad is a surgeon! Why would he believe that she'd need to ask ME about stuff like that?! Bhavin has made Dimple really do something thick. It's like men completely snog the clever bit of your brain out!

10.47 a.m.

Goose confirmed that Simon McKinnon fancies me, though he says he's a bit weird — in fact totally weird — and I should avoid him. Simon claims that he fixed his short-sightedness with the power of his own mind. Why would you bother doing that when there's Specsavers?

Goose seemed a bit jealous that a tall man who may not have a gecko but wears really cool boots fancies ME. GOOD. Perhaps deep down I have not killed all his pash for me.

1.38 p.m.

Jen is officially jealous TOO that Simon McKinnon fancies me as all the emos AND goths think he is a hero. They think he has special powers!

I don't believe this but I don't care. I just want Simon to have SUPERHERO LOVE SNOG ABILITY!

1.56 p.m.

I am a total doughnut.

9.23 a.m.

Just thought! This Simon McKinnon rumour might spur Goose into action. If he thinks someone else likes me he might actually DO something and I may get some love action! Perhaps good goth love will AWAKEN the GOOSE!

He'd have to REALLY have superpowers though to spur Goose into ANYTHING!

Sunday 21st February

4.38 p.m.

I went round to see Gran today to tell her that I had followed her advice. She said, "Hattie — it's about time you entered the world of men, but don't go the same way as your mother. Remember, if you stand up for nothing you'll fall for anything."

I assured Gran that I am not about to get pregnant by a boy called Keith who gets someone else pregnant at the same time!

Gran just said, "Good. Don't!" Then she carried on playing "Candy Crush Saga" on her iPad.

She also told me that she's decided to go to an art class tomorrow night as she feels she might have "hidden talents" and "needs to express herself". I don't think Gran has a problem with that! I don't think Gran has EVER had a problem with that!

Monday 22nd February

9.02 p.m.

UNBELIEVABLE!

MATFIELD runs Gran's new art class! SHE IS ALSO NICE to old people ALL the time! They even go to the pub for a drink afterwards! Over some gourmet beef-and-mustard crisps, Matfield told Gran that her CRAP stick men remind her of someone called "Lowry"!

9.21 p.m.

Just googled Lowry. He drew stick men! They are worth MILLIONS. This TOTALLY proves I have potential.

TUESDAY 23RD FEBRUARY

3.46 p.m.

There is now a MASSIVE rumour going around school about me and Simon McKinnon! Rebecca Pan has spread it that he fancies me and I've told her to spread it back that I like him. It's only a matter of time.

7.08 p.m.

Just had a humongous argument with Gran about Matfield. Gran says, "The school needs a woman like that. You could all do with a bit of discipline – it's not all hairspray and boys! Besides perhaps the woman has had a hard time in life, Hattie. You shouldn't judge." I yelled back at her, "We've all had a hard time, Gran! We do not all bully people about their collages!"

7.43 p.m.

OMG – I cannot believe Gran said "I shouldn't judge"! Gran judges everyone and everything. She told a security guard in Primark to keep an eye on a woman once because she was walking "funny". She wasn't at all! Gran admitted she thought she was suspicious because she had "red shoes – the footwear of a born shoplifter"(?!).

WEDNESDAY 24TH FEBRUARY

4.12 p.m.

FINALLY!!!

Simon McKinnon has sent me a note with loads of fantastic REALLY good doodles scribbled all over it.

OMG – PLAIN – private jet HERE I COME! I heard his parents were loaded.

4.26 p.m.

Jen says it means a SPIRITUAL PLAIN. That means you think the same thing.

5.38 p.m.

Wish it had been a plane. I don't want to be shallow but that would probably have made me probably like him more.

THURSDAY 25TH FEBRUARY

4.25 p.m.

I have replied to Simon McKinnon. I just said "yes". I didn't do any drawing as I'm rubbish.

Jen is really acting strangely with me. It's not my fault an emo does not attract a goth. Jen thinks I will have to go goth now. I asked for tips but she said it's not something you can learn. It's a state of being.

In my life one best friend is basically married. The other is getting cross that I might be.

6.26 p.m.
Jen texted. Apparently wearing black is a good start to being goth.

Like I didn't know that.

7.03 p.m.
I still love Jen though.

DATE TOMORROW! I am wearing black. And more black.

FRIDAY 26TH FEBRUARY

10.11 p.m.
I met Simon in the market place. We moved into Irongate where all the nice posh shops I can't afford are. He pulled out a blanket from his rucksack and put it over a bench. He'd brought a picnic! People were walking by either taking the mickey ("Bloody freaks!") or saying things like, "Ah! Young love!"

I couldn't decide if it was magnificent or just TOTALLY OFF THE SCALE strange. We had this picnic by candlelight and he kept asking me questions like, "Do you like bands like Frank the Baptist, A Spectre Is Haunting Europe and Cinema Strange?"

Do I? I'd never heard of them but I said "yes".

Then he said, "Do you believe in beings you can't see but can feel?" When I asked him, "Do you mean like a cushion?" he said, "Sort of. They may be of comfort."

Then we had this ... actually I don't know what it was! It was a sort of snog. I opened my eyes when we were kissing and he was staring at me. I shut my eyes quickly – but he SNOGS WITH HIS EYES WIDE OPEN. LIKE AN ALIVE ZOMBIE!

He eventually said, "Can I see you again?"

I think he can.

I don't know WHAT to think!

10.54 p.m.
Just listened to a bit of A Spectre Is Haunting Europe. It's just shouting noise.

11.38 p.m.
I can't text Jen about this because it looks like I'm rubbing it in. Dimple is probably having a Messenger love fest with Bhavin whilst she pretends to do some homework.

The truth is, I'm on my own with a goth who wants me but listens to really dreadful music. I thought Gran had bad taste.

SATURDAY 27TH FEBRUARY

8.23 p.m.

I think it's moving a bit too fast with Simon. He's asked me to consider committing to him in the afterlife as well as this life. It's apparently a goth thing.

Apparently he's committed to other girls but on different levels of being.

I said, "You're not a vampire, Simon". He stared at me for ages and whispered, "No – but I exist on different levels!"

Dear Simon – I think I just like this level and this life!

SUNDAY 28TH FEBRUARY

7.47 p.m.

I met Simon again this afternoon. He kept making me listen to goth stuff on his iPod!

For the record I think New Days Delay and Scarlet's Remains are AWFUL.

Honestly – I really just wanted a pizza and a DVD.

Then we had this conversation:

ME: Look, Simon, I don't really think we are suited. Do you like Jen?

SIMON: Yeah – but I thought she was out of my league!

ME: No – she's in your dark, semi-goth/emo league and she'd like to connect with you.

SIMON:	Oh – you couldn't arrange it, could you?!
ME:	Er … yes.

I expected a BIT more of a fight!

So I sort of dumped Simon the King of Goths in a soggy field near some tennis courts.

"She's out of my league." Well, Simon, I don't want to be IN your league.

8.09 p.m.
I have sorted out love for Jen. Dimple is having a secret relationship. But I am still SINGLE.

This is the price you pay for being a feminist woman of today who won't compromise. You end up watching the *MasterChef* final alone in your bedroom.

And has Goose rushed forward with his undying love? No – he's in his bedroom singing. I can't hear what Gregg Wallace thinks about someone's seared steak for the noise.

MONDAY 1ST MARCH

4.49 p.m.
TOTAL DEATH FROM RUMOUR!

It's going round school that it's ME who kisses with my eyes open. That's down to MGK! I do not kiss with my eyes open! It's Simon. I saw it with my own—

I can see their point now.

8.39 p.m.

Just had a shared homework night at Jen's. We didn't do any but we did talk ALL night about Simon McKinnon. His auntie has just died but he knows he will see her again in the next life. He's told Jen he really likes her but he needs to look after his dad too as they are like best mates.

Jen thinks he is VERY sweet and she can't wait to be with him more. I've warned her he kisses with his eyes open.

She snapped my head off: "That's fine — so do you!"

9.15 p.m.

Gran came back from Matfield's class with something she called a Mondrian. Matfield said Gran's picture was a "fantastic example of simple yet effective and powerful self-expression". They are TOTALLY just Lego blocks of colour, MATFIELD. If I did that you would say, "A 4-year-old could have done that — DETENTION!"

I am pretty fed up with everyone who has ever been in my life ever at the moment.

TUESDAY 2ND MARCH

5.28 p.m.

Came to see Gran after school and told her about Simon McKinnon's dead auntie. Gran said, "Well, we've all got to go someday, Hattie." Apparently Gran has Post-it notes

---

under everything in her house so "people can work out what is theirs when I cark it". OMG – that's so WRONG.

6.09 p.m.
Just checked her wardrobe – there's a Post-it note that says:

> Clothes and bedroom furniture to charity.

Thank GOD.

6.16 p.m.
Just checked her awful cuckoo clock – it says, "Daughter" aka Mum. LOL!

6.34 p.m.
OMG – the stuff she has left me is vile!

It's OK though because Gran isn't going to die for years!

WEDNESDAY 3RD MARCH

5.20 p.m.
Jen has been asked out by Simon McKinnon. I am officially Cupid! They can talk about Frank the Baptist and dead people together.

6.14 p.m.
Texted Jen tonight but she was too busy to talk. Dimple thinks Jen and Simon McKinnon could end up getting married they are so similar.

7.25 p.m.

OMG – has Jen checked that she isn't actually related to him? I'm living proof you can be related to anyone!

THURSDAY 4TH MARCH

3.40 p.m.

Jen has become a bit of an It girl at school because of her HOT relationship. Serious boyfriends mean serious popularity and she is getting it. Apparently it's so serious that Simon McKinnon has given up all other life forms on all other universes and committed to hers.

If an alien has more than 1 tongue – how do you kiss it?

4.02 p.m.

LOL! Mum says "with difficulty"!

4.11 p.m.

Since when is my mum funny?! Perhaps it's because we are getting closer in age that I understand her humour more.

5.19 p.m.

OMG – we are NOT getting closer in age. I'm getting older! So is Mum!

I'm convinced lack of love and pash is turning me really stupid.

Dentist tomorrow. Please take the braces OFF.

Friday 5th March

7.12 p.m.

My mad dentist has left. He has been replaced by Mr Winkler, who is German. He told me I have to keep my brace on for another 6 months. Apparently there's no point asking for a second opinion as it's "expensive"! Also because of his accent he said I should not "viggle" my electric toothbrush when I clean my teeth – I need to glide. When I started laughing he said, "I know I say it a bit funny but please don't laugh at my English, Hattie." He winked though so he's actually totally fine with me taking the mickey.

So no "viggling" or giggling – just more braces!

He was a brilliant dentist though – I didn't feel anything. Not like the one before. Mr Winkler had all his certificates on the wall. I wonder if the other one was an actual proper dentist? He just had a poster of a cartoon crocodile with big teeth on HIS wall!

7.36 p.m.

OMG – MGK has started hanging around Jen. Dimple and me are totally freaked out by this. What if she turns all MGK? She's got all our secrets. It would be like her joining a terrorist group!

8.04 p.m.

Actually not really.

8.49 p.m.

No way will Jen embrace FULL-ON MGK-ness — she's too emo and weird and basically wonderful.

SATURDAY 6TH MARCH

4.03 p.m.

Jen spent 12 minutes with MGK today getting boyfriend tips. Stuff like how to "keep your man interested" and "drive him wild". Jen already knows all this — it involves twisting a lock of your hair with his and putting a stone you've warmed in his bag. Jen says it never fails.

7.15 p.m.

Jen just texted. She wants to know if I have high heels.

Jen in high heels? No. No. No.

7.49 p.m.

MGK is like an evil disease that spreads and causes terminal girliness. Even Jen is not immune. MGK is like a superbug — but you can't even be cured at the doctor. She doesn't eat your flesh but she eats your personality.

SUNDAY 7TH MARCH

5.34 p.m.

Dimple and me just had the most uncomfortable afternoon EVER with Jen. I told a story about a girl leaving false eyelashes on a boy's shoulder when she kissed him. He freaked out as he thought they were caterpillars.

Normally Jen would LOL but today she said, "It's a bit immature to laugh at a girl who is just trying to look good — beauty does matter and accidents happen."

OMG!

It's MGK. Jen is infected. It's like her mind has been sucked out by MGK's brain hoover.

7.01 p.m.

Rang Dimple to have a total analysis of the afternoon. She was a bit weird and said her mum was "ill" and she "couldn't talk right now". Dimple can't talk because of her parents. Jen can't talk because she's a loved-up It girl of the moment. I can talk because the only thing I'm having a DEEP relationship with is peanut butter on toast.

MONDAY 8TH MARCH

6.35 p.m.

MEN!!! AGAIN!!!

Goose can't understand why I am so upset about Jen. I said, "Because she's had a personality transplant, Goose." Goose said, "Just don't hang around with her then!"

WHAT?!!

Men just give up on friends. Then they get geckos instead.

And they don't try hard enough to get YOU either!

9.28 p.m.

Gran just rang my mob. THE TOTAL LOVE AFFAIR between her and Matfield continues! Gran emailed me her "Rothko". It's worse than last week! It's 2 colours blurred together. I'm trying this on Wednesday with Matfield to see if she loves it when I do it too!

TUESDAY 9TH MARCH

8.24 p.m.

Mum and Rob went to the cinema tonight so I went round to Gran's to have pizza. She uses a knife and fork with takeaway pepperoni! Sort it out! I told her about Weirdo Jen and MGK. Gran hates MGK so I thought she'd totally be on my side.

Gran said, "You have a massive problem with jealousy, Hattie. You always have had. Like your mother."

Yes I have, Gran, but its genetic. I can't help it.

WEDNESDAY 10TH MARCH

5.17 p.m.

LEGENDARY DAY!

TODAY I PROVED THAT ALL TEACHERS TALK CRAPTACULAR BALLS OF NONSENSE!

Matfield asked us to paint how we felt so I just blended blue and red together. Matfield TOTALLY predictably said, "WHAT'S THAT?! My grandson could do better than that." I said, "Actually, Mrs Matfield, it's my ROTHKO — and when my gran did the same thing at art class on Monday night you said it was brilliant." Matfield just stared and started STUTTERING. Then she said, "Mature people bring an emotional maturity to art that young people cannot copy." We weren't quite sure what that meant but she was SWEATING and THEN had to "just nip out to get the mini guillotine". LOL! Bet she wanted to slice my head off and all she can actually chop is paper!

Nicky "bad boy" Bainton EVEN smiled at me!

1-0 to the HATTIE!!! GET IN!!!

THURSDAY 11TH MARCH

5.27 p.m.

OMG — Dimple's mum is NOT ill.

DIMPLE'S MUM IS PREGNANT!

worldfallingapart.com

Unbelievably Dimple is completely excited about her mum having a baby. What if it's a boy?! In fact I just know it WILL BE. Hasn't she known me long enough to realize the utter hell of brothers? Yes, he will be smaller but he can still cause DIMPLE hell!

Dimple says she has some serious thinking to do! Yes, you have, Dimple. Put everything you love away and prepare your actual mind for years of torture! At least Dimple

has grown out of Barbies. She won't have to go through
seeing her favourite doll with a completely shaven head
trying to ride the vicious dog that lives 3 doors away.

6.27 p.m.
Just want to say my brother put Barbie on the dog.
I wasn't saying she got up by herself or anything.

Brothers TORTURE TOYS.

4.19 p.m.
Dimple is totally upset about Jen because she texted Jen
with the news about her mum and she texted back:

> Congratulations! BTW, do you
> think I should go blonde?

Jen, what is going on?! No one in the underworld is blonde!

11.51 a.m.
Goose has invited me to the cinema tonight. OMG!
Perhaps this is it! I'm OBVIOUSLY going! He likes geek
films normally but it will take my mind off Jen and her
being a member of the MGK evil posse.

9.46 p.m.
Back from the cinema with Goose. OF COURSE IT
WASN'T "IT"! GIVE UP, HATTIE! STOP THE HEART
TORTURE! We saw a *Transformers* film. It was JUST

noise and machines banging each other on the head. We could only hear it a bit though because a group of boys at the back, including Nicky Bainton, were having a "Who can blow a piece of popcorn from their nose the furthest?" competition. The manager came in with this security guard and threatened to throw them out but not before one of them had moved on to trying to blow nachos out of his nose. He said he would sue them as the cheese was too hot and his nostril was "scarred for life"! THEN Nicky Bainton came and sat by me and Goose and started saying how good it was to see me out, and did I come here often? Goose looked cross but didn't say anything. He didn't say much on the way home either. I think if Goose could take Freak to the cinema he would.

Nicky is actually really funny when you get to know him.

SUNDAY 14TH MARCH

1.29 p.m.
Jen wants to see me and Dimple. She says it's URGENT. Perhaps she's having plastic surgery. Everything has gone mental.

5.28 p.m.
Jen has been brought to her senses by the moon phases. We have totally had an infiltrator in MGK's gang. We now KNOW the following:

* MGK thinks I am INTOLERANT!

---

* MGK thinks I HAVE BETTER LEGS THAN HER but THAT I WEAR CHEAP CLOTHES!
* MGK rings up her gang before they go out and makes them DETAIL what they are going to wear so she can make sure she ALWAYS looks best.
* MGK eats MINI TINS OF SWEETCORN COLD FOR LUNCH ON THEIR OWN LIKE THAT IS NORMAL.
* MGK hates her real name and would prefer to be another gemstone — say, "Diamond" or "Sapphire Slack" — LOL!

MONDAY 15TH MARCH

3.56 p.m.

I'm definitely being asked to process too much information at the moment (got that phrase out of Mum's *Psychologies* mag!). So basically, according to Jen, MGK talks about me all the time. It's like she fancies me or something. Yet she STILL ignores me in real life and spreads gossip.

6.35 p.m.

Gran says MGK is jealous of ME?! Jealous of what?!

* Braces.
* No wardrobe.
* An evil brother.
* A worse relationship with our real dad.
* A gran who still has some of Father Christmas's nose in diamantes on her backside.

10.02 p.m.

THE BEST BREAKING NEWS EVER! Gran has fallen out with Matfield. Her "Blue Period Picasso" didn't come up to the mark! Gran shouted, "I don't come here to be criticized!" Matfield suggested that art WAS about criticism and perhaps Gran should consider learning a foreign language.

Gran said, "I did tell her something in bloody French then and I walked out!"

That's her way of saying she swore.

<u>GRAN SWORE AT MATFIELD. LIVING THE DREAM.</u>

Gran is actually paying for my art crimes but I'm never telling her!

TUESDAY 16TH MARCH

5.46 p.m.

MGK TOTALLY knows Jen has been talking! She keeps death-staring me and then today, after Science, she came up to me and said:

```
MGK:    Have you heard from Dad?
ME:     You mean Keith?
MGK:    Yes - DAD. He emailed me the
        other day. It was a HUGE mail.
        I think he really sees me as
        someone he can talk to on his own
        level.
```

I just walked off. She means intelligence level. She's right – SLIGHT DOUGHNUT!

6.49 p.m.

Why hasn't he emailed me?

7.18 p.m.

He HAS emailed me – it was in the "junk" folder.

From: <keithkeepsitgreen@gmail.com>
Date: March 10, 8:23:12 PM GMT
To: Hattie Moore <helphattienow@gmail.com>
Subject: YOU!!!

Dearest Hattie,

How are you? Just want you to know I think of you often and how proud of you I am. You're an amazing young woman and it was lovely spending time with you.

How is school?

K xxx

Is THAT it?!

MGK gets an essay and I get 3 sentences?!

WEDNESDAY 17TH MARCH

5.32 p.m.

Came home to find my mum telling Rob and Nathan off for filling a rubber glove full of water and letting it off in the back garden. Apparently it was "massive".

ALL men are ALL 8 years old, ALL totally confusing and ALL RUBBISH.

THURSDAY 18TH MARCH

3.58 p.m.

OMG – INSANITY SPECIAL!!!

Dimple is ending the relationship with BHAVIN!

Dimple said, "Mum is pregnant, Hattie! She needs help". I said, "Dimps – you need to start putting yourself FIRST. Like Oprah says, you have to LOVE yourself before you can love anybody else!" Dimple says it's not fair to put an extra burden on her parents at this time. I shouted at her, "IT'S SECRET – HOW WOULD IT?!"

This is family loyalty gone mad. If I had a Bhavin, I wouldn't give him up for anyone!

4.34 p.m.

That's not true. I wouldn't want to hurt my family again for anyone. Except for you know who – and they all love him anyway.

FRIDAY 19TH MARCH

4.28 p.m.

Dimple was a bit down at school today. She told Bhavin it was over by text! He was really upset (he did about 20 sad faces) but he "understood"! UNDERSTOOD?! Those 2 were totally marriage material and they've given up their max pash without even a goodbye SNOG!

Dimple said clean breaks are good. *No, they are not.*
They hurt. You can't just give up on people – even
if your family need you or they do things that totally
annoy you.

7.46 p.m.

LOL!

Nathan is furious. He has been unemployed for so long that
they are making him do unpaid work. It's for "experience".
Mum thinks it's disgusting that Nathan is being forced to
work for free. She was cursing about the government.
Then Gran started saying all this stuff.

GRAN: It will do you good, boy! Your mum
spoils you rotten. She still buys
you Cheesestrings and Happy Face
biscuits!

NATHAN: You have no idea, Gran. It's
terrible out there. There are NO
jobs!

GRAN: Yes – you are right, Nathan!
There are no jobs for people who
get up past noon, go to bed at 4
in the morning, have hardly any
qualifications and want to be paid
£40 an hour!

NATHAN: I am prepared to go to work.

GRAN: I'm prepared to let you! It's about
time you paid for my pension.
In fact I might get a little job
myself. I fancy some company and
a bit of spending money.

<u>I LOVE GRAN</u>.

She clearly won't get a job but she's really upset Nathan!!!

SATURDAY 20TH MARCH

5.27 p.m.

Gran is applying for jobs. She has done her CV. It's about 3 lines.

> In my nearly 70 years on this Earth I have done every job known to man, had a child and managed a home with a husband in prison without any state benefits. There is nothing I won't do or try. I have a doctorate from the University of Life.

It's good to see her coming clean about her past and Grandad's criminal record but she's got no chance getting a job!

SUNDAY 21ST MARCH

8.35 p.m.

My brother is such a GO-GETTER!

HE got up about noon. That's like 6 a.m. for him! When I asked him what he was going to do for the rest of the day, he said, "What's it got to do with you, Tatty?!" (the not-funny name he calls me).

Then Nathan did NOTHING all day except eat 2-finger Kit Kats and watch the *Antiques Roadshow* while playing "Guess how much it's worth" and "Will the old bag bringing it be disappointed" with Rob!

I don't think that is a skills requirement for any job except for being a TV collectables expert AND they make you wash before you go in front of the camera. That means Nathan is out – LOL!

MONDAY 22ND MARCH

5.37 p.m.

We were talking about careers today at school. Dimple is definitely going to university. Can I even afford to go? Weirdo Jen wants to open her own "retail venture" (that's what you call a shop if you want to get a bank to give you money, her dad says). MGK wants to be a fashion buyer. Dibbo Hannah said, "You already are – you get stuff from the Internet, don't you?!"

LOL! We all agreed Dibbo Hannah should be a stand-up comedian!

6.43 p.m.

Dibbo Hannah wasn't trying to be funny, BTW – she was just being Dibbo Hannah.

I'm still not quite sure what I want to do.

8.09 p.m.

Nathan is watching *Lady and the Tramp* in his room.

The good thing is, Nathan has proved you can just stay here with Mum basically for ever until you decide what you REALLY want to do.

TUESDAY 23RD MARCH

6.12 p.m.

AMAZEBALLS!

Gran has an interview at the supermarket around the corner. The manager wants to see her as he thinks she's just the sort of person he's looking for!

So the manager is looking for old ladies with mad dogs who don't know what to do with vajazzles.

That doesn't sound good for Nathan.

WEDNESDAY 24TH MARCH

7.12 p.m.

Gran has got the job! Apparently the supermarket like people of a mature age as "they know how to work hard, whereas young people think it all arrives on a plate in life".

Gran is thrilled – she gets a 15% off discount staff card and has to wear BRIGHT red every day. She said, "My shirt is in 'Cherry Dream'. It makes me look fabulous. I may be nearly 70 but the truth is, Hattie, men still find me fascinating."

OMG – I WISH I WAS!

8.25 p.m.

I've just been to see Goose. He thinks Gran is taking a job off a young person who really needs it. This may be true but when I told Nathan that Gran had got a job he texted her a "Congratulations" message! He's not bothered that he has missed out on being employed. He's just glad he's not filling the fresh produce counter with carrots and Gran is!

Goose is grumpy a lot these days. A lot. I just seem to annoy him. Whatever I do. Why do I even bother?

9.01 p.m.

Gran just told me she won't be "replenishing stock" – she'll be operating the lottery machine and selling cigarettes in the kiosk. "I don't do heavy lifting, Hattie – I'll leave that to the tiny number of young people who have decided they do want to work!"

I've noticed everybody over 30 has a really nasty streak and thinks they have had it really hard. I'm never going to end up like that. I'll always be nice to teenagers. I'll never forget how MENTAL it all is. I will never forget the trauma of watching a gran make her dog pretend she is a customer wanting to buy a multi-entry lottery ticket on a triple rollover week.

9.36 p.m.

I just asked Gran what she will miss about her life whilst she is at work. Gran said, "I will miss going to funerals, Hattie. I go to funerals to get ideas."

Like I say, I will NEVER forget.

7.25 a.m.

Gran is being sent on a vegetable and fruit recognition course today. It's standard supermarket procedure apparently. No matter what department you work in you have to know a pomegranate from a sweet potato.

3.39 p.m.

Gran just texted:

> Hattie - what is the point of
> star fruit?

I should be thinking about MY future, not directing Gran on dessert.

6.45 p.m.

Everybody was talking today about what they are doing at the weekend.

Dimple – helping her mum put the new cot together.

Weirdo Jen – going out with Simon for a "paranormal tour" – aka "snogging".

MGK – clothes shopping with her mum and her "stepdad's big credit card".

She did a rubbish little giggle – ← ARGH!!!

Mum – hot Bath. *Good Housekeeping*. Glass of Pinot Noir.

Goose and Rob — boot sale.   ← Rob doesn't annoy him.

Nathan — playing snooker with his mate, Mo.

Gran — supermarket social night.

Hattie — nothing. NOTHING.

Just moaned to Mum. She said that the "world is at my feet" and I should go off and do something. Then she asked, "Are you too old to be a Brownie, Hattie?"

Yes, Mum.

She suggested Brownies after a bath and a red wine. Sometimes she can have 5 baths in one weekend.

7.47 p.m.
Dimple just messaged me a photo of a cot. I love you, Dimple, but it is just basically a cot. You put a baby in it. Whoop-de-doo.

I NEED PASH! I'm getting baby-bored middle-aged conversations before I've even had the HOT snogging.

8.56 p.m.
Just tried having a long bath. It's boring. I ended up looking at my feet for about 10 minutes. They are foul. I think I can live with my tiny boobs but my feet are TOTALLY deformed.

9.32 p.m.
OMG — according to a web page I just found toe cleavage is as important as breast cleavage and surgery CAN make my feet prettier.

The page doesn't give the price of the surgery but it must be more than the £12.68 I've got left from my Christmas money.

10.11 p.m.

Text from Jen:

> Think we just saw a ghost by
> the cathedral!

Ghosts may be dead but at least they just get to float without worrying about how their feet look in pumps.

SATURDAY 27TH MARCH

9.24 p.m.

Gran just rang my mob to say that the supermarket do was totally craptacular. For 400 people there were 3 plates of ribs, 2 platters of chicken and 2 bowls of fries. PLUS the Tom Jones impersonator only knew 3 songs. Gran had to leave — she was livid. She said, "If people pay good money they should get more than some middle-aged man in a wig threatening to make himself a prime contender for a hip replacement. I've had a better buffet at a..."

Funeral. YES, WE KNOW, Gran.

Why do old people talk about death ALL of the time?!

10.10 p.m.

Old people AND Weirdo Jen.

10.32 p.m.

Perhaps because everyone else is busy at the moment this is the perfect time to work on ME!

10.54 p.m.

I'm reading an article in a mag called "FEEL GREAT ABOUT YOU IN A WEEK!" I'll try it tomorrow.

SUNDAY 28TH MARCH

8.23 a.m.

"FEEL GREAT ABOUT YOU IN A WEEK!" suggests getting everyone round for a DVD night and between films asking everyone to write down what they love about all the other people in the room.

MAHOOSIVELY good idea. I'm going to do it!

9.25 a.m.

Dimple says her mum is really struggling with being pregnant at the moment and she can't really commit to a night for definite. She has to be around if her mum starts crying or wants a jacket potato (apparently every 5 minutes) but she'll message me.

11.04 a.m.

Weirdo Jen says she'll text me when she's got a date that she's free. She's spending all her time with Simon at the moment on "their planet".

Their planet is actually THIS planet. I saw them at the petrol station the other night buying a grab bag of Quavers.

Goose? *No* – no more disappointment. Fed up of dates that are actually just mates.

Boys and babies ruin everything.

MONDAY 29TH MARCH

7.02 p.m.

Nothing happened again today except for Gran taking over the supermarket social committee. The first thing she has organized is a bingo night. The under-30s aren't very happy. Gran said, "No wonder the parties have been so bad. The lady who used to run things had a beautifully made-up face but the dirtiest neck I have ever seen."

8.18 p.m.

No word today from Dimple or Jen.

I can't believe I am saying this: I wish I was at school.

TUESDAY 30TH MARCH

4.04 p.m.

The couple over the road were having a hell of a row this afternoon. They were swearing every other word! It was max chav! I had to go upstairs for a better look!

5.05 p.m.

OMG – I'm actually turning into Gran!

5.12 p.m.

No, I'm just bored. Can't show Mum I'm bored though – she'll make me clean the bath.

6.26 p.m.

I'm still stuck on Step 1 of "FEEL GREAT ABOUT YOU IN A WEEK!" I don't think it's going to happen.

7.47 p.m.

Weirdo Jen has just posted a photo of her and Simon in a tent in her back garden celebrating "Spring".

It's definitely not going to happen.

I have too much time to think and my thinking leads to a Goose cul-de-sac every time. The cul-de-sac of dashed hopes, exotic pets and ... stuff.

WEDNESDAY 31ST MARCH

6.28 p.m.

Gran was called into the supermarket office today and asked by Roger the general manager if she'd seen "anything strange" whilst she was on the morning shift the other day. She said she hadn't. Roger then showed her some CCTV footage. A man shoplifted 5 bottles of whisky, a widescreen TV and 12 pots of yoghurt at exactly 11.12 a.m. during Gran's morning shift.

Gran missed it all because she was doing Irish dancing with Elsie in the kiosk.

On the footage you could see Gran and Elsie flinging their arms in the air whilst the bloke walked out with a massive trolley. Scott from security was on a cigarette break — and the kiosk is meant to take "extra care" when he is

---

not around. They didn't. They did what Roger called "a carefree jig".

They don't think Gran is "in on the scam" (they MUST suspect a bit — she was married to a thief) BUT she's in trouble for not paying attention.

Roger said that the company was "very sensitive to other cultures, including Celtic traditions — but there's not really a place for cultural expressions when stock is at risk".

Gran decided she's only up to working part-time. Roger agrees it's a good idea.

THURSDAY 1ST APRIL

11.25 a.m.

OMG!

OMG!

OMG!

Goose and Rob bought an ornament from the boot sale on Sunday for £2 and it's worth £150,000!!! Rob says they've had it valued. It's Ching Dynasty China — you can tell on the bottom!

Mum is screaming, "Finally I can get the dishwasher fixed!" She is LOONY happy. She keeps breaking her nails washing up.

1.25 p.m.

Gran is THRILLED. She said, "I told your mother they'd strike gold. She just thought Rob was avoiding doing the crazy paving in the garden."

Hattie is thinking, "HELLO, VERSACE – OR SOME DECENT CLOTHES!"

3.37 p.m.

April Fool AGAIN.

Goose and Rob have just admitted it's an April Fool. Of course it is. NOTHING that good could ever happen. Gran and Mum are livid. Mum had already been to the shop and bought some Finish "diamond standard" Powerball dishwasher tablets. "I had dreams of unloading that machine," she said. She looked like she was about to cry!

4.23 p.m.

Goose and me have just had a MASSIVE ROW...

ME: Thanks for the MASS DISAPPOINTMENT SESSION, GOOSE!

GOOSE: It was just a joke, Hattie.

ME: Well, you got our hopes up and let us down. You're actually very good at that.

GOOSE: WHAT?!

ME: It's becoming a bit of a habit!

GOOSE: You're a FINE one to talk, HATTIE MOORE!

ME: Meaning?

GOOSE: Meaning?!

```
ME:      Goose … just … I don't care any
         more…
GOOSE:   ME NEITHER.
ME:      Fine. Right, I've got to go and
         wash up. Mum is too gutted to face
         it tonight – she thought she was
         getting a dishwasher. Thanks for
         that TOO.
```

And no, I'm not apologizing. Not this time.

6.17 p.m.

Gran has asked Nathan if he wants to take over some of her shifts at the supermarket. Nathan didn't think it was really "him". What IS Nathan? That is a question I have been asking all of my life?

I'm going to the library tomorrow. I KNOW! GEEK AHOY! BUT it's free, they have good films and it's not next door to Goose.

Oh, Goose.

I'm sorry.

But I'm sick of saying it.

FRIDAY 2ND APRIL

4.12 p.m.

BREAKING NEWS!

TOTAL LIBRARY SHOCK!

Was just minding my own business in the library when I saw Nicky "bad boy" Bainton. He was reading *Of Mice and Men* in a big chair! That's the sort of book school MAKES you read! He didn't see me but he looked AMAZEBALLS. He's had a massive haircut – in aid of a cancer research charity apparently. He has gone from grubby boy to TOTAL chiselled fitty! I can't believe it! I told Mum, "ALL the boys should now get the chop." Mum laughed but Rob just looked odd and said, "Don't say 'the chop' – it means something else. And I've had it. Hair grows back, Hattie."

Men talk another language. They are totally from Jupiter!

5.04 p.m.
MARS! Men are from Mars! It's all planets! The point is it's miles away and we haven't got a clue what language they speak there!

5.26 p.m.
OR if there is any intelligent life there at all!

Goose is from another black-hole galaxy worm-hole thingy – the sort of mental thing that Brian Cox goes on about.

SATURDAY 3RD APRIL

6.12 p.m.
I went to see Gran this afternoon. She was moaning about her weight again. She is on the Postnatal Diet – even though she had her baby nearly 40 years ago! She says Mum made her "stick on weight" and now she looks "chubby in her cherry shirt".

How long can you blame your family for your terrible life?

6.49 p.m.

Answer – FOR EVER.

SUNDAY 4TH APRIL

10.02 a.m.

EASTER – new starts and all that. And thanks, MUM – 2 eggs this year ... and one is a Crunchie. The bits get stuck in my braces but who cares?!

12.34 p.m.

"FEEL GREAT ABOUT YOU IN A WEEK!" has failed but at least I've found out that the library is actually a not completely dullster place. Mum told me it was a good place when I was 7. What else is she right about?!

2.13 p.m.

Going to the library again tomorrow. Perhaps it's good that Dimple, Jen and me are spending some time apart. We can't be together for ever. Mum never talks to people from her school!

That makes me want to cry.

3.03 p.m.

OMG – think of a time when MGK is not THERE EVERY DAY! HEAVEN!

MONDAY 5TH APRIL

11.23 a.m.

The library is shut on a bank holiday! Why do interesting places shut on a boring day?!

5.45 p.m.

Just been round to see Weirdo Jen. I told her about Nicky. She didn't seem that shocked. She says that Nicky Bainton spends a lot of time out of his house because his parents are a TOTAL NIGHTMARE. When I said, "Aren't everyone's!?" Jen sort of whispered, "No – they really are. His mum shouts at everyone and his dad is always in slippers."

Then she said, "OMG – you don't fancy him, do you, Hattie?! He is BREAKING BAD NEWS CENTRAL!"

I told her "no". But the truth is, I'm ... just not sure.

I feel bad now. I'm not sure what for but I do. Gran would tell me to stop moping.

Goose might get it but hasn't said sorry for the April Fool's non-joke and I am NOT really feeling like speaking to him.

TUESDAY 6TH APRIL

3.12 p.m.

Nicky "bad boy" Bainton has slightly broken his ankle! I helped him up the stairs at the library. He looked at me sort of embarrassed and said, "Thanks Moore-on – without

my hair I lost my balance." He looks sexy with crutches.
I like vulnerability.

4.01 p.m.

Did I just write "I like vulnerability"?!

I may be a bit of an idiot.

I am an idiot. I haven't spoken to Goose for nearly a
week. I miss him. I even miss Freak.

WEDNESDAY 7TH APRIL

8.12 a.m.

UNBELIEVABLE! An email from Keith:

> **From:** <keithkeepsitgreen@gmail.com>
> **Date:** April 6, 11:09:47 PM GMT
> **To:** Hattie Moore <helphattienow@gmail.com>
> **Subject: Summer**
>
> Hats – are you coming in the summer? I need to book
> your flight.

Dear KEITH – thanks for getting in touch with another
tiny email that is almost certainly smaller than MGK's.
Love,
Hattie x

1.27 p.m.

Am I going? In situations like this, Gran always says make
a "for and against" list.

FOR	AGAINST
✓ It's abroad.	✗ What if I hate it?!
✓ He's my dad.	✗ What if I've found the love of my life by then and a long-distance relationship won't work?!
✓ Australia looks amazing.	
✓ He will like MGK more than me if I don't.	

4.26 p.m.

Gran has looked at my "for and against" list. She just said, "It's an experience, Hattie."

That's what she said when Mum had her gall bladder out.

5.12 p.m.

I should give Keith more of a chance. He's not like Nicky's parents. I suppose he's trying to do something a bit good.

THURSDAY 8TH APRIL

6.12 p.m.

Unbelievable!

I went to the library again today. I saw Nicky and just nodded at him. HE CAME OVER!

FULL CHAT:

Not Moore-on!
↓

```
NICKY:   Hello, Hattie. What are you doing
         here?
ME:      Oh, just … looking at stuff.
NICKY:   Do you read a lot?
ME:      A bit.
NICKY:   What sort of stuff?
```

ME: Mice!   ← WHY DID I SAY THAT? WHY DO I NEVER GET IT RIGHT?

NICKY: Er... Do you want to come
           to the cinema? 'Cos I'm on
           these I can get the comfy   ← He wobbled crutches
           disabled seats.

ME: Yeah, OK. Text me.   ← I sounded cool with that!

I think I may fancy him. He's mysterious and there's just a bit of danger about him.

8.08 p.m.

Just told Dimple about Nicky. She said being in plaster does not make you dangerous. It just makes you stupid.

I could get cross but I think she STILL misses Bhavin.

FRIDAY 9TH APRIL

4.15 p.m.

I just think I could help Nicky bring out his sensitive side. His deep side. The side that reads classics underneath his jumper.

7.04 p.m.

Told Gran about Nicky. She reckons I am trying to change him already and changing a man takes a "military mission" and "usually ends in total defeat for the woman — it's kamikaze, Hattie, trust me."

8.07 p.m.

Kamikaze were pilots who went on suicide missions. OMG — there've been total nutters in the sky for over 80 years!

SATURDAY 10TH APRIL

2.35 p.m.

Jen and me had a ~~row~~ debate about Nicky. She thinks it's
ethically wrong to use the disabled seats at the cinema
BUT she agrees it's fine at Asda for my mum to use the
"mother and baby" parking spaces when she goes shopping
with Gran.

Why aren't my friends HAPPY FOR ME? It's apparently
FINE for THEM to have boyfriends but NOT me?! Is
THAT FAIR?! NO!

SUNDAY 11TH APRIL

9.32 p.m.

Nicky has asked me to the cinema tomorrow. It's the
first day back at school but Mum says she appreciates I
haven't seen many of my friends and I can go as long as
I'm back early.

10.28 p.m.

OMG – I think Mum feels sorry for me! That's tragic.

MONDAY 12TH APRIL

BACK TO SCHOOL.

5.39 p.m.

It was great to be back with Dimple and Jen today but
Dimple was mainly moaning about her mum and Jen was
mainly mooning about Simon. I was a bit bored by lunch.
Then both of them started going on about Nicky again
like he is a major criminal, and "Why didn't I go out with

someone a bit nicer?" When I said, "Like who?!" they just looked at each other. Helpful. NOT.

I can go out with WHO I like. Everyone deserves a chance. Weirdo Jen reckons she is so open to different beings but she is NOT. Apparently they don't want me to get "hurt". BUT it already hurts feeling like such a single doughnut.

MGK has got a new boyfriend with a CAR. Everyone agrees she's a cow but brilliant at the same time. She IS a cow and she IS brilliant and she is STILL my half-sister. Why can't I have her attracting-men jeans?!

6.03 p.m.
GENES not jeans. Actually I'd like her jeans too. She only has Levi's. Her bum looks amazeballs in them.

6.11 p.m.
Gran says MGK is like a Venus flytrap. Men get sucked in by the sweetness and die. She's a teenage-boy trap!

I'd like to be a carnivorous man-eating plant!

10.12 p.m.
BEST NIGHT EVER!

Nicky took me to the cinema. The attendant woman said it would be OK to sit in the disabled seats but if a really disabled person came in we would have to move. They didn't. The film was OK but Nicky was GORGEOUS. He's REALLY funny. He knows ALL the boys at the back who throw popcorn and he's REALLY popular. At the end −

I didn't even expect it to happen – we had this really odd fantastic kiss. I had to partly prop him up because of his crutches. He leaned against a fire exit and we snogged. We had to be careful though as we were worried that the fire exit would accidentally open and Nicky would break his arms too.

10.57 p.m.

Could I go out with someone from the Paralympics? Yes. If I loved someone I would even pick their nose for them.

11.06 p.m.

I can't get over how Nicky kisses.

He could be THE ONE! SERIOUSLY.

TUESDAY 13TH APRIL

5.39 p.m.

Weirdo Jen asked me all about the date. I told her he was actually really sweet. THEN she asked if Nicky had any scars. Simon has no scars and Jen likes them. She is dark that way. She said she was basically trying to find ways to like Nicky. I told her he actually made me HAPPY and THAT should be enough.

There was a massive pause and then she said she liked Nicky's crutches as they are cyber-punk.

I am better at thinking about other people's feelings than people are at thinking about mine! EVEN JEN!

Certainly better than Goose, who STILL hasn't been in touch.

WEDNESDAY 14TH APRIL

7.12 p.m.

Nicky came round tonight. He couldn't get upstairs on his crutches so we spent (TOO MUCH) time in the lounge with Mum asking ridiculous questions. I didn't even warn or tell her about him earlier because I KNEW she would interrogate him anyway! Mum seemed to think he was OK but said, "Be careful, Hattie – he's from a tough side of the tracks. That's not his fault but it can make him a bit – unpredictable."

I KNOW, Mum. I KNOW! THAT'S what makes him SO FIT!!!

8.45 p.m.

I want to go and tell Goose about Nicky.

We need to make up. I miss him and just because he doesn't want to be lovers doesn't mean we can't be friends. Telling him about Nicky will put him at his ease a bit and I don't think he'll feel ... lust pressure. Though part of me still wants HIM TO BE AS JEALOUS AS HELL.

That is a bad part of me. But I need to go and sort it out. Men never say sorry. I'll have to say it first. It's not feminist but it's life.

Thursday 15th April

7.53 p.m.

It was weird with Goose today. His mum looked really pleased to see me and said, "Just go up, Hattie." But when I did we had this really weird conversation...

ME: Look, Goose – I'm really sorry. I said some horrid things. And you know I don't really mean them.

GOOSE: Are you going out with Nicky Bainton?

ME: Well … yes … I suppose so. Yes.

GOOSE: Well, I could see THAT coming when I took you to the cinema. You know what – when someone takes you out you should actually speak to THEM, Hattie.

ME: You hardly say anything any more though unless it's about your gecko or boot sales or… Look, I'm sorry. I just thought you and me…

GOOSE: Look. Let's just forget about it.

ME: What, me and you?

GOOSE: What do you mean, "me and you"?

ME: I mean, me and you. You know the old Power Rangers team. Good friends. I know that … I know…

GOOSE: Oh.

ME: So me and you are OK?

GOOSE: Yes, me and you are fine.

ME: Oh, Goose, I'm so glad because I've actually really missed you.

GOOSE: I've missed you, Hattie.

But he didn't seem very happy at me and him being friends again. I don't get it. It's like a tiny part of him might in a tiny way fancy me but there is a wall in his head that stops him thinking that we can. Or this might be nonsense. He just never does ANYTHING about it. He never COMMITS. Nicky is on crutches and that hasn't stopped him snogging me.

Anyway we are friends again. I think.

I don't know. Who knows? I could read every book about boys going and not be able to understand this one. I would fail my boy GCSE.

FRIDAY 16TH APRIL

7.21 p.m.

Nicky asked me this afternoon, "What's going on with Goose?" I said, "Er... NOTHING!" Then Nicky said, "I want you to spend less time with him." I shouted a bit, "No, Nicky! Goose has been my friend since I was basically zero years old! I'm actually a feminist. I see who I want!"

What's that about?!

8.05 p.m.

Gran says, "Nicky is jealous, Hattie. Men are very territorial. They are like tomcats."

I think I like jealousy when it's over me.

SATURDAY 17TH APRIL

3.52 p.m.

Nicky can't see me tonight. He's busy. I get that. I'm an independent woman. I'll do something else exciting.

5.09 p.m.

I'm going round to Gran's to watch *Britain's Got Talent*.

8.12 p.m.

Gran has a crush on David Walliams! She said, "He's a lovely boy! All that swimming for charity – and he takes his mum everywhere!"

SUNDAY 18TH APRIL

5.19 p.m.

I've decided that me and Nicky are <u>serious</u>. Jen has MAX reluctantly given me the full MGK list of tips on how to treat a boyfriend. Basically back off and snog hard. You can try to change them but you have to do it gently – they don't notice if you do it slowly. I don't know if I can do that. It took Mum years to get Rob to put the toilet seat down. It's better to get things sorted now!

MONDAY 19TH APRIL

7.13 p.m.

Nicky is SO mature. He plays poker. He says he's a high-stake gambler. My gran wants him to come round for a game. How can Gran afford to gamble?! She says she's too poor these days to eat fresh vegetables!

7.49 p.m.

Then again I have heard her say, "I'd rather live on Aldi baked beans than miss bingo." Food means nothing to Gran when it comes to the regional full-house jackpot.

TUESDAY 20TH APRIL

8.23 p.m.

Gran is now actually taking jobs and money off young people! She won £5.36 tonight off Nicky at poker. She said he was too easy to read. She's been giving him lessons in her poker face. She says he's perfected it too quickly. She whispered at me, "Watch him, Hattie – he plays his cards close to his chest. Too Close!"

Anyway Gran has invited Nicky to Skegness on Sunday. I don't think I want Nicky to see my family at the seaside. They turn even more mental than normal! My mum still thinks she can get on a donkey. She can't.

8.55 p.m.

It's a bit weird. Normally Goose comes with us to Skegness.

He used to.

That makes me sad.

Does it matter that Nicky holds his cards close to his chest? What does that mean?!

Wednesday 21st April

5.23 p.m.

Gran didn't mean literally. She meant he was a private person. Gran doesn't understand people who don't gossip. If she gets a juicy titbit she actually has a special list of people she rings.

5.45 p.m.

To be fair so do I!

6.04 p.m.

Perhaps slagging people off is genetic. I hope hairy nostrils aren't. How do you wax the inside of your nose?!

8.42 p.m.

Tonight I told Nicky I loved him. I am fully in control of my feelings and can share them openly. It's not pathetic. Nicky didn't answer back but I'm sure he will.

Thursday 22nd April

5.24 p.m.

Today at work Gran told a trainee in the supermarket to wear a top that "didn't show her lungs" (that means her breasts in Gran-speak) and she got away with it! She says a woman cannot be taken seriously when the entire shop is talking to her boobs. The trainee THANKED Gran for her careers advice! This is Gran, not Alan Sugar – her employment history includes sewing the elastic into knickers and packing Marmite into boxes. AND WHY CAN'T A WOMAN WEAR WHAT SHE WANTS?!

6.33 p.m.

Gran is now considering becoming a union representative. This means you get to shout at your boss and NOT get sacked! Nicky thinks this is really cool as authority needs to be challenged at every level. I'm just thinking, "Will she lose her discount card and have to pay full price for DVDs?"

Stuff the workers, as Gran calls them! I want everything with Robert Pattinson in for £7.

FRIDAY 23RD APRIL

5.52 p.m.

Dr Richards set the essay question "I love" today. He called it an exercise in self-discovery. Dimple said, "I bet MGK's answer is one word – ME!" LOL!

Then Jen looked across and saw the first part of MGK's answer!

> I love my friends. They've got my back and I've got theirs. I love shopping and my fave label is Prada.

Superficial or what?!

Florence Morse – ultimate rebel – wrote:

> I love the way teachers set these exercises thinking that we'll tell them everything about us so they can control us via emotional blackmail and mind control. No. I cannot be enslaved by the

modern tactics of mass education. I am a riddle, wrapped in a mystery, inside an enigma.

I know she is always in trouble BUT she always sounds dead clever.

What do I love? I LOVE NICKY! But I can't write that. He's busy again tomorrow. Doing what? Not asking. I am not turning into a psycho-girlfriend.

7.12 p.m.
Gran says Florence is copying Winston Churchill. Bet the teacher doesn't notice.

SATURDAY 24TH APRIL

3.23 p.m.
Went to see Goose but he seems to be in a bad mood constantly at the moment. It's like a massive man period. If I mention Nicky at all he changes the subject or says, "She just wants kissy-kissy with her boyfriend." It's almost nasty. It's so not like Goose. He's doing well at school, his mum is lovely and his gecko is eating properly — what's the problem?!

I think the problem may be... No. I am SICK of going OVER and OVER it in my mind.

You think Nicky holds his cards close to his chest, Gran! Goose has swallowed his cards!

We are going to Skegness tomorrow. I'm slightly dreading it. Rob isn't coming. He was born in South America and knows what real beaches are like. He's taking Goose to a boot sale.

(Skegness Day Trip)

5.05 a.m.

Gran has just turned up 2 HOURS EARLY. She says she can't sleep these days anyway so she'd rather wait. This actually means sitting on the sofa like the queen, saying "Are we going yet?" and looking at her watch every 5 minutes. Sorry, Gran – I'm going back to sleep.

5.35 a.m.

Just woke up to Gran at the end of my bed staring at me. She said, "When are we leaving, Hattie?" When I said, "Don't know – I need more sleep..." she started talking about how you can get 3 for 2 on flavoured sardines in her shop. I don't need to hear about cheap Omega 3 before 6 a.m. in the morning – if EVER!

5.49 a.m.

Dear Princess – please stop eating my pillow. I will get up.

6.13 a.m.

We are leaving early. Mum can't put up with Gran talking about special offers any more. We are picking up Nicky on the way. I've never been to Nicky's place. Basically because I've been playing it cool. Better text him to tell him we are going to be almost an hour early.

9.52 p.m.

OMG – I AM NOT GOING TO SKEGNESS AGAIN.
EVER.

To start with Mum forced us all to go to "Natureland",
which was EMBARRASSMENT TO THE MAXIMUM.
Gran freaked out like she normally does in the butterfly
house. I always forget they have lovely wings but big fat
hairy bodies. THEN Mum made me and Nicky have our
photos taken with the goat in Pets' Corner. Nicky thought
it was LOL! It was not. The goat had a massive slobbering
tongue and I am not 6. All I could hear was Princess
whimpering outside for Gran. We couldn't take her in. If she
saw a seal perform she'd jump in and try to catch the fish.

Gran and Nicky kept giggling at everything. They played
mini golf and then spent 4 hours in the arcade, gambling.
Nicky knows EVERY fruit machine and how to get the
best from them. Gran and him spent about £40 but got
£26 back! With our sort of winnings we all had fish and
chips, though we had to leave Princess outside. Gran took
her out some bread and butter.

At one point I said to Gran, "Any chance I can have some
time alone with Nicky?" Gran was really moody and said,
"You know he's had a tough time, Hattie. Why not give him
a nice family day out? Bet he's never had one in his life."

She's right but I wanted a bit of snogging.

Nicky does seem to be a bit ashamed of his family. When
we went to pick him up he was looking for us through

an upstairs window and sprinted down before we'd even stopped the car. I thought he was going to let me in and introduce me to his parents — but he didn't. He couldn't wait to get out. I think his parents are a nightmare.

10.53 p.m.

The worst thing my mum did today was paddle in the sea and scream how cold the water was.

11.02 p.m.

Oh, and put candyfloss on top of Princess's head and pretend she had hair.

It was quite funny. Princess didn't think so — she doesn't like anything pink. Mum let her eat it though so she was fine!

11.41 p.m.

Gran just called me. Apparently Princess has been chasing her tail and barking for the last 2 hours. She said I was always the same after Skeggy — they could never get me to sleep.

I have just been compared to the world's most mental dog.

11.53 p.m.

Text from Nicky:

Gr8 day. Thanx XXXXXX

6 KISSES!!! 6!!! I love him.

MONDAY 26TH APRIL

5.18 p.m.

Dr Richards DID notice that Florence Morse has quoted Churchill! She got bonus marks for quoting the greatest Briton on Earth.

Nicky was off school today and hasn't texted. Perhaps I need to be less Skegness and more Vegas.

Tried to tell Dimple and Jen about Sunday but they just seemed bored and kept giving each other strange looks. At one point I think I saw Dimple roll her eyes! It was totally rude. I have had to listen to them go on and on about their boyfriends but apparently I'm not allowed to go on about mine. Thanks very much, my so-called 2 best friends!

TUESDAY 27TH APRIL

4.19 p.m.

IT ALL KICKED OFF TODAY.

Dimple and Weirdo Jen admitted they have tried but they actually HATE Nicky.

Jen said, "Look, Hattie — he has a really negative vibe. You can feel it through a wall. Dimple feels the same." Dimple nodded and started going on about how she doesn't like the way Nicky speaks to me and that he "picks me up and leaves me where he wants to".

Dimple thinks because she has been out with Bhavin she knows everything about relationships. Bhavin, who just let her DUMP him because her mum was having a baby!

As for Jen! She goes out with a total freak who has picnics in public, with aliens. Or something. I'm TOTALLY furious! How dare they tell ME that Nicky treats ME badly. They don't even see us together. They are BOTH too busy these days with their own lives and their own families. Nicky is lovely to me in his way. Just because he's not buying me presents every week like Simon (VOM!!!) or "being respectful". That's not what I want. I want a REAL FULL-ON RELATIONSHIP and sometimes love does cause you a little bit of unhappiness. That's NORMAL. Someone who makes it OBVIOUS he likes YOU and takes a bit of control of the situation. Unlike ... other people.

I didn't say all this. I just said, "Well, I love him and he's from a difficult family."

5.08 p.m.
I know they just say all this because they love me.

5.15 p.m.
I'm sick of being understanding.

5.43 p.m.
Dear Gran – I am so bored with the saga of your hedgehogs. I don't care that you can hear them "doing it". Prickly porn is not what a nearly 70-year-old woman should be talking about. I do not care!

I need to know about men! Not "Bertram the spiky bull and all his girlfriends"!

I didn't say all this when Gran called me. I just thought it.
I am OFFICIALLY calm and restrained.

7.02 p.m.

I'm fed up with being safe and nice. I need to be more edgy.
I think I'll start with my hair. Nicky will like it.

7.28 p.m.

Just told Mum I was shaving my head completely. She was
fine with it.

8.03 p.m.

Gran says most boys don't go for totally bald. That's why
Mum would be fine with it.

That's a NO GO then.

WEDNESDAY 28TH APRIL

1.38 p.m.

It's on! Today I was talking about going more edgy over
lunch and Jade Montgomery said her sister needed models
for her college course. She says I would be perfect as a
model. So she's cutting my hair straight after school. She's
only 4 years older than me but apparently she's really
good and does a lot of stuff for magazines.

When they say "magazines" she was actually in the
local paper once. When I said, "What for?" Jade said,
"A drawing competition when she was 7" – but it's all
artistic. That's the thing. If you can draw a castle and a
knight well you can do a decent haircut!

I've told Jade to ask her sister to be experimental.
I think my face shape can take it. Jen thinks it's exciting
but Dimple said she likes my hair the way it is. It's all
been a bit tense since they told me they didn't like Nicky.
How can I trust people who've got him SO wrong?!

5.52 p.m.
OMG – it's pretty OUT THERE.

6.08 p.m.
OK! OMG – it looks FOUL.

I can't go out looking like this. If you want to achieve the
Hattie Moore look...

*   Put a bowl on your head.
*   Close your eyes.
*   Use blunt scissors.
*   CUT!!!

I just sent a photo to Jen. She thinks it's "brave".
I daren't show Dimple.

7.28 p.m.
Mum says, "Amputees doing the London Marathon are
brave, Hattie – not someone with a bad haircut."

So it's officially a BAD haircut.

Thanks, Mum.

THURSDAY 29TH APRIL

6.31 p.m.

Today I found out what it must feel like to be a celebrity with a wardrobe malfunction. Everyone was staring at me. Some were giggling in their hands. Some were LOLing (MGK – PREDICTABLE!). Dimple said, "If you don't like it you can just wait till it grows back." How long will that take??!

Didn't see Nicky. I was pleased about this fact. I haven't heard anything from Nicky. I am not happy about this fact.

7.37 p.m.

My brother thinks I look like a medieval monk! He keeps singing hymns behind me and every time I finish a sentence he says, "Amen".

The sooner he goes travelling and gets stuck for ever on a bungee jump off a bridge in Thailand, the better. The idea of my brother boing-ing up and down for ever is a beautiful thought!

FRIDAY 30TH APRIL

6.25 p.m.

My hair is not the main thing people at school are talking about any more. It's the fact that there's a film of Laura Tynan doing a One Direction song at her mum's wedding and screaming, "Harry, I LOVE YOU!" over and over. She has to be helped off stage by the best man as she "gets emotional".

Rob said, "Hattie, your haircut is just a drop in the ocean."

8.03 p.m.

Found out tonight that Gran has an arrangement with Mrs Braun over the road. If Gran's curtains are not open before 8 a.m. she's either dead or seriously ill. Mrs Braun knows to call an undertaker or a doctor.

She'd be dialling 999 every weekend if it were me! Why do old people get up when they don't have to? When I retire I'm going to stay in bed for ever with my laptop and a box of crisps.

My husband can wait on me!

8.32 p.m.

Gran says, "Men don't live as long as us. Always marry them younger, Hattie!"

Apparently male immaturity is a small price to pay for toast and marmalade in bed every morning.

9.14 p.m.

TEXT FROM NICKY!

C u tomorrow x

1 kiss?!

SATURDAY 1ST MAY

4.11 p.m.

I don't want to write this ... but Nicky is acting ... horrible.

He came over, and the first thing he said was that I've put on a bit of weight. He called me Fatty 3 Seats.

I think he was sort of joking.

Then he hated my hair. He says it makes me look more masculine and less cosmic sexy goddess.

I don't think he was joking about this. When we were kissing there was less tongue and I caught him looking over his shoulder at *The Great British Bake Off.*

I might just eat apples for the rest of this weekend.

Sunday 2nd May

9.57 a.m.

I can't diet. It goes off your breasts first and THERE IS NOTHING THERE TO START WITH.

6.28 p.m.

And Rob did his spicy chicken and rice thing today. My body needs it. My A-cups NEED it.

Monday 3rd May   BANK HOLIDAY

10.34 a.m.

Just spoke to Dimple. She's gone mad at even the thought of Nicky saying I'm putting on weight. She said, "Hattie, you are like a stick insect – this is JUST what we tried to tell you about him. He's all mixed up. Dump him!"

2.12 p.m.

Nicky wants me to go boarding with him on Wednesday at the skate park.

I'm sure he was just joking.

Tuesday 4th May

6.12 p.m.

I can't even think past THIS week and school are MAKING us "consider our LONG-TERM futures". WHY?!

Today we had to write our CV. Florence Morse – ultimate rebel – wrote a pee-take one!

> I can breathe through my nose, I mastered walking at 18 months and can turn off my mind in order to carry out a brain-dead job every day. In my spare time I enjoy juggling kittens and pretending to be a moth.

Bet they all think it's fantastic!

Nicky wasn't at school today to write his CV. He hardly ever is! He says the future will "just happen".

8.39 p.m.

Nicky just rang my mob. He wasn't joking about the skate park. He wants me to meet him there after school tomorrow!

WEDNESDAY 5TH MAY

5.46 p.m.

I met up with Nicky at 4 p.m. He kissed me when I turned up and then spent the rest of the time basically grunting and stunting. I shouted, "Well done!" when boys did big loop things but I felt like such a doughnut standing there. In the end I just said goodbye and got Rob to pick me up after an hour. Rob said, "Getting into skating, Hattie?!" Er, no, Rob. I'm not getting into snogging either!

6.16 p.m.

Nicky sort of ignored me tonight. It was a bit bad.

6.39 p.m.

Or perhaps he just respects the fact that I can cope on my own! He may well respect me as an actual woman.

7.02 p.m.

Actually I just think he likes doing half-pipe aerial thingies more than he likes me.

THURSDAY 6TH MAY

4.12 p.m.

OMG! SCHOOL SHOCKER.

The school do not think Florence is brilliant and have said she has to have special career lessons. I can't imagine Florence ever in a job. Unless there's a job where being moody and grumpy is a good thing.

5.09 p.m.

Rob says the people who do these jobs are always miserable:

* People you have to deal with when you're trying to claim insurance.
* People who work in banks when you are asking them for money.
* Traffic wardens.
* Moody people with guitars who sing about death from war, death from climate change, death from a broken heart or death in general.

I think Florence could do the last one REALLY WELL.

6.11 p.m.

Thinking of it, Florence and Nicky are quite similar...

6.54 p.m.

No. They shouldn't go out together. I still like him.

FRIDAY 7TH MAY

7.29 p.m.

I went round to see Gran after school. She was out the back watching her new young gardener in action. She said, "My engine has gone but my headlights still work, Hattie." She is getting more happiness from Tyson planting some bulbs than I am from an entire relationship with Nicky.

SATURDAY 8TH MAY

1.48 p.m.

I met Dimple at her house this morning. I started to cry. The facts are that I have a rubbish haircut, a boyfriend who doesn't treat me very well AT ALL and a gran who wolf-whistles at good-looking young men and then pretends it wasn't her when they turn round. My life is a mahoosive MESS.

Dimple couldn't really argue. It's all true. She saw Gran whistle at the men who are working on the new shopping centre in town. They saw it was her, leant over their scaffolding and cheered.

Anyway Dimple gave me a big hug and promised to try and cheer me up. She's asked her friend Nita to come over and give me some henna art on my arm this afternoon. It's only temporary! I'm having a rose. It symbolizes growth, beauty and strength. Plus I know that Nicky likes tattoos on women.

6.02 p.m.

My rose looks like a cabbage. Nita said she thought petals were a bit of a "challenge". They were. I've got leaves!!! Nita said, "Perhaps vegetables are a sign of dignity and rebirth."

No, they are not, Nita — vegetables are sign of your actual dinner!!!

8.02 p.m.

I just rang Gran. She understands things going wrong on your body. She tried everything on her Father Christmas diamante vajazzle bum. She said, "You'll have to wear long sleeves, Hattie, till it fades." That could be all summer!

SUNDAY 9TH MAY

10.45 a.m.

It's quite warm today but I'm covering up. I've got no choice.

11.38 a.m.

Mum just said, "You're quiet, Hattie. Is anything the matter?"

What could I say?! I just told her I was feeling like I was "getting something".

Actually I've already GOT something. It's a cabbage!

4.38 p.m.

I tried everything in the kitchen AND in the bathroom to fade my tattoo. Nothing is working. My arm now smells of Radox and Cif cream cleanser.

10.24 p.m.

Dear Nicky — you haven't replied to any of my texts or called me and now I have a vegetable on my arm.

I am not happy. At all.

Every time I have texted Goose recently, he seems to be BUSY. When did HE get so busy?

MONDAY 10TH MAY

4.19 p.m.

People at school today were begging to see my crap body art! Dimple said she totally did not tell anyone. Nita did! AND she blamed me and said she couldn't draw properly because I didn't sit still!

MGK was saying that she wants a tattoo with "Hattie Moore is not my sister" on it. A permanent one. She says she will NEVER regret it.

7.12 p.m.

What I have I turned into?! I'm not a feminist – I am a TOTAL DORK DOUGHNUT!

Things I have done for Nicky:

* Got a new haircut that's craptacular.
* Got a henna tattoo that's craptacular.
* Spent time with his grunting skateboard friends.
* Let him come to Skegness.
* TOLD HIM I LOVED HIM!

Things he has done for me:

8.35 p.m.

I'm going to go to the doctor tomorrow morning to see what he can do about this henna thing. It's not fading. I'll tell Mum I'm going because I'm getting headaches.

8.51 p.m.

Told Mum I was going to the doctor's tomorrow. She said, "You've not moaned about headaches. What are you really going for?"

When I said, "Headaches – honestly. Perhaps I need contact lenses", she looked at me with her "I don't believe a word you are saying" face.

Mum has a TOTAL radar when it comes to my lies.

TUESDAY 11TH MAY

8.55 a.m.

I've been ringing the doctor for an appointment since 8.29 a.m.! 26 minutes AND it's still engaged!

9.17 a.m.

Finally got through and the receptionist bit my head off! She wanted to give me an appointment in 2 weeks' time till I told her it was an emergency. She asked what sort of "emergency" it was. I said, "An arm one." Then she laughed and said, "See you at noon!"

NOON! My arm could have fallen off by then!

9.45 a.m.

Mum is NOT happy that I am missing school today but then she said, "Better to go than to .... not go, I suppose. With your .... head."

3.01 p.m.

The doctor's was a nightmare. Everyone there was sneezing or coughing or huddled up in a ball of pain. There was 1 magazine in the entire waiting room and that was *Agriculture Today!* I now know everything about the new breed of tractors and what to do if your cows are depressed.

Why are cows depressed? All they have to do is eat grass, hang around with their mates and get milked whilst they listen to Radio 2. I'd love to be a cow.

Except for the ones that become burgers. That's bad.

Anyway the doctor said I was stupid for having a henna tattoo and even more stupid for treating my arm like a kitchen worktop. I've got a special cream and a bandage that covers it all.

Got home and Mum was practically WAITNG by the front door (she must have finished at the cafe early). Then we had this really weird "chat".

MUM:	WHAT DID YOU GO TO THE DOCTOR'S FOR?
ME:	Headaches.
MUM:	Don't lie, Hattie. I need to know about the big things that are

happening in your life. We need
to talk about any ... big decisions
that you've made. Big decisions
have consequences, you know, and
some things ... well, you have to
take them REGULARLY for them to
work. Perhaps I could remind you
every morning so you never ← WHAT IS SHE ON ABOUT??!
forget. Medicine is important!

ME: OK – I had some henna art done.
MUM: What?! Show me!
ME: It's terrible. Don't yell at me.

Then I showed her and SHE LAUGHED and said, "Oh,
Hattie – only you could have a vegetable painted on your
arm. Don't worry – it'll fade. My friend's little boy had
a dolphin done on holiday in Mykonos. It only lasts a few
weeks!"

She almost seemed RELIEVED! I will NEVER understand
my mum.

WEDNESDAY 12TH MAY

5.17 p.m.

OMG – Nicky has SENT me flowers and written me a
song. He emailed me the file! It's him rapping.

Give me love, Hattie,
I'll fight your corner.
I just want to hold you.

I let Goose listen because he of all people should
understand OTHER men.

194

He just said, "It's Ed Sheeran's 'Give Me Love'. I could do better than that... Anyone could."

He'll never get over his anti-Nicky-ness.

9.12 p.m.
OK – I was checking Goose for jealousy. There wasn't any. He was just slagging him off and checking his phone lots.

THURSDAY 13TH MAY

5.34 p.m.
Goose was checking his phone lots?!

WHAT FOR?

Gecko tips OR TEXTING A GIRL?!

Gecko tips I hope.

And what do I say to Nicky? He's a TOTAL pig then he does the HUGE, BIG, MAX ROMANTIC stuff I have ALWAYS wanted.

FRIDAY 14TH MAY

7.52 p.m.
I told Gran tonight about the song. She said, "Don't mess with a man's heart, Hattie. When you have them in your hand you don't play with them." Gran clearly thinks I'm some sort of evil boy-controlling queen. She started wagging her finger at me! "In my day men didn't write a

song — they bought you chips and, if you were lucky, a decent piece of cod."

Fish is NOT romantic!   🐟 ≠ ♡

SATURDAY 15TH MAY

8.01 a.m.
Nicky has emailed me again. Did I get his song?

I don't know what to write back!

1.13 p.m.
Gran says NEVER in the history of time have men splashed out on flowers saying, "Well done. You're quite nice." She says Nicky LOVES ME but, like many men, can't say it.

Like all the men in my life ever.

SUNDAY 16TH MAY

5.35 p.m.
Gran thinks I should give Nicky a chance just like you should "try the curried mushrooms on the salad bar before you opt for the coleslaw".

She's STILL spending too much time at the supermarket.

MONDAY 17TH MAY

6.27 p.m.

Email from Keith. He has a special sensor in his head that knows when I LEAST want to hear from him and when it's the WORST possible time.

> **From:** <keithkeepsitgreen@gmail.com>
> **Date:** May 16, 3:23:12 PM GMT
> **To:** Hattie Moore <helphattienow@gmail.com>
> **Subject: YOUR visit here!**
>
> Hattie – I NEED to know now if you are coming over.
> I will pay for the ticket. It would be great to spend the summer with you.

Typical of Keith to complicate everything by doing actually NOTHING!

7.12 p.m.

Gran thinks this would be the chance of a lifetime.

7.34 p.m.

Mum says she'd miss me A LOT.

8.09 p.m.

OMG – is MGK definitely going?

I've got massive coursework this week – WHY IS THIS HAPPENING NOW?

TUESDAY 18TH MAY

3.46 p.m.

Of course MGK is going. She'll probably wear a bikini on the plane.

5.45 p.m.

Mum says I should go and see Keith. Why does she want to get rid of me?

6.02 p.m.

She says she doesn't but she thinks it's important I have a relationship with my father.

I have to make a decision on Australia, work out Nicky and do some stupid homework about my body.

I wish humans were just heads with wheels. Life and exams would be so much easier.

WEDNESDAY 19TH MAY

7.34 p.m.

I just asked Gran for more of her advice. All she could go on about was how her foot lady is moving and how the new chiropodist has had 2 husbands — both of whom have been in wheelchairs. She kept saying, "I won't trust her with my feet, Hattie."

I said, "Gran. Please help me. I can't decide what to do about Keith."

Gran said, "Let me have a think about it. I'll call you later once my ingrown toenail has stopped throbbing."

8.49 p.m.

Gran rang to give me her advice. Apparently "love can wait" and I will be a "more attractive" woman if I travel the world. HOW DOES THAT WORK?

I can't even think.

I need to concentrate on my insides. Not feelings – the actual squishy kidneys and stuff.

THURSDAY 20TH MAY

5.23 p.m.

Handed in my stupid work today. Who cares about hormones regulating the function of organs?! Their real role is to make you a total mental. You can't concentrate on major life decisions!

6.56 p.m.

I've decided I have to tell Nicky it's over. He doesn't treat me well and he's NEVER at school. I've become a craptaculatar pathetic girl that just wants to make her boyfriend happy. Plus there's someone else complicating matters. I'm avoiding them both!

FRIDAY 21ST MAY

6.31 p.m.

I have made 2 MAHOOSIVE decisions with the help of Dimple and Jen today.

BIG DECISION 1:

Firstly I have made the decision NOT to finish with Nicky OR go out with him either. I have asked Nicky for space. It's easy as he is NEVER usually at school or even anywhere near me.

BIG DECISION 2:

I've also decided to GO to Australia. Dimple had a month in India and she says she definitely came back thinking how lucky she was and how great her parents were. PLUS it's better than working in Mum's cafe over the summer or listening to Gran talk about her "corns".

7.18 p.m.

Nicky has agreed to give me space. He texted:

    OK :-)

NO KISSES?!

8.59 p.m.

Goose just emailed me.

> **From:** <goosegeekwhatever@live.co.uk>
> **Date:** May 21, 8:57:49 PM GMT
> **To:** Hattie Moore <helphattienow@gmail.com>
> **Subject: Are you ok??**
>
> Heard about Nicky. I'm here if you need me. xx

Bet Dimple told him.

Oh, Goose.

2 kisses!

You are sweet but you mess my head up SO MUCH.

Saturday 22nd May

9.01 a.m.

Princess is involved in a relationship with a mangy dog. Mum keeps saying to Gran, "Have you had her done?" Mum is obsessed with accidental pregnancies! Just because she had one!

I am concentrating on Princess's love life because I can't think about my own. Mine is too complicated.

Sunday 23rd May

5.49 p.m.

GREAT!

MGK is coming to Australia because it is full of hot boys. I don't mean hot as in "too hot" (though they probably are) – I mean hot as in "FIT". And they wear cut-off T-shirts and stuff.

PLEASE, MGK - DON'T COME. Get something serious but not life-threatening like pneumonia.

6.32 p.m.

Gran says pneumonia is life-threatening.

Weak pneumonia then.

Monday 24th May

4.34 p.m.

OMG – Princess has been seen cavorting with Doug the Pug!

Gran has given me the full list of dogs that Princess is involved with:

* Bouncer the Staffy
* Ralph the Dalmatian
* Prince the Terrier
* Dfor the Labrador
* Patch the Staffy
* Ben the ? (no one knows)

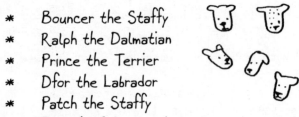

7.42 p.m.

NEWS FLASH – Princess is now hanging out with Marmaduke the ginger cat.

She just doesn't care!

TUESDAY 25TH MAY

4.45 p.m.

Told Keith I am going to come to Australia and he is booking the tickets. I have no idea where he is getting the money from! Perhaps he has busked 24 hours a day and finally created some half-decent clothes. Perhaps he has robbed a bank. LOL!

5.35 p.m.

OMG – hope Gran hasn't given him any tips on bank robbing. She once said her building society was held up by a man with a cucumber that was disguised as a gun! Perhaps Keith could grow his own weapon in his organic garden – then eat it!

7.04 p.m.

Just found out that because we are under 16 we have to be escorted as unaccompanied minors! I hope this doesn't mean they give me colouring books. I hope it does mean they give me a bodyguard – like a major celeb. OMG – what if they put me in first class?! Who could I meet?! MGK can stay in economy whilst I talk dresses with MAJOR CELEBS.

7.43 p.m.

Dimple just rang. Her mum's baby really moved today during a conversation about mortgages. Everybody is taking this as a really good sign. The baby is SUPER intelligent ... OR perhaps it just did a massive YAWN.

8.04 p.m.

Asked my mum about when I first moved. She couldn't remember. "Nathan was a bit of a handful at the time, Hattie." So I get ignored because my brother is a doughnut? NOTHING has changed.

WEDNESDAY 26TH MAY

4.03 p.m.

Princess has received a death threat – it was pushed through Gran's door. It said, "Keep your *%*#ing dog inside OR ELSE!" but it was signed by someone called "Petra". If you're going to make a threat do it anonymously! It's why people have usernames, so you can say terrible stuff without people knowing!

5.19 p.m.

I have never done that, BTW. Weirdo Jen says the US government knows what EVERYONE is doing and can trace everything. When they put you in prison they give you your favourite foods to freak you out. If you've EVER mentioned you like Big Macs in an email you get them for breakfast and the US government people say, "We heard you like them!" They don't tell you in a nice way though. They tell you in a "we know what burger you eat and we know you are a terrible person" kind of way.

8.01 p.m.

Just checked my emails. I've never mentioned how much I love KFC anywhere!

8.19 p.m.

If I'm in prison though I will want to have my favourite food every day!

8.53 p.m.

Just emailed Dimple randomly and asked her if she fancied a Bargain Bucket on Saturday.

9.24 p.m.

Dimple says "no". It doesn't matter — the US government now know I would like chicken strips for breakfast.

10.12 p.m.

I miss Nicky. I'm writing it here to get it out. I need the space but I miss him.

10.44 p.m.

Can I actually handle space?

THURSDAY 27TH MAY

6.34 p.m.

Gran has gone on the warpath about Princess! She's rung the police and said she's had a death threat. The police said, "No – your dog has." Gran said, "Me and Princess are a team. A threat to her is a threat to me." The policeman said the law does not recognize canines as having the same rights as humans.

Is Princess a liberated feminist woman in charge of her own sexual destiny or is she just a tart? Perhaps she is just good friends with these dogs?

FRIDAY 28TH MAY

8.12 p.m.

Gran says platonic relationships cannot exist between female and male ANYTHINGS. When I said, "What about Goose and me?!" Gran looked at me for ages like I was doing something wrong. I changed the subject and said that Princess was a modern dog taking charge of her own life and rejecting the constraints of society.

9.03 p.m.

Perhaps she IS just a bit of a tart.

Saturday 29th May

10.09 a.m.

Choosing a bikini for Australia starts now! Yes, I have got a million weeks before I go but this is still a major decision. I wish Dimple or Jen could come to Australia. Especially to keep me company on the flight. It's bad enough going with MGK. What if I get seated next to someone really dull on the other side?

12.34 p.m.

Dimple DID get trapped next to a man on the plane from Delhi who had a collection of airline sick bags. He went through every one of them alphabetically. She said that by Air Canada she was losing the will to live and was asleep by Air Slovakia.

6.28 p.m.

Looked at every bikini EVER on the Net for HOURS. I can't find 1 I like. I wish you could buy the body with the bikini.

7.34 p.m.

Mum just came up and said, "Forget boys. Forget bikinis. Hattie, if you do well in your exams this year I WILL TAKE YOU SHOPPING and YOU can CHOOSE what you like!"

I WILL TAKE YOU SHOPPING AND YOU CAN CHOOSE WHAT YOU LIKE!

I will start revising tomorrow.

8.04 p.m.
OMG – what if Mum's entire clothing budget is £5?

8.36 p.m.
Mum has confirmed her budget for me is £100!

£100!!!

That's more than my ENTIRE wardrobe is worth now, including my school uniform!

SUNDAY 30TH MAY

11.31 a.m.
This year with exams I am going to be completely different. I am going to make an actual revision plan like Dimple and I am going to stick to it like major dorks do.

1.15 p.m.
How can you revise when Jen is on Skype being pee-funny over the fact that cows are the world's most psychically sensitive animals – that's why they get mutilated in fields by aliens.

7.12 p.m.
Gran thinks Princess may be pregnant and isn't sure who the father is! I have some experience of this – not the pregnant bit – MORE YOUNG PEOPLE BEING BORN NOT KNOWING WHO THIER DAD IS! Well not people – puppies. But they have feelings too.

BANK HOLIDAY
AND HALF-TERM

MONDAY 31ST MAY

As Mrs C
calls it.

8.04 a.m.
REVISION PLAN – A PLAN FOR SUCCESS

9 a.m.	BREAKFAST
10 a.m.	Dance/Drama rehearsal (in bedroom or with group at school)
11.15 a.m.	Coffee break
11.45 a.m.	Resume Dance/Drama
1 p.m.	Lunch
2 p.m.	Dance/Drama theory
3 p.m.	English
3.10 p.m.	History
3.20 p.m.	Science
3.30 p.m.	Maths
3.35 p.m.	Break
3.40 p.m.	French
3.50 p.m.	Geography
4 p.m.	FINISHED!!!

TUESDAY 1ST JUNE

7.49 a.m.

I am sticking to my revision plan today. I have told
everyone I am NOT HERE. I've just turned my mobile to
silent. I feel sick doing it but IT IS my future. I'm worried
about Dance/Drama. It's my most important subject and
our play is all about "conflict" – domestic arguments and
wars between countries. We're struggling with only having
6 people in it. It's easy to do a performance of a couple
arguing but not so easy to represent thousands of men in
a battle with big guns.

WEDNESDAY 2ND JUNE

4.39 p.m.

In our group Dance/Drama rehearsal today Dibbo Hannah
dropped the chair that represented conflict. It fell
brilliantly and I shouted, "WAR!" Everyone thought this
was fantastic and we are going to add it to the entire
performance. We have also worked out how to give a
feeling of more people. Each of us is going to wear a hat
with a face on it during the battle scenes. That will make
the stage feel more "alive".

THURSDAY 3RD JUNE

4.43 p.m.

I have stuck to my revision plan – even Mum came up and
said, "I am so proud of you, Hattie. I could never manage
to revise!"

There is no way I can fail! I have fully revised everything that it's possible to revise, I think.

7.29 p.m.

Is Mum being so nice to me because she's worried that Keith is making such an effort by paying for me to go over?

Perhaps that's the worst thing I've ever thought.

8.19 p.m.

Perhaps it's true.

8.34 p.m.

No, it's one of the worst things I've ever thought.

8.53 p.m.

Mum just looked at my revision plan and thought it might be "a bit Dance/Drama heavy". Dear Mum — are you doing my life? No. Please go away.

9.59 p.m.

Just been making my Dance/Drama hat. It's pretty spooky but really good. I look like I have a massive soldier towering over me.

FRIDAY 4TH JUNE

7.01 p.m.

FULL Dance/Drama group rehearsal!

Dibbo Hannah misheard what we said about making a hat with a face on it. She has made a TANK! I think she

---

looks RIDICULOUS! It looks like a really rubbish papier mâché Dalek. Everyone else though agreed with Becca that it added "depth" to the battlefield scene. So it's staying!

SATURDAY 5TH JUNE

5.21 p.m.

I have stuck to my revision timetable today but I spent most of my Dance/Drama time getting really cross about Dibbo Hannah's stupid tank. How can other people think that is good?! Not one person mentioned how REAL my hat soldier looked. I gave him wrinkles and everything! Perhaps I should make something that adds something "more".

I am making a machine-gun hat.

SUNDAY 6TH JUNE

12.22 p.m.

I can't get a machine gun to work so I've made it into a missile.

4.19 p.m.

Mum couldn't work out what my missile was and said it looked a "bit odd". Mum, though, hasn't got much of an imagination so you can't really count her opinion.

Back to school.

MONDAY 7TH JUNE

5.12 p.m.

Becca and Jade have made missile hats too. We have
agreed to hold our "missile" hats in our hands as we walk
and put our "people" hats on our heads. It's going to look
BIG.

TUESDAY 8TH JUNE

7.45 p.m.

FINAL DRESS REHEARSAL.

It seemed to go really well. I think once we get the hang
of holding our hats and having them on our heads too we'll
be fine!

WEDNESDAY 9TH JUNE

5.12 p.m.

ACTUAL PERFORMANCE OF *BATTLES – HOME
AND AWAY.*

It went OK except for the following – minor – points:

* Dibbo Hannah forgot to drop the chair
  representing conflict so I just shouted "WAR"
  randomly.
* When Clare was meant to shout, "You're not my
  dad!" during the domestic argument scene she
  yelled, "You're not my dog!" – and giggled.

* I slipped on a script that Hannah had left on the floor but I think I made it look like I'd been shot. A bit.
* Jade got really nervous and forgot her lines. Instead of saying, "War is the very worst that mankind has to offer. It is tears and bloodshed for *NOTHING!*" she said, "War's a bit bad really."
* Dibbo Hannah cannot hold and wear a hat at the same time.
* Nor can Becca or Jade.
* Or me. Must be a missile thing. And a Dibbo Hannah thing.

I think we'll get at least a "B" though – everyone does!

THURSDAY 10TH JUNE

3.42 p.m.

History.

Since when did we study Russia?! I know lots about Germany.

I think I might have put a bit too much time into Dance/Drama.

FRIDAY 11TH JUNE

4.39 p.m.

Geography.

Erosional landforms?!!

Dimple was writing like mad. She says erosional landforms are different to depositional landforms.

I have definitely put too much time into Dance/Drama.

7.31 p.m.
YES!!! I got fold mountains right.

SATURDAY 12TH JUNE

9.12 a.m.
I am FULL-ON revising today.

I am now officially determined to be AMAZING at French, Maths, Science and English.

It's just to get some decent clothes, not to be a total geek.

7.45 p.m.
LOL! Gran saw MGK buying swimwear in Debenhams today. Gran said, "I know she's tiny but she was picking way too small sizes. Her backside looked like a gorge with a tiny hammock strung over it."

YES!!! MGK will look STUPID!

8.13 p.m.
Or like a beach queen of hotness in hardly anything.

SUNDAY 13TH JUNE

7.44 p.m.

Dear Charlotte Brontë – *Jane Eyre* is depressing and Mr Rochester sounds horrible. I've been out with a moody boy with secrets and it's no fun. Oh, and thanks for letting Helen die of coughing. I actually liked her.

MONDAY 14TH JUNE

6.34 p.m.

English and French! I may have done slightly well actually. I worked out what Raoul and his monkey wanted to do in the French listening test! They both wanted to go marching. Perhaps it's a French army thing.

7.01 p.m.

Jen says it wasn't marching. It's WALKING! It sounded like marching.

7.29 p.m.

Why was a monkey going walking anyway?! Raoul must be a weirdo.

TUESDAY 15TH JUNE

4.12 p.m.

Science and Maths.

I may have done very badly. I don't understand redshift.

7.35 p.m.

If the Big Bang and the Universe is still expanding, how do we know that we won't expand till we snap?

7.59 p.m.

It's depressing that the Earth may twang and break like an elastic band but at least no one would care about my exam results then!

8.10 p.m.

Except Mum. She'd find a way to nag me from the nothingness of space! LOL!

EXAMS FINISHED – **YES!!!**

WEDNESDAY 16TH JUNE

4.21 p.m.

UNBELIEVABLE!

They are MAKING US GO IN FOR PE on Monday. Why do we HAVE to do PE when we have finished our exams and basically everything else?! We are doing easy stuff in other lessons. It's so UNFAIR. Mrs Cob and Matfield say it's good for our brains but why is swimming doing anything except giving us massive shoulders and smaller breasts?!

THURSDAY 17TH JUNE

6.23 p.m.

MAGNIFICENT PLAN AHOY!

Today Becca said we should totally all pretend to be ill to get off swimming. I said, "THAT is a GENIUS idea! Shall we all rush to the toilet?" Jade thought that was rubbish and it would be far better to pretend to faint all at the same time. A FLASH MOB FAINT! It's like synchronized swimming but formation fainting! It's like a flash mob but we don't dance — we just fall over! I think we can totally do it. They will stop the lesson immediately and they might ban PE totally for health and safety reasons!

We are agreed that we are going to do it on Monday. As soon as Jade says, "I feel a bit funny", we're all going to fall down just outside the pool. We need to be hardened up so we don't break anything.

FRIDAY 18TH JUNE

4.02 p.m.
We had a practice today on the crash mats in the gym. We can pretend to faint brilliantly. Not laughing afterwards is hard but if we can keep that up PE will be gone for ever!

SATURDAY 19TH JUNE

2.32 p.m.
Dimple says swimming actually helps to keep breasts in shape and "uplifted" by working the chest muscles. Then she said, "*Breast stroke, Hattie?*" like I was Dibbo Hannah. She's not taking part. It's "not fair" on her mum

---

to think Dimple might be ill. AGAIN Dimple puts family before her mates who need her to pretend she might be dead to stop unfair treatment of students!

I'll let her off though because I love her and her dad does shout VERY loud.

SUNDAY 20TH JUNE

10.32 a.m.

Weirdo Jen has texted us all to say we should think of death as we faint and that will stop us laughing.

11.15 a.m.

Just tried it. I still laughed.

2.13 p.m.

I won't tomorrow though. I will be deadly serious.

MONDAY 21ST JUNE

 ## FLASH MOB FAINT!

5.31 p.m.

It went so well that the PE teacher thought there had been a chlorine leak and rang some ambulances and the fire brigade. Why do they have a deadly gas thing making the swimming pool cleaner?!

When the ambulance men came to prod us Dibbo Hannah felt guilty, started to cry and said, "We are just pretending."

We all have to see Mrs Cob tomorrow.

I miss Nicky at times like this the MOST. He understands trouble.

TUESDAY 22ND JUNE

5.32 p.m.

OMG – Mrs Cob went more MENTAL than I've ever seen a person go MENTAL before. She started going on about, "Wasting the time of our brave emergency services." Then she said, "I need to show the rest of the school how despicable this prank was. So I'M BANNING YOU FROM THE PROM."

BANNED FROM THE PROM?

BANNED?

WE ARE BANNED FROM THE PROM. The one actually decent thing school DO!

WEDNESDAY 23RD JUNE

3.58 p.m.

Exam Results!

English	Maths	Science	History	Geography	French
B	D	C	C	B	C

DANCE/DRAMA
D

A "D"?!!

Apparently we were "a bit of a shambles and unintentionally comedic".

Whatever. Who cares? I'm banned from the prom.

5.02 p.m.
Mum is pleased with my exam results. In fact she is so pleased that she wants to buy me a dress for the prom. I told her I'm not going. She laughed and said, "Don't be silly!" I said I was totally serious and I just didn't fancy it.

7.11 p.m.
Mum has found out from Weirdo Jen's mum the real reason why we are not going to the prom. She says she doesn't have to punish me as I have had the worst punishment possible.

She is right.

THURSDAY 24TH JUNE

6.23 p.m.
MGK is apparently helping to organize the prom on a specially set-up student committee.

The school have TOTALLY set it up to make our punishment WORSE.

I even heard MGK ordering her car for the prom at school today.

I really honestly hate her and her stretch limo in classic black not "chav hen-night pink".

FRIDAY 25TH JUNE

8.02 p.m.

Found out from Weirdo Jen that we are now known as "The Prom Rejects".

I am a Prom Reject.

In 30 years' time, when everyone is talking about school, that will STILL be what I'm remembered for. It's like a scar. And not a cool one either.

SATURDAY 26TH JUNE

2.35 p.m.

I haven't shaved for 5 days. What's the point? I can have hairy legs. Everyone will be too busy a) preparing for the prom, b) actually at the prom, to notice I've turned into a gorilla.

SUNDAY 27TH JUNE

10.21 a.m.

Message from Nicky:

> I'm not going to the prom either! Shall we meet up?

Dear Nicky – you have barely been to school your entire life. Go away! Love, Hattie.

I didn't say that. I just ignored the message.

6.12 p.m.

Goose is still going to the prom. Probably with a girl in a really amazeballs dress.

I might go round and say I need him on prom night.

No – that's not fair. He didn't do something STUPID.

MONDAY 28TH JUNE

7.18 p.m.

YES!!!

You can't keep brilliant people down!

The Prom Rejects are having their own party at Jen's house on Friday. We are calling it the WRONG PROM. Even people going to the REAL prom have admitted it sounds really cool. We are going to eat what we want, drink what we want, dance like nutters and DO WHAT WE WANT!

TUESDAY 29TH JUNE

4.03 p.m.

Who actually wants to go to a thing AT school organized BY school?! Matfield will be there!

Dimple is NOT going to the prom – she is coming to Jen's! She said she'd rather be with her best mates. YES – Dimple would rather be at THE COOLEST party this Friday.

MGK has bought the most gorgeous dress ever. REALLY glad I'm not going.

WEDNESDAY 30TH JUNE

5.09 p.m.

Just asked Mum if I can get a limo to Jen's house on Friday.

She said, "Sod off! Rob can take you and put the back seats down to make it feel more spacious!"

Thanks.

THURSDAY 1ST JULY

4.03 p.m.

We have all agreed that tomorrow we are just going to go casual to Jen's house. We don't need to glam up to feel amazing!

FRIDAY 2ND JULY

END OF SCHOOL!

5.02 p.m.

It was hard seeing everyone really excited today but I know we are going to have an AMAZING night tonight. We don't need Mrs Cob and MGK to organize our fun! We can have a REAL laugh at the Wrong Prom!

11.19 p.m.

Had a Chinese. Watched a DVD.

At 10.12 p.m. Dimple said, "Shall we call it a night then?" and everybody said, "YES."

Came home.

I'm not happy.

11.46 p.m.

Goose just got in and he was laughing on the phone. I banged the wall. He shut up.

SATURDAY 3RD JULY

8.49 a.m.

Apparently the prom was amazing. Unbelievable. The best night ever and the photos on Facebook look...

They look GLAM-FABULOUS.

9.44 a.m.

OMG – there's a photo of Matfield doing the conga. She's laughing.

It's 9.45 a.m. and I'm going to bed again. Goodnight.

4.09 p.m.

I went to see Gran this afternoon. She said I should just get over it. "They had a good night, Hattie – you didn't. That's how it goes sometimes. Sometimes you win the jackpot. Sometimes you don't even get a line. Life is a lot like bingo." Then she gave me 10 quid for doing well in my exams.

I feel better. The prom will be forgotten by tomorrow.

SUNDAY 4TH JULY

10.36 a.m.

Dimple said that Kate Friars tried to snog Tom Lacey at the prom – and SNEEZED instead. There's a film of it going round. Even Kate thinks it is LOL!

The prom will probably be forgotten by about Wednesday.

9.35 p.m.

FULL DRAMA!

Dimple's mum used a birthing ball as a space hopper bouncing toy at the antenatal class this afternoon and was admitted to hospital. Dimple says she's usually so sensible but this pregnancy has made her go mental. Last week she spent 2 days in her pyjamas watching the box set of *Downton Abbey* with the TV on mute and old '80s albums on. Apparently she started crying during a song called "True" by Spanx Ballet or something.

10.14 p.m.

Spandau Ballet. Spanx is what she needs after giving birth. Mum says your belly is never right again. I know that, Mum. I've seen Gran. She's like a massive deflated balloon after a party.

A hairy massive deflated balloon. She doesn't even have Brazilians any more. The college where she had it done cheaply stopped doing them. Apparently they had a record number of people leaving last year in the middle of the course. I wonder why! LOL!

MONDAY 5TH JULY

6.23 p.m.

Mum says my exam results are good enough for a
CLOTHES BINGE! I'm a bit worried she will want me to
buy a full-body burka swimsuit. She'll pretend it's to shield
me from the sun but it's actually to shield me from boys.

TUESDAY 6TH JULY

7.25 p.m.

Gran has crocheted me a bikini.

Mum is going to use it as a tea towel. She'll hide it when
Gran comes round.

WEDNESDAY 7TH JULY

11.21 a.m.

Mum has asked me to make a list of clothes I need for
Australia. I am compiling it today with the help of Dimple.

At the moment it is:

1. A very brilliant bikini that makes me Queen
   Gorgeousness.

THURSDAY 8TH JULY

1.01 p.m.

My brother has given me a book about dangerous
Australian animals! There's an OCTOPUS that can KILL
you and you don't even know it's stung you till you are
actually dead! Scary!

3.21 p.m.

MY CLOTHING LIST:

1. 6 bikinis
2. 2 cut-out swimsuits
3. A wetsuit
4. 2 pairs of sunglasses
5. 4 halter necks
6. 3 vintage-style dresses
7. 4 pairs of skinny jeans
8. 5 pairs of shorts
9. A boogie board
10. An inflatable boat

It's probably better to get the boogie board and the inflatable boat in Australia.

FRIDAY 9TH JULY

9.13 a.m.

MGK has tweeted that sun and salt water make your hair really dry and can be prematurely ageing.

She knows I want to go sailing and surfing in Australia. She tries to ruin everything by threatening beauty DOOM. Bet she's lying!

10.24 a.m.

No – I've googled it. She's right! Perhaps she was trying to actually HELP me!

10.49 a.m.

No. She wasn't. She was just showing off her glam knowledge.

11.29 a.m.

I think I'd rather have a laugh and worry about the wrinkles later.

OMG – I am now naturally feminist and often think brilliantly without trying!

4.03 p.m.

Someone has made a YouTube prom photo compilation.

The prom will NEVER be forgotten.

SATURDAY 10TH JULY

4.55 p.m.

SHOPPING DAY!

Mum had a totally predictable meltdown over EVERY bikini I liked. She said they were too revealing! Eventually I said, "No problem, Mum – I will go nude. It's the only way to get an all-over tan."

After I said THAT we finally found one that she thought was "appropriate"!

5.49 p.m.

Just want to say I would NEVER go nude in real life. I can stuff a bikini full of Plenty kitchen towel to give me more boob if I'm desperate. I've tried it before.

6.39 p.m.

Trouble is Plenty would try to soak up half the sea – I'd end up with soggy, uneven double-Fs.

7.04 p.m.

OMG – DOUBLE-Fs WOULD BE AMAZEBALLS!

SUNDAY 11TH JULY

1.48 p.m.

I have looked through the full list of Australian killer creatures that Nathan gave me. I shall not be going to the beach, the bush, near any trees, long grass or sheds. Or near water. Except taps.

2.36 p.m.

Apparently Tasmania has fewer killer things than most other killer places but there are still killer things everywhere. There's even something called a devil!

MONDAY 12TH JULY

6.32 p.m.

Mum has come home with another decent bikini. It's really sweet of her but I told her not to worry as I'll not be wearing it due to death creatures.

TUESDAY 13TH JULY

3.36 p.m.

OMG – our summer is winter in Australia. That is mental! What is even more mental is that Tasmania gets

ANTARCTIC blasts. I don't need to be buying swimwear. I need a suit of armour and a massive jumper.

5.11 p.m.

Even the cute things seem to have massive teeth in Australia. They need my dentist – I'm seeing him tomorrow for a brace update.

Please don't let my mouth set off the security alarms at the airport. MGK will spread it EVERYWHERE.

WEDNESDAY 14TH JULY

4.35 p.m.

My teeth have moved back!!! Mr Winkler said I was "very disciplined and patient". YES!!! Can you hear him, Mum?! I have to keep the brace on but I've made "great progress".

I saw MGK coming out of the dentist. It's like she waits till something good happens so she can RUIN it! She says my teeth do not look any different after months of wearing my brace. "That's odd," I said, "because despite years of wearing a Wonderbra your boobs don't look any different either!" LOL! I win!

THURSDAY 15TH JULY

12.19 p.m.

MGK is spreading it that I am a boob-watcher. And seriously, they are suggesting that I spend 26 hours NEXT to this person on a plane?

FRIDAY 16TH JULY

2.49 p.m.

MGK is also telling everyone she is going to be upgraded to first class – she is turning up to the airport in her designer gear. Apparently Prada gets you immediately into the celebrity lounge.

Genuinely I would prefer to be on the WING of the aeroplane – rather than next to MGK in ANY class.

SATURDAY 17TH JULY

2.25 p.m.

I am now ready to go to Australia or die in a horrific plane crash. Why do I watch *Air Crash Investigation?*

6.23 p.m.

OMG – just got a text from Nicky!

> Hats, Miss ya. Have a great time in Oz. Don't die by being bitten by crazy stuff. See you PLEASE, PLEASE for snogs when you get back. NXXXXXXXXXXXXXX

1. Please, please...
2. So many kisses it's actually difficult to count.

Dreading saying goodbye to Gran tonight.

8.48 p.m.

Gran and me just cried. She said, "Skype me when you can. I don't tell you but you're my best friend."

9.01 p.m.

Just cried again.

9.34 p.m.

Just rang Dimple and Jen. They cried. I told them they HAD to keep me up-to-date on ANY gossip.

I've been trying to see Goose but he's always out at the moment. I feel I should say goodbye. We aren't as close as we used to be. Or are we? I don't even know any more.

9.52 p.m.

Rob just cried. Mum just cried. I cried. AGAIN.

10.02 p.m.

Nathan said, "See ya!"

PURE evil. PURE lazy evil.

10.17 p.m.

Mum just came up and said through sobbing, "Your brother can't help it, Hattie. He feels rejected."

Er, Mum – HE rejected Keith! Keith did try. He rescued a sausage.

SUNDAY 18TH JULY

Somewhere in the world somewhere...

I don't even know what time it is!

MGK did not get upgraded. She started shouting at the airline man then looked at me and said, "DON'T TALK TO ME UNLESS YOU HAVE TO."

I am on a plane squashed between MGK and the most boring couple known to the world. The guy and his wife started telling me exactly how Tesco's in Crawley works. Apparently they think this is more interesting than the 100 films on the plane's entertainment system. I DON'T CARE HOW YOGHURTS get distributed. I want to see Taylor Lautner in the buff!

I think it's 6.45 p.m. but it might be 6.45 a.m.

Just landed in Bangkok. The boring couple got off. Please don't let them meet many Thai people. They will think all British people are dull. Weirdo Jen said to be careful of people trying to plant drugs on you. But Gran has sewn up my pockets, so I'm fine.

Why do they always seat our row last?

AUSTRALIA AT LAST!———————⟶

When we landed an Australian Customs man asked if we had brought any food, wine, fauna, eggs and dairy products in as Australia is a "unique ecological space that we wish to protect from ravaging pests and other environmental disasters".

We both said, "No."

The Customs dog went completely mad at MGK's bag and she looked really guilty. I looked at her and said, "What have you done?!" She said, "NOTHING." Anyway we were dragged over to a special table and this man rifled through

ALL her clothes until he found a Waitrose carrier bag full of FOOD.

MGK had only sneaked some diet yoghurts and some Yakults in because she "didn't know if Australia did them or not" and she needed them to be sure that she "maintained her good figure" and "didn't bloat".

The Australian man said, "So let's get this straight: you not fitting in your jeans is more important than bringing foot-and-mouth disease into the country, resulting in the slaughtering of millions of Australian cattle?"

MGK didn't apologize – she just said, "I think you're overreacting a bit."

The Customs official just stared at her and said, "If you were an adult we would fine you – you're lucky you're just a girl!"

"Just a girl!" – LOL! For MGK this is the worst punishment ever.

My bag didn't arrive. We waited for ages near the conveyor belt then Keith and his hippy girlfriend met us. She smells of soup but seems really nice. Apparently my luggage is in Bangkok. The boring couple are probably telling my suitcase about the best-before dates on bread.

TH JULY

OMG – what day is it? Today has gone. It's like *Doctor Who.*

Monday 19th July

10.23 a.m.

Keith's girlfriend offered to lend me some of her clothes. I now smell of soup too. We are sight-seeing tomorrow. I just want to sight-see my bed.

10.41 a.m.

OMG – Keith's girlfriend's name is Butterfly.

11.05 a.m.

She was born Tracey though – she had a renaming ceremony when she was reborn. In a forest.

12.34 p.m.

Keith had a renaming ceremony – he didn't tell us because he thought it would freak us out. His name here isn't Keith – it's Storm.

He is right. It would have freaked us out!

Me and MGK tried not to laugh.

To be fair even Keith did laugh a bit till Butterfly/Tracey said, "There's nothing to be ashamed of, Storm."

THIS MADE MGK and ME COLLAPSE WITH GIGGLES. Keith didn't say anything – just smiled. He actually seems really pleased to have us here.

Tuesday 20th July

8.32 a.m.

I've been asleep all night!

OMG – it's 8.32 p.m. not a.m!

Keith has just been in and told me the time. They said I looked so peaceful they didn't want to wake me up.

<u>And I'm STILL tired.</u>

Tasmania is mad from the window. It looks like *Jurassic Park* but without the dinosaurs. It's not like the Peak District at all. There are these massive plants and ferns everywhere and it smells like a massive cough sweet. Keith says this is because of the eucalyptus in the trees. It's the most foreign place I've ever been to. It's like landing in prehistoric Britain but with really nice houses and a massive casino.

Keith and *Butterfly's* house is the ultimate in shabby chic. MGK says it's actually just shabby but as usual she is being a tremendous cow bag. There are lots of wood thingies, armchairs with mad patches of fabric on them and compost bins everywhere. It's very … homely.

OK, it is a bit shabby but they've made our bedroom look really nice. Our bedroom. We are sharing. MGK was more horrified at this than me. She has her own walk-in wardrobe, remember. Now she has a walk-in clothes rail. LOL!

WEDNESDAY 21ST JULY

11.56 a.m.

I just heard MGK telling Butterfly and Keith that I should have put my body on to Australian time like SHE did.

I can't help needing sleep.

Keith has put the Internet in specially so we can Skype.

Thanks, Keith, but right now I don't want to speak to anyone unless I'm dreaming about them.

7.35 p.m.
Just dreamt about Goose. All his teeth had fallen out and I was trying to fix them back in with Blu-Tack.

He looked really good in the dream. Even with saggy gums.

Perhaps I should email him to check he is cleaning them for 2 minutes twice a day.

Perhaps I should get an actual life instead and stop thinking about Goose head-mess fest.

Thursday 22nd July

2.32 a.m.
According to MGK, I SNORE. She says she just had to turn me over to stop me "making a noise like a pig". I'd better tweet that I do not snore before she tweets that I do!

OMG – my phone doesn't work here! Apparently because I'm "pay as you go" I need a new SIM card.

6.35 p.m.
MGK DOES have a phone that works here. There you go, Mum – now the whole world knows I make snorting noises

because you are too tight-fisted to pay for an iPhone with global roaming!

6.49 p.m.

To be fair I don't know if MGK has tweeted that I snore yet.

FRIDAY 23RD JULY

10.37 a.m.

I HAVE A SIM CARD!!!

11.01 a.m.

MGK has NOT tweeted that I snore yet. Perhaps she's frightened I will tell people her secrets.

I haven't found out any yet but it's only a matter of time.

1.35 p.m.

OMG – they've arranged a welcome party for us! It's a green party.

7.35 p.m.

WEIRDO JEN, WHERE ARE YOU? YOU'D LOVE ALL THIS!

All the food was from their garden and everything had peas in it. They have a really boring artist friend called "M" who just went on about his art and himself and the fact he hasn't got a girlfriend (surprise!) because women affect his productive vibe.

Then all these women arrived from Butterfly's creative poetry group. None of them wear make-up but they look quite good. They were talking about the death of trees and global warming. They sounded like Weirdo Jen before we tell her to give it a rest! Basically we are all going to die unless we go vegan and ban plastic and mobile phones.

MGK and me agreed – we will die without a mobile anyway. What about emergencies?!

9.54 p.m.
OMG – MGK and me actually AGREE on something!

SATURDAY 24TH JULY

7.32 a.m.
I've just watched Butterfly try to wash up with really rubbish eco washing-up liquid. It apparently "helps the seas".

7.51 a.m.
I just Skyped Gran. She thinks if we have to use eco washing-up liquid dolphins should be trained to help her wash up. She thinks they could do it with a rubber glove attached to the end of their nose! LOL!

8.48 a.m.
Told Butterfly about Gran. Butterfly does NOT believe in training animals to do anything and would never commit a dolphin to domestic slavery. In fact she once got arrested for trying to free one of the beagles that sniff for illegal stuff at the airport. She particularly hated the fact

that the dog was in a special jacket with its name on. Butterfly said, "It's a dog not a policeman — it should be smelling for its own pleasure!"

I said, "Butterfly, I was only joking. A rubber glove would fall off a dolphin's nose unless you used elastic bands!" She's really sweet but she takes everything very seriously. She said dolphins have been abused for too long.

How can jumping through a hoop and getting a treat and a round of applause be abuse?

10.34 p.m.

Butterfly showed me a book where dolphins had been militarily trained. She thinks they will eventually take over the world when "mankind has destroyed itself". Not very cheerful!

SUNDAY 25TH JULY

7.35 p.m.

I've realized that when people swim with dolphins at Disneyland the dolphins are just taking notes on humans. They will know all our weak points and make us do tricks eventually.

8.13 p.m.

I explained to MGK about it. She doesn't like dolphins because supermodel Tyra Banks has a phobia of them and apparently, "What Tyra says goes!"

MGK then tried to teach me to "smize". This is what models do – they smile with their eyes. MGK can do it brilliantly. I just look like I've had a nasty shock. MGK told me to do it every day in the mirror and I will NEVER look bad in photos ever again.

9.23 p.m.

Keith and Butterfly use craptacular washing powder. I have to go to a laundrette tomorrow as I have no clothes thanks to my lost luggage. I have to use chemicals. I can't live in the Stone Age. I have grown up with Gran – Queen of Stain Removal and fantastic washing that is always really soft!

MONDAY 26TH JULY

5.31 p.m.

OMG – there was the fittest boy in the laundrette today. He was waiting for his pants to dry – that's what Australians call trousers. It was really hot in the laundrette and I was sweating in a jumper. This boy could see me sweating and he looked at my feet and asked me if I'd brought my thongs. I thought, OMG – he wants me! But thongs are Australian for flip-flops. I think he liked me though because he *did* wink at me. He told me he loved my accent – especially the way I said "bus". I am making sure I come to this laundrette every day!

7.35 p.m.

Keith's boring friend "M" is here. He's telling Keith and Butterfly that he had been eating lots of keenwah (?) and could probably outrun a tsunami if he had to. I hope he can't.

8.10 p.m.

Keenwah is spelt "quinoa". I googled it for about 20 minutes before MGK told me. It's a super food. She eats it regularly. Of course she does. Why can't she just eat lasagne and chips like the rest of us?!

TUESDAY 27TH JULY

3.01 p.m.

Keith/Storm (what do we call him?) has suggested we go camping at the weekend as it would be good to "get" with nature and have the opportunity to "bond". Butterfly is going to make us a vegan meatloaf. I had a bite of it before – it's a bit like eating cornflakes and nuts. MGK smiled at Butterfly but behind her back she started to make really bad vom faces. It was actually LOL!

WEDNESDAY 28TH JULY

11.03 a.m.

Nicky has messaged me:

> Did you get there OK?

I'm not even answering.

---

1. *NO KISSES AND I'M 10,500 miles away.*
2. *Obviously, I did, Nicky. You would have heard about it on the news by now if I hadn't.*

12.46 p.m.

I just asked MGK about Nicky. She looked at me for ages then said, "You totally went mental over him. I don't know why. You look good and you're all right."

You're all right?!

Perhaps her jet lag has just hit.

4.32 p.m.

Keith is very excited about camping. We are not.

THURSDAY 29TH JULY

6.29 p.m.

Me and MGK went shopping today for some camping gear. I helped MGK buy some tracksuit bottoms as she would not normally be seen dead in them even if they were "Juicy Couture". When she tried them on when we got home she thanked me and said they didn't look too bad. When I told her she looks good in most things she said, "Says the girl who's got a figure like a model." I shouted, "Yeah – skinny, no tits." Then she looked at me DEAD SERIOUS and said, "No – athletic and would probably look good in an all-in-one jumpsuit."

I really, really don't think she was being sarcastic.

Friday 30th July

12.53 p.m.

OMG – reading back on this I think there are some times when MGK may be OK. MAY be OK. Actually there are flashes of really quite lovely.

It can't be jet lag now. OMG – perhaps it's a long-haul thrombosis blood clot!

Saturday 31st July

7.29 p.m.

CAMPING – this is hell. MGK and I agree. You cannot use straighteners in a tent. No TV. No Internet. Even 3G doesn't work. It's like Gran's childhood without meat AND with the threat of snakes. I keep seeing massive spiders out of the corner of my eye when it's just a bit of sleeping bag and a hairbrush.

10.34 p.m.

Keith just had a massive chat with us, explaining how grateful he was that we had come over and that he really wanted to get to know us as "individuals". Then he said, "I'd like to think this is an opportunity for you 2 to become friends too."

I know this place has been a place of real change for you, Keith, but let's not expect a miracle.

11.01 p.m.

I must say though MGK is NOT being the total nightmare I'd thought she'd be. She's being quite ... OK.

Sunday 1st August

1.34 a.m.

OMG – there's something moving in my sleeping bag.

1.46 a.m.

It's fine – it's just my actual other foot.

2.36 a.m.

There is something moving outside. It's HUGE.

2.45 a.m.

It's Butterfly – she is going to wee in the bush as it helps the flora and fauna grow.

3.03 a.m.

Me and MGK are holding everything in till the morning – we'd rather be uncomfortable than suffer a comedy death being bitten on the bum by a poisonous something or other.

4.10 a.m.

Even MGK cannot sleep. She just asked me if blue-ringed octopuses can walk inland (she's been googling dangerous stuff too). I told her I didn't think so. Then I told her snakes give them a lift – it has been known.

She believed it. She's put her towel around her head.

I've told her I was joking but she has kept the towel around her head. She says she is now doing it for a laugh. I can't actually believe how much we are ... ~~gettting on~~ giggling.

I can't write any more. While I'm writing I could be attacked by something!

MONDAY 2ND AUGUST

10.34 a.m.

We are back from camping. We slept all day Sunday and all last night. Keith was a bit upset that we didn't connect with nature more but MGK told him that we did connect with our sleeping bags AND HE LAUGHED!

To be fair it was a bit LOL.

I've offered to take the washing to the laundrette.

12.35 p.m.

NOW MGK is coming with me too! She has Butterfly's green washing powder and the chance to ruin everything.

5.35 p.m.

The fit laundrette boy is called Lachlan!

How do I know? Because he talked to MGK for 4 HOURS.

4 HOURS of watching gorgeous people flirt and listening to tumble dryers. We are meeting again tomorrow too! It's either go with MGK or join Keith and Butterfly for a meditation morning.

You never know — there might be ANOTHER fit boy in Tasmania!

TUESDAY 3RD AUGUST

2.35 p.m.

Lachlan is completely in love with MGK. While they were "getting to know each other", I got lumbered talking to an 85-year-old called Janet. Apparently she helps out at the local old people's home, even though it sounded like she should actually be living there. She had perfect eye make-up but mahoosive chin hair. That makes no sense to me! Whilst she was telling me about Mr Stephanopoulos (who has eaten nothing but sweet-and-sour-chicken every day for 6 years) Lachlan and MGK had already arranged to meet the same time tomorrow. GREAT.

Another boy lost to someone more beautiful. When will my love life explode? When will someone want me more than their skater mates or their gecko?

Goose would love it here. It's full of lizards. They run off when they see you though. Good. It's not like I'm their Number 1 Fan. Reptiles are the reason – OH, GOOSE, GET OUT OF MY HEAD!

WEDNESDAY 4TH AUGUST

2.30 p.m.

Lachlan is going to see his brother who lives somewhere with a name I can't pronounce tomorrow. MGK and him had a massive goodbye snog when the washing machine was on its spin cycle! I started LOLing because it sounded like they were making all the sloshing noises with their actual mouths.

They both stared at me as if I had officially ruined their farewell love session.

HA!!!

5.24 p.m.

Texted Gran. Apparently fighting facial hair when you're over 50 is like fighting weeds in the garden. It's a constant job and sometimes in bad weather you can't be arsed.

I don't ever want to get old. Ever.

THURSDAY 5TH AUGUST

4.32 p.m.

2 MASSIVE things happened today:

1. I SAW MY FIRST BIG AUSTRALIAN SPIDER this morning. Butterfly spoke to it like it was a dog. It WAS the size of a dog. MGK was asleep. She was probably dreaming about Lachlan.
2. I had a massive conversation with Keith.

KEITH: I know I haven't earnt the right, Hattie, but can I give you a piece of advice?

ME: Er … go on.

KEITH: You're a great kid … sorry - young woman. I love how you can take the mickey out of yourself.

ME: Er…   ← SINCE WHEN?!

KEITH: But just one thing: don't miss out on relationships - love,

friendships. Don't ignore ← I HATE HEAVY
it like I did.   ADULT CHATS.

ME: Sounds like you've got someone you
         are thinking of…

KEITH: Well, take Ruby, for instance.

ME: OMG! You seriously don't know the
         history. She has made my life
         actual HELL.

KEITH: Well, I haven't got the best
         record either – and we've managed
         to become friends, haven't we? I
         mean, I know there's A LOT to do…

ME: That's different. You're my dad.
         She's my…

KEITH: Sister. Let her in, Hattie.

Why is it ME who has to do the letting in? Why is it ME
who always has to do the running and the chasing and the
asking?

Slightly – in fact TOTALLY – sick of it.

FRIDAY 6TH AUGUST

5.38 p.m.

At the laundrette today I met a man who was in the
Vietnam War (there was a war there apparently). He
narrowly missed a "bomb in the bunker" and ever since has
lived "day to day". He was really friendly – but why is it
that people want to tell you their entire life story when
they're cleaning their pants?! In fact everyone here wants
to tell you their entire life story. They are very, VERY
friendly. At first you think, "Are you weird?" or "What

249

do you want?" and then you realize they are actually just being Australian and NORMAL.

Whilst he was telling me about nearly dying MGK was slurping Lachlan's face off. It's wrong to hear giggles and kissing when a man is telling you about jungle rations.

YES! I am jealous.

SATURDAY 7TH AUGUST

5.53 p.m.
Finally there's ANOTHER fit boy in the laundrette! He's called Wayne! I know Wayne is the worst name on Earth BUT he has invited me out for coffee and cake in the mall on Monday. It's the best invite I've had since I got here!

10.12 p.m.
I can't believe I'm writing this but I just had a lovely night with MGK, Keith and Butterfly playing Scrabble. We had pizzas made with VEGAN CHEESE on the barbecue and then played a board game. It sounds like DULLSTER VON DULLSTER but it was really funny. MGK made the word "tooch" – which is another model word and means "to stick your bum out". Keith said, "That's not a word." I said, "I've hardly got one and therefore I am banning it anyway!" and MGK started laughing like CRAZY but not in a horrible way. WHAT IS GOING ON?!

Sunday 8th August

4.23 p.m.

MGK disappeared TOTALLY today. Keith let her. He thinks you should trust adolescents completely and they will "surprise and reward you".

Keith has clearly never brought up anyone! Good job he's had nothing to do with my brother!

8.01 p.m.

MGK has been with Lachlan all day. Apparently it's serious. It always is with her till it's not and she's dumped them!

Monday 9th August

4.21 p.m.

Met Wayne in the mall! We didn't really do anything but it was good to have a look round. I don't think we fancy each other. I think we are both a bit ... bored.

7.34 p.m.

Keith said today he'd like to spend more time with us and that maybe we're spending a little bit too much time with other people instead of him. I said, "I know how you feel! We've had 15 years of it!"

MGK wet herself.

This might be the greatest comeback EVER.

Keith wasn't cross. He just said, "Fair enough, Hattie — but let's move forward, shall we? How about we just spend a bit more time together. What woud you say to another Scrabble night?"

It WAS mahoosively hilarious.

8.10 p.m.
Mum called – am I having a good time?

I am actually. I told her me and Ruby were getting on quite well sometimes.

8.55 p.m.
OMG – I just called MGK "Ruby"!

TUESDAY 10TH AUGUST

7.18 p.m.
Wayne may have THE worst name in the world BUT 1) he can surf (he keeps falling off but he also stays on a bit), 2) he has his OWN CAR! FINALLY A POTENTIAL BOYFRIEND WITH 4 WHEELS AND A MOTOR!

WEDNESDAY 11TH AUGUST

7.12 p.m.
Wayne introduced me to his car. He put newspaper on the floor when I got into "her" as he didn't want any dust on the floor. I'm used to this. Rob is precious about his car. It's totally the sign of a good man.

Wayne dropped me off at home. MGK— Ruby thought he looked a bit "rough". She means SEXY.

I think I might fancy him. Might. He's not ... he's not my type.

He's not a geek.

OHHHH, WHY CAN'T I GET THE BOY OUT OF MY HEAD?!!

THURSDAY 12TH AUGUST

9.05 a.m.

OMG – Keith and Butterfly have just dropped a BOMBSHELL.

THEY ARE GETTING MARRIED AND WANT US TO BE BRIDESMAIDS!!!

Apparently they've been thinking about it for a while and now we are here and "fit in so well" (?!) they want to celebrate their love with the people they love the most!

I'd better tell Mum.

10.01 a.m.

Mum doesn't care. "He can do what he likes!" she said. Then she said, "Hattie, it's lovely to hear from you but couldn't this have waited till the morning?"

I forgot! It's night back home!

I'd better tell Gran.

10.32 a.m.

Gran doesn't care either. She said, "Congratulations but I can't chat, Hattie. I'm playing 'Words With Friends' on my iPad with a man from around the corner. I've not met him but I think he's got more chance with his marriage than Keith has. Goodnight."

Well, Ruby and me are pleased for them. They are quite sweet really.

5.23 p.m.

Wayne picked me up in his car. He does not want to be seen as a "hoon" (boy racer) so he drives sensibly. This means very slowly. He says he is cruising and he needs to "treat her right". He polishes her ALL the time. He calls HER "Adrienne the car".

Adrienne?

It's after the cat he had when he was 7.

Is that cute or really freaky?

I daren't ask Ruby.

FRIDAY 13TH AUGUST

5.21 p.m.

Wayne was late today as he was polishing "Adrienne the car". I am beginning to understand how a mistress feels. Wayne is married to Adrienne. I'm a bit on the side. I've seen this on soaps — it never ends well.

And I'm thinking all the time ... If I had JUST perhaps said 1 sentence my life could be so different right now. I COULD be about to Skype someone who I just really LOVE and FANCY and LIKE and ALL OF IT. I could be in snog city not car mistress mist.

I'm talking crap but I know what I mean.

Saturday 14th August

9.24 a.m.

Wayne rang my mob. Adrienne the car is ill. He couldn't get her started this morning. I said, "No worries." I'm going on a nature hike with my dad. Ruby is off with Lachlan – Dad is starting NOT to trust her. LOL!

9.32 a.m.

OMG – I just called Keith "Dad"! What is going on?

6.32 p.m.

Please note: leaves, ferns and fungi are more appealing than being with Wayne and Adrienne. That's not a good sign, is it?

Sunday 15th August

7.12 p.m.

Wayne and I were going to kiss tonight but I accidentally scuffed Adrienne's handbrake with my trainers. Wayne pretended it didn't matter but said he had to deal with it immediately or it could be permanent.

MONDAY 16TH AUGUST

5.32 p.m.

Wayne doesn't think he can come to Dad's wedding — whenever the date. He can't get Adrienne near the venue. He doesn't want to leave her somewhere that isn't monitored.

This is getting weird now. I thought geckos were weird. They are not. They are fine. Gran was right — world travel does open your eyes.

9.24 p.m.

I have seen Butterfly's wedding dress. It's made of eco-friendly material. It's sort of ... brown.

OMG — what if our bridesmaid dresses are like that? Ruby won't wear it.

9.45 p.m.

If Ruby doesn't then I'm not either. I'm just going to say it's SISTER SOLIDARITY.

Also Ruby is basically *Vogue* and I am NOT.

TUESDAY 17TH AUGUST

3.23 p.m.

Wayne has put a "Ninja Love Machine" sticker on the back of his car.

This is not going to work.

WEDNESDAY 18TH AUGUST

1.32 p.m.

Wayne says he has to replace Adrienne's engine.

I told him I understood and to contact me when he's finished.

Hopefully it will take a long time!

Cars are just grown-up skateboards. Wayne is just an Australian version of Nicky. I have swapped one disinterested boy for another.

I know who I want really.

Just came home to find Lachlan and Ruby having the world's biggest snog.

2.34 p.m.

It is still going on!

3.34 p.m.

It is STILL going on! Don't they need actual AIR?!

6.14 p.m.

Ruby has been kissing for HOURS. Occasionally they eat, drink and giggle. Then they start again!

7.39 p.m.

After Lachlan went tonight Dad asked Ruby if she wouldn't mind NOT seeing him for a couple of days as he wanted to spend time with us!

Ruby got a bit annoyed but agreed.

11.35 p.m.

I can't sleep. Ruby has been talking to Lachlan for 3 hours since she just gave him "a quick ring" to tell him she couldn't see him for a few days.

He calls her "KB" – it's short for Koala Bear. VOM!!!

THURSDAY 19TH AUGUST

8.23 a.m.

We are having an eco-friendly hen night tonight for Butterfly. I am actually scared what this might mean.

11.12 p.m.

The eco-friendly hen night consisted of a vegan buffet and homemade alcohol created from potatoes that me and Ruby were not allowed to drink!

After Butterfly and her friends tried it most of them ended up singing about how the sky gives women strength, sisters are doing it for themselves and a song called "Mary was meant to be hairy – be brave, don't shave".

Ruby could not understand this. She asked Butterfly's friend Sky if she'd ever had a Brazilian. She said, "No, but I travelled with a man from Peru once who owned a llama farm."

Then one of Butterfly's friends did fortune-telling. They told Butterfly her marriage would be very happy as she transforms others and brings a healing love to everything she is near. Yes, total crap, BUT she actually is really sweet and you can't laugh at someone on their hen night.

Butterfly then told everyone she was desperate for a decent steak. The atmosphere turned a bit weird. I said, "She only wants a bit of meat — it's not like she's having an affair or anything." One of her friends said, "Better to engage in free love than to eat the soul of a living creature."

No wonder my dad fits in here! LOL!

No that's not fair. Dad HAS changed. He's actually lovely and that's everything you could want in a man. Someone you can depend on and you're good friends with and — OH— WHY HAVE I BEEN SUCH AN IDIOT?! YES! YES! YES!!! I KNOW!!!!

Friday 20th August

10.02 a.m.

Butterfly thanked me this morning for sticking up for her when she was really drunk. She actually remembered what she had said about steak! I told her not to worry — it would all be forgotten now. Butterfly said it wouldn't be — Rosehip didn't speak to her own mother for 6 months when she caught her eating a tin of tuna. These people are SERIOUS. Apparently it's better to say f*** than veal.

What is veal?

11.13 a.m.

It's baby calf. It's expensive and a delicacy. That's why I don't know about it. We live on economy mince.

Just read about how they keep some of the calves
andthey do have a point.

2.13 p.m.

Ruby and I have agreed that when we get home we are
jointly spreading it that Matfield has veal for breakfast.
RAW. LOL!

SATURDAY 21ST AUGUST

5.24 p.m.

OMG - FASHION DOOM!

Our bridesmaid dresses ARE made of felt and hemp.
Please let the happy couple be against cameras too
because they are not environmentally-friendly or something!

6.34 p.m.

They are not. These photos are going to end up
everywhere.

7.12 p.m.

Ruby just said something actually lovely.

Ruby, previous Empress of Cow and fashionista
extraordinaire, just said, "These dresses are vile but both
of us can rock them with some well-placed accessories. I
will help you."

YET AGAIN, I'M BLOWN AWAY.

11.24 p.m.

DAD IS MARRIED!!!

It was a pagan ceremony. Jen would have loved it!
Butterfly came in covered in flowers. She didn't carry
them — they were ALL over her dress. She actually
looked really beautiful. The wedding ceremony was
WEIRD though! They mentioned "emotionally
and physically honouring each other" (VOM!!!).

Dad looked OK. He had mad hair but his purple velvet
suit looked quite cool. He gave a speech at the reception
and said the most special thanks goes to Hattie and Ruby
for travelling all this way. He said, "I am so proud of my
2 daughters, who are so different yet so special in their
own way." Everyone applauded this.

Basically we got a clap for sitting on a plane for a long
time and being born.

MASSIVE SURPRISE!!! Wayne actually arrived in his car
to see me. He found somewhere secure to park and was
even really apologetic that he missed the wedding.

We kissed but I'm not bothered — the person I have
missed most on this holiday is Goose. That's the truth.

Just realized Lachlan didn't turn up yesterday either.
Perhaps he was working.

Monday 23rd August

9.34 a.m.

Dad and Butterfly slept under the stars last night. They're still out there looking at the sky and pointing at nothing and laughing. It's half sweet and half VOM!

Oh, it's sweet. They are really in love.

12.35 p.m.

OMG – just went into the bedroom to find Ruby sobbing.

I said, "What's up?" She couldn't talk for a while as she was crying so hard and then she said, "Oh, Hattie. I've been dumped!"

OMG – RUBY HAS BEEN DUMPED. SERIOUSLY THIS IS MAHOOSIVE!

She cried for another hour then she managed to say, "I really liked him. We ... we .... did stuff. Stuff I've never done with anyone before. Stuff."

OMG TO THE MAX! Does she mean what I think she means?

I didn't ask. I gave her a cuddle.

She is my sister. And she lent me the loveliest belt ever to save my felt dress from fashion doom.

I know what it's like to be dumped.

5.32 p.m.

Dad and Butterfly are still laughing at clouds. Ruby is still crying.

I don't want to spoil Dad and Butterfly's camping honeymoon so I am looking after her. She has gone through 4 toilet rolls already!

7.21 p.m.

I am actually quite lovely in a crisis.

TUESDAY 24TH AUGUST

7.34 a.m.

OK, I am officially not lovely in a crisis. Ruby has now been crying all night and I am sick of it. It's not like she was married to Lachlan!

11.32 a.m.

OMG, OMG, OMG!

Just had this conversation with Ruby:

ME:	Come on – it's not like you were married to Lachlan!
RUBY:	Shut up. It was special. It was…
ME:	What?!
RUBY:	I think I might…
ME:	Might what?
RUBY:	Be pregnant!
ME:	OMG! RUBY!

Then we had a massive hug for about 10 minutes. Then I said, "What happened?!"

Ruby told me! OMG!

I shouted at her. "YOU CAN'T GET PREGNANT DOING THAT! URGH! TMI — but you definitely can't get pregnant doing that!"

Then she said, "People think I know a lot about boys and stuff, Hattie, but I don't know everything."

No, Ruby — you actually know less than I do.

Then she made me swear that WHATEVER happened I would never tell anyone that she was mixed up about the actual act of doing it.

I have sworn.

3.44 p.m.

Is it wrong to keep information like this from your best friends though? Isn't it like lying to them?

4.56 p.m.

No. I am never going to tell anyone ever.

Except perhaps Dimple in 2 years' time when it doesn't matter any more.

No — not even then. Ruby is family.

7.25 p.m.

Dad and Butterfly just came in to have some dinner. They thought Ruby looked a bit "red around the eyes". I said, "She's got hay fever." At EXACTLY the same time Ruby said, "I got flies in them." We looked slightly suspicious but I think they fell for it!

Wednesday 25th August

12.26 p.m.

Ruby just said, "Thanks for yesterday, Hattie. I just wanted Lachlan to like me. I want people to like me."

I said, "Don't be such a stuck-up cow then. You're actually all right really."

Ruby snapped back, "It's all right for you. People LIKE YOU LOADS!"

All right for me?! ALL RIGHT for me?! Ruby has got a REAL Miu Miu handbag! THAT'S all right!!!

Thursday 26th August

9.23 a.m.

Text from Wayne:

```
Patty. Engine replacement hard.
Perhaps C U b4 u go back.
```

I replied:

```
It's HATTIE. U can't actually
snog cars. Bye.
```

LOL!

6.34 p.m.

Dad wants to have a goodbye dinner. He says him and Butterfly want to give us a proper send-off. Dad and Butterfly came inside for some lunch then went and sat in the garden again all afternoon and sang songs by this bloke called Van Morrison!

I've realized they are not having a proper honeymoon because every day of their lives is actually already like a honeymoon!

FRIDAY 27TH AUGUST

5.34 p.m.

Dad just said how much closer he feels to the both of us.

I DO feel closer to him. I get him more, I think. And I can see how this place could change him. It is totally OFF IT ... in I think a good way.

SATURDAY 28TH AUGUST

5.32 p.m.

Mum just rang my mob. She said, "Keith and I made a mess and perhaps you didn't have the easiest start but you can't blame us any more. Rob has done a great job, Hattie. The BEST. We aren't the reason why you are rubbish with boys!" Typical out-of-the-blue Mum randomness.

When I said, "What made you say that?" Mum told me that "Ruby's mum told me you'd been dumped by a boy called Wayne. I just want you to know we love you and we want you back here, HAPPY!"

UNBELIEVABLE!

Bet Ruby hasn't told HER mum what SHE has been up to!

7.09 p.m.

Just asked Ruby. She said, "Sorry, Hattie. I just didn't want to talk about myself so I told Mum about you — I was in a panic."

I will let her off.

SUNDAY 29TH AUGUST

11.54 p.m.

We had a goodbye meal tonight. Dad kept crying, and saying, "I do hope you'll see me as a kind of dad." The odd thing is I DO but in a sort of "will never be around, vague but lovely man really" dad way. Ruby feels basically the same way. Her stepdad is her REAL dad. And her REAL dad is a "will never be around, vague but lovely man really" sort of dad.

It's complicated.

The real revelations from this holiday have been:

1. The fact that my half-sister is actually MAX sweet underneath all the Prada fake RUBBISH.
2. I know who I really LOVE. Now I think I need to go home and tell him.

In bed and dreading the journey, sorting out men and never sleeping again.

MONDAY 30TH AUGUST

6.13 p.m.

Goodbye Butterfly, Dad and Tasmania. You are very weird but I think I may slightly, in a very mental way, REALLY LOVE you.

(LATE AND HOME!)   ## TUESDAY 31ST AUGUST

Ruby was asleep before we took off. I was sat between her and a woman who told me her husband's dying words were: "Have you given the cat his worming tablet?" She hadn't. She thinks that might have finished him off but at least now he was gone she had more time for knitting.

Then she got off and the woman who got on kept telling me that her son was in the chorus line of Les Misérables and if the lead's understudy was ill and his understudy was ill he'd be the star in the Wednesday matinee.

I think I finally fell asleep over Afghanistan according to the map.

OMG – Afghanistan! Isn't that dangerous?! How close was I to actual death?!

Ruby woke up when the doors were opened at Heathrow. We landed at – I can't even remember. We had to walk through the airport – about 26 miles. Collected the suitcases (mine was now back from Bangkok) and Mum saw me and would not let go of me! I was hugged for about a million hours. AND she cried!

Then Mum said I had to sleep in the car so I was ready for school. It's on Thursday*!!!* Thursday*?!* I need a week to recover!

WEDNESDAY 1ST SEPTEMBER

2.12 a.m.

I can't sleep.

1. How do I say it?
2. How do I even start to say how I feel?
3. And how do I tell the other one that I'm probably over him?!

6.12 a.m.

Just was awake all night. Watched YouTube – I've seen every cat video ever. I've even see people pretend their cats are beards. You can't do that with a gecko, Goose! It would make such a rubbish goatee!

Goose. Goose. Goose. Goose.

I HAVE to tell him how I feel. Who cares what happens? I HAVE to put it out there.

THURSDAY 2ND SEPTEMBER   Back to school.

4.35 p.m.

Mum made me go to school today. It was AMAZEBALLS to see Dimple and Jen again! I nearly had a nap on Dimple's shoulder though when she hugged me. She just felt so comfy – like a human pillow. I told her she felt like a lovely bed. She didn't look ever so happy about that.

Then I fell asleep in the paint in Matfield's class. Jen suggested that I could paint with my forehead as that's what Salvador Dali probably did (who's HE? Jen knows some WEIRD stuff). This made Matfield go predictably mad as she worships the great artists and says they had more ability in the womb than I have at 15. I ended up having a lie-down on Mrs Kirton the school nurse's fold-out bed.

I was only allowed to stay there for an hour then I had to get up for Maths. Who cares? Data representation?! Dear Data — I do not want to represent you EVER.

Nathan grunted a "Hello" to me when I got home tonight. No — he did NOT ask me what Australia OR Dad were like as he truly does not care.

7.22 p.m.

No, Gran, I cannot come to yours and sit with you for a few hours and tell you everything that happened. I am an official zombie. I'm not dead but my head is!

10.31 p.m.

Gran has just been round. She quickly realized I was too tired to talk so she hugged me for 5 minutes then spent 2 hours telling me about her life. I fell asleep whilst she was telling me about the deli counter at her shop. Hungarian salami is not very exciting. Not even when

Vera from checkouts is slipping on it and dislocating her shoulder!

FRIDAY 3RD SEPTEMBER

4.32 a.m.
PLEASE LET ME SLEEP.

6.12 a.m.
Mum has agreed it's actually pointless going to school. Goodnight.

6.34 p.m.
I have slept all DAY and I have had no contact with anyone on Facebook/Twitter/my mobile/MSN – anywhere any time! Mum says it was like this when she was growing up. How did people do anything? How did love actually happen? What if you were late and your mate was waiting there for ages – what did you do? It's MENTAL.

7.56 p.m.
OMG – just got up to a message from Nicky:

> Hats, I've really missed you.
> I've had a bit of a hard time.
> Please see me. I can make stuff
> better if you help me become
> less of a total doughnut.

NO KISSES AGAIN. DOES NICKY KNOW HOW TO WRITE A TEXT?!

"I've REALLY MISSED YOU"? Gran is right – the more you ignore men, the more they like you. They are CRAZY-

WEIRD. If a girl ignores a girl it's because she hates her, is deadly jealous of her or she wants her to be a friend and is frightened of making a bit of a tit of herself. Men are very complicated. Someone needs to write a guidebook about men.

Anyway I don't want Nicky. I want Goose.

8.12 p.m.
I just told Gran. She said, "Oh, you're awake now that you need to know about the opposite sex!"

I told her that Nicky had said he had missed me but that I really wanted Goose. Gran said, "WELL, TELL HIM THEN! What do you want him to do? Fly a plane over your house with an 'I LOVE HATTIE' banner dragging behind it?"

I'll do it tomorrow. I'll go for it tomorrow. Tomorrow I'll just explode the Goose love.

SATURDAY 4TH SEPTEMBER

10.18 a.m.
I swear God hates me. Or someone does.

Dimple came round this morning and looked really serious. Before I could tell her anything about Australia she said, "I've got something to tell you – Goose is seeing Megan Fenton!"

GOOSE IS SEEING MEGAN FENTON?!

MEGAN FENTON?!

I shouted at Dimple, "Why didn't you tell me before?!"

Dimple said, "Because Jen and me decided that you had more important things to think about with your dad and we didn't want to spoil your holiday and then you had really bad jet lag at school and you couldn't think straight..."

MEGAN FENTON?!!

HATTIE MOORE fails again. Well, you lost him, Hattie. You played it cool and froze to actual love DEATH.

11.35 a.m.

You know what, Goose? That's cool. That's cool. That's really cool.

And it is cool because I'm going to see Nicky. HE wants me. YOU don't.

SUNDAY 5TH SEPTEMBER

12.45 p.m.

BAD. BAD. BAD. BAD.

Just as Goose and Rob were gettng back from the boot sale this morning Nicky came round. Goose gave him this really horrible look! I could see it from my bedroom window. He looked like he was going to hit him. Luckily Rob shouted, "Come on, mate! Early bird gets the worm and all that!"

Nicky just marched past Mum and mumbled, "Hello, Hattie's mum!" She tried to say something back but she had a mouthful of muesli and started choking on a sultana. Nicky came up to my room and said:

NICKY:	Hello.
ME:	Hello.
NICKY:	Missed ya, Shorty.
ME:	Good.
NICKY:	I'm a doughnut.
ME:	Yeah, you are.
NICKY:	Can we have another try? I think you get me.
ME:	I don't know. You've got to … just be nice.
NICKY:	I am all right honestly – I just can get things wrong, you know. I think I sort of love you, Hattie.

HATTIE PLAYS IT SUPER COOL – EVEN THOUGH TO BE FAIR HE LOOKS SUPER HOT.

OMG!

I didn't say anything but then we just had this huge snog till my mum rushed in and said, "Nicky, it is traditional to be invited into someone's house."

Nicky said, "Sorry, Mrs M. By the way, you've got Alpen on your chin."

Mum went a bit red and walked off.

NICKY AND ME ARE BACK ON AND HE CAME AFTER ME!!!

SEE! WHEN MEN LIKE YOU THEY TAKE CONTROL AND DO SOMETHING.

MONDAY 6TH SEPTEMBER

6.20 p.m.

Just thinking about it. I'm pretty sure Goose was snogging Megan Fenton before I even went away. He was always on his phone looking totally suspicious.

But it's still OK because I'm with Nicky.

And I can still be friends with Goose. I will have to be. He's next door and he's basically Rob's best friend. So I will keep it...

What's that word Gran uses when you want to ACTUALLY KILL SOMEONE but you have to be nice to them?

6.44 p.m.

Just texted Gran...

Civil. I am going to be civil.

As "civil" as I can be.

TUESDAY 7TH SEPTEMBER

7.38 p.m.

I went round to see Goose after school today. He asked me if I'd heard about him and Megan. I said, "Yeah, it's cool – I'm really pleased for you. Did you hear about me and Nicky?"

Goose just said, "Yes – Meg used to have a terrapin so she understands how much time exotic pets need."

I REALLY DON'T CARE ABOUT MEGAN'S PREVIOUS PET HISTORY.

8.34 p.m.
Just asked Gran if you can base a successful relationship on animals. Gran shouted, "Of course you can! Hattie, people who breed cocker spaniels always marry other cocker spaniel breeders. Sharing passions is the key to a long-term relationship. I know a couple who had their dogs as bridesmaids."

If Goose wants to marry Megan and have a gecko crawl with her down the aisle that's FINE BY ME.

WEDNESDAY 8TH SEPTEMBER

8.19 p.m.
Dimple just rang. Her mum is in labour but the hospital have told her to go away till she's more "ready"!

8.45 p.m.
Nicky says labour can go on for ever. His mum was in labour and he went to the cinema. He says after the fourth baby it becomes as normal as "going to school".

Nicky doesn't go to school very often. How would he know?!

Thursday 9th September

5.01 p.m.
Dimple wasn't at school today and her mobile was off. Nicky says you're probably not allowed to text when your mother is giving birth.

7.32 p.m.
OMG – Nicky was actually with his mum when she had his little brothers Javier and Nemanja. He said she just shouted even more than normal but weirdly swore less.

8.03 p.m.
Dimple just texted. Her mum had a little boy at 3 p.m. They've called him Amitabh – it's after another film star!

Nicky says his brothers and sisters are named after Manchester United players. His dad thinks it's lucky.

9.42 p.m.
Nathan is singing something very loudly and very annoyingly in his bedroom. Dimple is really happy about having a brother. She has NO IDEA!

Friday 10th September

5.23 p.m.
Dimple was telling us all about her mum today. As soon as Mrs Rathod had got home she had to go straight back to hospital again! Labour sounds horrendous.

It's unbelievable what people will go through for a family!

Dimple's mum had forgotten how bad labour was — apparently you block it out. Apparently adults can block out lots of things, I've noticed — actual children being born (Dad, prior to last year!), the pain and agony that their children are going through (Mum!) and the TOTAL embarrassment that their grandchildren experience whenever they are around (Gran!).

7.03 p.m.

Nicky says it's all worth it in the end as "family is the most important thing in the world".

Nicky IS kind.

9.23 p.m.

Dear Megan Fenton — STOP GIGGLING IN GOOSE'S BEDROOM NEXT DOOR. THEN STOP GOING QUIET. That means you are obviously snogging and you make me sick.

I don't have to be civil in this diary to ANYONE.

SATURDAY 11TH SEPTEMBER

1.35 p.m.

According to Dimple, all Amitabh does all day is eat, cry and sleep occasionally for 15 minutes at a time. It's the worst jet lag ever on Earth!

3.23 p.m.

Nicky has invited me round his house tomorrow. I'm a bit nervous because his family sound completely crazy.

7.34 p.m.

Gran just called my mob and asked if she could have a leg of lamb for her birthday instead of flowers.

My family is also mental. At least at our wedding everyone will get on!

SUNDAY 12TH SEPTEMBER

7.34 a.m.

OMG – Megan has gone car-booting with Goose. How sad is that? Does she even have a personality of her own? She was wearing a really nice vintage-style print dress too at 7 a.m. in the morning. She's going to be freezing in the middle of a field wearing THAT! I am going round to Nicky's house today and I am wearing a COAT. I am a feminist and dress for warmth as well as fine glam style, Megan. You ought to try it!

6.54 p.m.

Nicky's house is total CHAOS. Nicky seems to have about 20 brothers and sisters. They were all playing on an old washing machine in the back garden, pretending it was a space station. Nicky's mum was shouting that they had used "all her bloody tin foil making a rocket". We heard her from down the street before we even saw the space station. When Nicky actually got in the front door all the kids charged up to him for a hug – at one stage he had 5 children hanging off him! He just acted like it was totally normal.

We didn't stay long because Nicky doesn't really have any personal space (Nicky doesn't have ANY space) and his dad had just got back from the supermarket IN SLIPPERS. Neither his mum nor his dad seemed to notice I was there. Or that Nicky was there. He just comes and goes as he wants.

Nicky said, "Come on — I am going to take you to my favourite place." We ended up at Peartree Railway Station! Nicky whispered, "I come here to read. It's really quiet. Hardly any trains stop here and it feels sort of like the countryside." At that point a massive Virgin Train came thundering past us and blew its horn! According to Nicky you get used to that.

I don't want Peartree Station to be where I go on dates!

Nicky was saying, "Sorry about my house. It's just my mum is really busy with the kids and my dad is busy working and getting shopping and they don't always notice who I bring home." I told him it didn't matter but I was a bit freaked out by it all. I was also a bit freaked out by the railway station too. There were about 14 CCTV cameras and they all seemed to be pointed at us. When we were snogging it felt like I was doing something REALLY wrong. I couldn't concentrate on getting a decent kiss rhythm because I kept thinking of MY mum sitting at the main police station shouting, "She said she was going round Nicky's house — NOT kissing in him in the middle of nowhere." The cops could totally show her the footage if they wanted to. Nicky started to get a bit annoyed at me being nervous. "I come here all the time — I've never got in trouble. I doubt those cameras are even on!" Then one of the cameras moved and Nicky decided it was a "bit cold to be out".

Nicky showed me his graffiti tag on the way home. He'd put it on the side of phone box. He was really proud of it but it just looked like a big load of triangles to me.

Now I'm sitting here feeling guilty but I don't know exactly what for.

7.36 p.m.

A full snog at a railway station is not against the law — even when it's caught on camera.

8.45 p.m.

Hope I don't look weird when I kiss.

9.03 p.m.

Perhaps if you ask them, the police will show you the footage so you can improve your snog technique!

Nicky is a bit … I don't want to get in trouble. I didn't know he did tagging. That's proper graffiti. Proper crime.

MONDAY 13TH SEPTEMBER

4.10 p.m.

Ruby at school today cornered me by the canteen and said, "Hattie — WHY are you going out with Nicky Bainton again?"

When I told her it was because I liked him she said, "Hattie – HE IS TROUBLE. You helped me when I was in trouble, now I'm helping YOU. Give him up. I know why you are really doing it too – everyone does – and it's not fair." Then she stormed off.

Good to see Ruby can still do a MAHOOSIVE MGK flounce-off when she needs to.

And what does everyone know? They haven't seen how brilliant Nicky is with his family and how great he is to his brothers and sisters.

YOU HAVE TO GIVE PEOPLE A CHANCE. JUST LIKE I DID WITH DAD. And that's what I'm doing. I'm not using him or anything!

7.12 p.m.
I just rang Gran to ask her about Nicky. She said, "Hattie – I can't talk now. I'm going out and it takes 10 minutes for me to put my support tights on." There's no one I can speak to here and Dimple and Jen would FREAK at this. I'm just totally worried. Nicky is out for the next 2 nights. I know what he's doing and I can't stop him.

I hope he doesn't start writing "Hattie" anywhere so people think I'm actually involved!

9.01 p.m.
Just been practising my tag on my Science textbook. It's rubbish but you can't get arrested for it.

Tuesday 14th September

4.10 p.m.

Mrs Field saw my tag on my Science book. Apparently I am scribbling on school property and I should "stop immediately". I get told off for doodling 1 scribble on 1 book. Nicky has tagged 7 park benches, loads of walls, a fence on a house AND 5 buses (one of them was actually moving at the time!) and NOTHING happens. I AM CURSED.

7.32 p.m.

Dimple rang. She says that newborn babies are a living HELL. Apparently her mum is crying every 5 minutes and last night they had CHIPS for tea. They NEVER have takeaway. Dimple's mum had a kidney stone once. She was in AGONY and she still cooked dinner! All that is left in the cupboard is Pot Noodles. I'm surprised Dimple's family even have them.

Apparently Dimple's dad has a secret Pot Noodle addiction but I can't tell anyone as it could damage his reputation as an upstanding member of the community. Dimple's dad needs to chill out. Even the prime minister lives on Pot Noodles, plays "Fruit Ninja" all the time and cries every night about how hard the job is. It's a well-known fact!

8.12 p.m.

Tell you what, I would rather listen to Amitabh's SCREAMING than Megan Fenton's crap girlie giggle. I am tempted to knock on the wall and tell her to ACTUALLY

SHUT UP but I'm worried that would be seen as being a bit ... something.

She lives at Goose's house. It's ... NOT ON.

WEDNESDAY 15TH SEPTEMBER

6.34 p.m.

Nicky went round with me tonight to see Amitabh after school. As soon as he picked the baby up he stopped crying. It was UNBELIEVABLE. Dimple doesn't like Nicky but even she had to admit it was like *Supernanny*. We've been invited again to go tomorrow. Nicky understands families and babies. And writing his tag on electricity substations' "Danger of Death" signs. That's what he was doing last night.

THURSDAY 16TH SEPTEMBER

8.14 p.m.

Went round to see Dimple again. Every member of the family looked really pleased to see us.

Dimple's mum jokingly asked Nicky if he's considered becoming a professional nanny. Nicky said he'd had a bit too much of babies. Mrs Rathod giggled and said, "Shame!" She looked really disappointed though.

Dimple's mum has admitted she's having trouble coping! I'm not surprised. Being a mum is dreadful from moment 1!

8.54 p.m.

Although I reckon my mum doesn't have it too bad... She is asleep AGAIN before 9 p.m. and Rob is doing everything!

I can't decide whether she's a proper feminist or actually just completely lazy.

FRIDAY 17TH SEPTEMBER

8.34 p.m.

I told Gran about Dimple's mum. Gran has been in touch and offered to help Dimple's mother — she has theories about babies. Apparently years ago babies were shoved all together in a full-time nursery and a big scary matron gave you the baby at feeding time and then the rest of the time just left them to cry!

Gran believes that the reason that so many young people are not prepared to work hard all stems from the fact that babies are not left to scream nowadays!

BARKING!

9.21 p.m.

Asked Mum if she left ME to cry as a baby. She said, "Never, Hattie. You slept in my bed most nights till you were 4."

THAT'S why I can't finish my homework!

SATURDAY 18TH SEPTEMBER

5.34 p.m.

Gran has been round to see Dimple's mum today!

Apparently Amitabh stopped crying after Gran wrapped him up like a mummy. Mrs Rathod got 3 hours' sleep. This apparently is a MIRACLE!

3 HOURS' SLEEP IS A FORM OF TORTURE!

I can see why Mum didn't let me cry now!

SUNDAY 19TH SEPTEMBER

2.18 p.m.

Dimple wants to hire Gran as a part-time nanny. Gran now has the choice of 2 jobs! ARE YOU HEARING THIS, NATHAN?! Gran has written down a few things she believes in:

1. Groups of mums should not be allowed to meet in public places. Gran is sick of going to Starbucks and hearing squawking. She says, "I want to be able to enjoy a latte and a blueberry muffin in peace."

2. Children should not be given felt-tips until they are 18. They are potentially more damaging to your wallpaper and your health than cigarettes.

3. Dummies dipped in brandy should be used when babies are teething.

4. Children should be at school 52 weeks a year as brains go stale in the holidays.

Has Gran actually ever heard of Social Services?!

Monday 20th September

6.23 p.m.

Apparently Goose and Megan went to see Amitabh today. He cried. He was really trying to say, "Megan, stop wearing little vintage dresses on very cold days and PUT SOME MORE CLOTHES ON!" LOL!

6.41 p.m.

I find Megan THE MOST annoying woman ON EARTH – even though EVERYONE ELSE, including Dimple and Jen, thinks she's "quite sweet really".

6.53 p.m.

I should be kind to other women.

7.01 p.m.

Sometimes it's difficult being a feminist.

Tuesday 21st September

4.35 p.m.

Gran's worried about Princess. She's really lethargic and has started piddling on the carpets. And she won't even touch the gourmet chicken that Gran cooks for her every day. Gran's going to take her to the vet's in the morning – even though it costs an arm and a leg. Why doesn't the NHS extend to man's best friend?

Wednesday 22nd September

3.27 p.m.

Princess has been diagnosed as "jealous of a newborn". That's why she is depressed. Apparently first-borns often regress when a new baby comes into the mix.

Nathan has been doing it all his life.

4.35 p.m.

Princess has been referred to a pet psychologist. Gran thinks she needs it. This is Gran, who thinks psychiatrists who treat humans should be banned and that people "need to just pull themselves together like a decent pair of curtains".

Thursday 23rd September

4.49 p.m.

OMG — pet psychologists are NOT available on the NHS either. You have to PAY for them! AND they cost a fortune. Gran says she wants Mum to consider remortgaging the house just to help her out.

Friday 24th September

7.19 p.m.

Mum says she refuses to help "the diva pooch". Gran then had this MASSIVE row that the whole street must have heard.

GRAN: I've lent you money in the past!
MUM: That was to feed my children.

GRAN:	BUT this is to save the love of my life.
MUM:	I thought Dad was the love of your life?!
GRAN:	He wasn't as loyal and he didn't sit when I wanted him to!

When you hear conversations like this you can tell why I mess up EVERYTHING with men.

SATURDAY 25TH SEPTEMBER

6.26 p.m.
Gran has decided to sell her jewellery to pay for Princess's treatment. THAT IS MY INHERITANCE. HOW DARE SHE?

7.04 p.m.
Just remembered what Gran's jewellery is like. She can do what she wants!

SUNDAY 26TH SEPTEMBER

3.23 p.m.
Gran didn't get much for her bracelets. She's using some of our savings. Since when did we have savings?! I've been asking to go to Florida since I was 6. Mum always says, "When we win the lottery!" So there is no money for me to meet the Little Mermaid. There IS money for a dog that has actually chewed through 2 microwave ovens.

Perhaps if I actually ate the kitchen I would get spoilt!

MONDAY 27TH SEPTEMBER

6.25 p.m.

I can't work Nicky out. One minute he's fine with me. The next minute he's acting all "Mr I Am the Biz" with his friends. His tag is everywhere now! His mates are daring him to tag a teacher's car. I don't want him to get in trouble but PLEASE do Matfield's. PLEASE. She would hate street art on her car. She says everything that has been painted since 1960 is total rubbish.

7.32 p.m.

Email from Keith and Butterfly. It just said:

From: <keithkeepsitgreen@gmail.com>; <butterflymeanstransform@gmail.com>
Date: September 26, 2:32:08 AM GMT
To: Hattie Moore <helphattienow@gmail.com>
Subject: Now that you're back

How's it going, Hattie?

So I replied:

From: Hattie Moore <helphattienow@gmail.com>
Date: September 27, 7:25:19 PM GMT
To: <keithkeepsitgreen@gmail.com>; <butterflymeanstransform@gmail.com>
Subject: Re: Now that you're back

Fine, thanks. Thank you for a lovely holiday and for being so welcoming. Ruby and me are even sort of getting on and I am going out with a lovely boy called Nicky!

That's it!

I didn't say what I'm really feeling. I don't even want to write it.

TUESDAY 28TH SEPTEMBER

4.32 p.m.

OMG – Mrs Cob's car was tagged at lunchtime! Everyone knows it's Nicky but no one is dobbing him in. He is a school LEGEND now. I am going out with the coolest boy that ever lived. Only geeks were weird about it. Geeks like Goose. Goose said, "But Cobsy is all right! Why is he being horrible to her?!" I told Goose she is a teacher and therefore the enemy. Goose thinks I've become really immature since I've been with Nicky. No, Goose – since I've been with Nicky I've actually GOT A LIFE.

WEDNESDAY 29TH SEPTEMBER

3.17 p.m.

Dimple's mum has asked me and Weirdo Jen to babysit on Saturday as she desperately needs some sleep. Things must be bad if Dimple's dad has officially unbanned Jen from the Rathods' house. He once described her as "a very dangerous girl who messes with dark powers and talks total rubbish". Now she is allowed to look after his only son. Tiredness drives people totally mental. I'm going to make sure I have mahoosive lie-ins ALL my life.

THURSDAY 30TH SEPTEMBER

4.40 p.m.

Jen and me read up on babies after school and what they need.

Babies basically need EVERYTHING ALL of the time!

7.27 p.m.

Nicky and me ended up at Peartree Station again tonight. We mainly snogged. Nicky kept talking about how he could only stay out for an hour as he had to babysit. I asked him if he wanted to go round Dimple's house on Saturday. He said he didn't because he was sick of kids by the weekend and just wanted to have a laugh. How selfish can you get?!

FRIDAY 1ST OCTOBER

4.07 p.m.

OMG – we've had more sex education at school! I knew MOST stuff but I had NO idea about the full details of babies and birth. Why do they let people go through it?! Why don't they cure birth?! They say it's natural – but so is swine flu!

7.45 p.m.

Gran thinks you should practise putting a condom on a gherkin – people say a cucumber but Gran says that's unrealistic for 99.9% of men!

TMI, Gran. TMI.

9.01 p.m.

Nicky has decided to come to help babysit tomorrow after all. It will be good for him to spend time with Dimple and Jen as they are going to be my bridesmaids.

9.17 p.m.

Not that I am definitely going to get married.

9.25 p.m.

And if I do, I am keeping my name.

9.54 p.m.

No, I'm not! I HATE it.

SATURDAY 2ND OCTOBER

10.21 p.m.

Things I have learnt tonight:

* When your best friends are there too you can't really snog your boyfriend.
* You will end up having girl conversations.
* Your boyfriend will end up getting bored and going "for a tag".

Amitabh cried solidly for hours. He was only happy when we put Sky News on and there was a war on somewhere. There was gunfire, bombs and lots of flashing and he loved it.

You can't do anything with a baby crying. No wonder Nicky wants to get out of his house! At one stage I gave baby formula to Dimple's cat. TOTAL DISASTER!

11.05 p.m.

Just want to say though I was never going to give Amitabh Whiskas Senior.

Weirdo Jen thinks that Amitabh may have been a freedom fighter in a past life.

11.23 p.m.

Gran says that "freedom fighter" and "terrorist" are often the same thing.

SUNDAY 3RD OCTOBER

5.23 p.m.

Dimple's mum has said to Gran that the supermarket probably needs her more and she doesn't want to drag her away from manning the lottery and managing people's dreams. So Gran is going to just "help out" when she can.

No wonder Mum is such a mess and ALWAYS asleep. She didn't stand a chance with Gran!

6.20 p.m.

I wonder what will happen to Nicky when he's older. He comes from a bit of TOTAL MADNESS. No wonder he's a bit moody now.

8.29 p.m.

Dimple called to say that Amitabh fell asleep on his baby gym whilst Mrs Rathod was doing her post-birth yoga. She left him on top of a mini lion that played "Twinkle Twinkle, Little Star" for 3 hours. Dimple said by the end she was slightly mental and put the electric kettle on the gas hob to make a cup of tea. I think Amitabh has a mad look in his eye.

Boys. Men. Males. They cause trouble from the moment they open their actual eyes!

MONDAY 4TH OCTOBER

4.32 p.m.

Apparently Ruby has had the worst outbreak of zits ever – her mum is taking her to a spot specialist. I feel dead sorry for her. I texted her and told her that they would soon clear up. That was a lie though. Some people can have really bad acne for YEARS. Sometimes you have to lie to protect people from the hurtful truth.

5.34 p.m.

THAT sounds like my MUM. And how she "protected" me for all those years. I am doomed.

TUESDAY 5TH OCTOBER

5.29 p.m.

OMG – Ruby said to her mum that she felt ugly and she didn't want to go to school AND HER MUM LET HER OFF!

WEDNESDAY 6TH OCTOBER

7.39 a.m.

I told my mum I felt ugly. She said, "You'll feel better at school. There're uglier people than you there."

Thanks for your sympathy, Mum.

Why can't I have a thick, soft mum?!

THURSDAY 7TH OCTOBER

6.39 p.m.

RUMOURS GOING ROUND SCHOOL THAT I AM NOT GOING TO TELL RUBY:

* MGK (everyone still calls her that) is having laser treatment that is costing 3 GRAND!!!
* MGK got called by *Boots* – they want to put her in an advert for their new skin treatment.
* MGK is going to the health farm where all the celebrities go to recuperate from the stress that is causing her zits.
* MGK can never eat chocolate again or she will turn into 1 massive spot that can never be cured. Literally 1 Mars bar could kill her.

FRIDAY 8TH OCTOBER

7.38 p.m.

Ruby came back to school today and I TOTALLY HAD A GO AT THE SEEMINGLY SWEET AND LOVELY MEGAN FENTON.

Apparently Megan Fenton told Dibbo Hannah that Ruby is going out trick-or-treating as herself AND that she has asked for her school photos to be airbrushed in future.

I AM NOT HAVING MY SISTER SLAGGED OFF.

I stormed up to Megan Fenton and said, "Do yourself a favour – STOP being a cow about Ruby Slack. Spots are

---

296

NOT a big deal and YOU are ONE NASTY PIECE OF WORK."

Megan just smirked and said, "Don't make out this is about your sister, Hattie. You've wanted to have a go at me for AGES and we all know why!"

I just said, "WHATEVER! LEAVE IT!" and stormed off.

I went to Ruby's house tonight and said, "You're still totally pretty even with massive zits." She didn't look that happy when I told her that, which was a bit ungrateful. I didn't tell her about Megan COW Fenton. I'm tempted to tell Goose. Bet he wouldn't love her half as much if he realized that she was EVIL.

SATURDAY 9TH OCTOBER

4.34 p.m.

Dimple is worried that the baby monitor is revealing how much she talks to herself. Her dad heard her pretend she was being interviewed by Graham Norton about her latest film. He must know she's secretly completely Bollywood under all her "A" grades.

My WHOLE family is going to Amitabh's sort-of-christening tomorrow. Gran wasn't invited but she has sort of invited herself. She gets one sniff of a free sandwich and mini apricot slice and there is seriously NO stopping her.

Nicky is going too.

297

Megan and Goose are NOT going. GOOD.

SUNDAY 10TH OCTOBER

8.39 p.m.

Amitabh's naming ceremony was AMAZEBALLS. The food was unbelievable. It was really lovely too. Dimple has got this amazing huge family and they were all hugging Amitabh AND telling Dimple what a great daughter and sister she is. Loads of them were crying. It was TOTALLY emotional and TOTALLY lovely. Everyone was getting on with everyone else. Only Gran caused a little row by asking for some "non-spicy meat" for Princess and then pushing in the queue for the toilets. She shouted, "I've got an irritable bladder, Hattie – I can't queue at a social function!" and went to the front. People tutted but they didn't argue.

At the end Nicky went out for a cigarette and gave me a puff. It WAS HORRIBLE. I coughed like a mental but Nicky thought smoking suited me and that I looked "sort of cool". I might smoke. Just for a bit. Nicky has given me half a packet. I know it's totally wrong but it's only for a little while.

MONDAY 11TH OCTOBER

7.19 a.m.

I can't believe it's raining on my first day of smoking!

7.35 a.m.

OMG – cigarettes?! WHAT AM I DOING SUICIDE-BOMBING MY ACTUAL LUNGS?!

3.54 p.m.

I had half a cigarette with Nicky at lunchtime. He thinks it's cool. I don't want him to think I'm not my own woman and that I just do what society says I should. As a feminist I can give myself pneumonia if I want to.

9.42 p.m.

It's still raining. I'll have a cigarette when it stops.

TUESDAY 12TH OCTOBER

7.32 a.m.

It's still raining! Smokers must spend their entire lives feeling soggy.

3.45 p.m.

I refused to go out for a smoke with Nicky at lunchtime. He got really moody and said, "If you'd prefer to be dry than spend time with me then fine."

I have to practise smoking. No one is home. I'll go on the decking.

4.10 p.m.

I've made a slight burn mark on Mum's sun-lounger but she won't notice. It's got flowers all over it. The burn just looks like a stalk! No one is going to go out there till next summer. If summer ever happens again!

6.38 p.m.

LOL! Mum came in and just flopped on the sofa. She said she felt REALLY tired and could we all make our own tea. Thank you, people wanting fry-ups in Mum's cafe! You have saved me from MUM LECTURE ACTION!

WEDNESDAY 13TH OCTOBER

4.58 p.m.

I had a smoke at lunchtime. I can't inhale yet but I've stopped choking every time I do it! I'm going round to see Gran tonight.

9.23 p.m.

Gran smelt the smoke on my breath as soon as I got in the door and went mental. She started RANTING at me like I was about 4 years old.

GRAN:	Why are you bloody smoking?!
ME:	Everyone experiments, Gran! Nicky smokes. It's sort of a thing we can share!
GRAN:	Well, I thought you had more sense, young lady, than to make yourself ill and give yourself wrinkles for a boy. You stink like an ashtray! There are men at my social club that smell sweeter than you and they don't wash unless their wives tell them to. What on Earth do you think you're doing?

When I said th[is] I knew it sounde[d] a bit pathetic.

ME: I just want to be a bit … I just
         want…
GRAN: You just want your boyfriend to
         like you. You are fine as you are.
         Don't you start changing to suit
         men!
ME: I'm not!
GRAN: Yes, you are. Now – I won't bother
         your mum with this IF you give me
         the cigarettes now and PROMISE me
         you are not going to smoke again.
         Nicky OR NO NICKY!

I've promised her.

Princess growled at me. Gran said, "She doesn't like smoke either! Plus she is a bit fragile after her trip to the pet psychologist today. He taunted her with some chorizo sausage. Of course she snapped. What dog wouldn't? He doesn't have to beg and play dead for his lunch. Why should she?"

10.13 p.m.
I am now an ex-smoker. I've texted Nicky to tell him. I'm glad really. Cigarettes are foul and make you smell like an old woman with too many cats. That is not sexy.

10.43 p.m.
I was doing it for Nicky. Am I a mental girlie sap fest?

10.56 p.m.
Or am I in love and that's the sort of thing that you do?!

I don't think I'm in love with Nicky.

THURSDAY 14TH OCTOBER

4.09 p.m.

Nicky spent ALL lunchtime smoking. When he is at school he does English, Art and "standing behind the canteen having a ciggy". He treats it like he should treat coursework!

8.35 p.m.

Gran just rang my mob. "Hattie, if you're grown up enough to smoke you are old enough to hear the truth... I'm in a relationship with a man called Barry. He's a lorry driver."

OMG – my gran's broken biscuits do come from her secret lover!

FRIDAY 15TH OCTOBER

8.32 p.m.

I've spent ALL evening with Barry and Gran!

They are actually really sweet. He rubs her feet and makes her cups of tea. He's about 10 years younger than her, comes from Wolverhampton and calls everyone "pet"! When I walked in he said, "Hattie, pet, would you like a custard cream with some strawberry-flavoured milk? I've got plenty of biscuits. Always!"

I hope Barry is not after Gran's money. She hasn't got any.

SATURDAY 16TH OCTOBER

5.12 p.m.

Took Nicky round to see Barry. Nicky told Barry he doesn't really go to school. Barry kept saying, "What you need is a job, Nicky. Forget about school. Qualifications don't count for anything. With haulage it's just you and your lorry. You're King of the Road! Plus there's cheap fags and lager in Calais." Gran shouted at Barry for this.

Nicky looked excited.

I don't think Nicky ... is "me".

BUT he likes me.

SUNDAY 17TH OCTOBER

7.32 a.m.

Goose and Megan are going to a boot sale again. They look TOTALLY loved up. He wouldn't look loved up if he knew what she was really like under her stupid, flouncy bird-print skirt.

9.12 p.m.

Gran wanted to know all the details tonight about what Nicky meant when he said he doesn't really go to school. I told her he doesn't really actually go that much. She death-stared me and said, "Don't you get any ideas, Hattie. Get those qualifications. I don't want you working in a cafe all hours. You're a smart cookie! Don't waste anything for a man!"

WHERE DID ALL THAT COME FROM? I yelled, "Gran, that won't happen. I'm a FEMINIST!"

Gran laughed and said, "Germaine Green never started smoking because a bloody boy wanted her to!"

Who is Germaine Green?!

10.16 p.m.
Weirdo Jen says Gran means Germaine GREER. She basically invented feminism. Before her, women just wore big dresses, baked cakes, looked after children, painted pictures of kittens and fainted in hot weather.

MONDAY 18TH OCTOBER

5.23 p.m.
Nicky can't see me tonight. He's going tagging with all his mates.

There's nothing left to tag. He'll have to start tagging people as they sleep!

9.36 p.m.
Would Germaine Greer go tagging with a man or would she go tagging on her own?

10.03 p.m.
Germaine Greer would not tag. Tagging is a boy thing. Germaine Greer would do feminist things like not taking her clothes off OR taking her clothes off and not letting *FHM* take photos!

10.15 p.m.

Just want to say there's more to feminism than just whether you're in *FHM* or not.

10.27 p.m.

And if you are in *FHM* you can still be a feminist. Just a feminist in pants.

TUESDAY 19TH OCTOBER

6.32 p.m.

OMG — Jen has just rung me. She was out with Simon being goth and they saw Nicky come out of the police station. He was caught tagging a police car in the city! The policeman thought it was a cry for help as "only someone who wanted to get caught would tag a patrol vehicle with 2 law enforcement officers and a shoplifter in it". Even the shoplifter, who had just been caught with some yoghurts and a widescreen TV, had a go at Nicky for being a mindless vandal!

8.39 p.m.

OMG — I wonder if the shoplifter was the same shoplifter who nicked the yoghurts and the telly from Gran's supermarket?

9.04 p.m.

My brother said all shoplifters steal tellies and yoghurts because people always want them.

Then he asked why I asked him.

I said I'd just seen something on telly!

But I hadn't! I am the girlfriend of someone on *Crimewatch*.

I've texted Nicky. He hasn't replied. Perhaps the shoplifter took his phone.

4.42 p.m.

Everyone is talking about Nicky the criminal at school. Hardly anyone gets arrested at our school. He is officially totally hard. People are asking ME to tell HIM that HE is REALLY COOL.

I don't think he is cool. I think he's a doughnut.

5.32 p.m.

As long as Mum doesn't find out about Nicky I'm OK. Luckily she's been working really hard and is still falling asleep at stupid o'clock every day. It's a good thing – like Gran says, when she's dozy she's not nosey.

3.58 p.m.

Apparently, the rumour is Nicky is going to be excluded from school! Mrs Cob will not tolerate vandalism in or outside the building. Nor will she tolerate repeated absenteeism (she means bunking off). Nicky does both of those things. I'm going out with a major problem character now.

6.13 p.m.

Rob called me into the kitchen tonight. He'd been doing his last lesson of the day on Tuesday. During an emergency stop he saw Nicky getting arrested.

I begged him not to tell Mum. Rob just said, "Hattie, is he really the right boy for you? He's already getting into trouble."

It's actually a good question.

7.32 p.m.

He still hasn't texted me since he did it.

And do I REALLY love him? No.

No.

I don't think I do. He's hotness but even the tingles have gone. Tagging cancels out my tingles.

And really wasn't I on the sort of rebound? Even though I wasn't actually rebounding from anyone?

This is hard.

FRIDAY 22ND OCTOBER

6.38 p.m.

Barry is taking Gran to Europe! An OAP is having an officially more exciting life than her grandaughter!

Gran got really cross when I told her about Nicky! She of all people should understand loving a man who makes mistakes. She said, "Graffiti today! Armed robbery tomorrow. I know he's from a tough background but that's no excuse! Anyway – I need to get ready. Barry and me are going to Calais. He's staying in his cab – I'm in a Holiday Inn. You don't rough it at my age, Hattie. Neither should you be slumming it at 15. Get yourself a nice boy!"

Gran! Independent women like me do not want a "nice boy". They want boys with strong personalities who also let us be our own women and who do lots of stuff on their own but also take control and say what they mean.

9.32 p.m.
I hardly see Nicky and when I do it's because HE wants to.

I am not a strong independent woman. I am a bit rubbish.

SATURDAY 23RD OCTOBER

2.34 p.m.
Nicky FINALLY rang. He was really horrible! He said, "Tagging is my right. It's like art. It's just a scribble, Hattie. Get over it. If you don't want my heat get out of my kitchen!"

I didn't have a chance to talk. He just shouted at me about how he "wasn't actually in the wrong" for about 10 minutes. Then he said, "If you really want me I'll be around!"

I don't think I want to be around.

Sunday 24th October

10.12 a.m.

Why am I so useless in love?

2.14 p.m.

No, Mum. Roast lamb will not cheer me up.

4.44 p.m.

It did a bit. But I still don't know what to do!

Monday 25th October

HALF-TERM

9.23 a.m.

Mum just asked me how it's going with Nicky.

I said, "Yeah. Good."

Even through Lemsip and Berocca cocktails she can TOTALLY tell there is something wrong.

7.34 p.m.

Spent all day in my room listening to music wondering what to do about Nicky. I think it's got to end but am I deserting a man in actual need of my help? Perhaps I can help him stop drawing on everything.

Tuesday 26th October

7.23 p.m.

Mum knows! SHE WENT MENTAL. And the best thing — not?! Goose told her! He's apparently "worried" about me. He never worries about me these days — he's too busy snogging flimsy-dress FAKE woman.

What a grass!

What business of HIS is it anyway? Why does HE care?

WEDNESDAY 27TH OCTOBER

5.23 p.m.

Nicky has had a meeting with the police. They say next time they catch him they are not going to hold back. They are going to tag him. Tags for taggers. They are suggesting his parents give him a curfew, which they've done. His dad turned up to the station IN SLIPPERS and promised that Nicky was going to stay in at night from now on.

Nicky said, "I'm not. I might go to Manchester when I'm 16 and start squatting. Hattie, you can come. My mate is already there! We can find an empty place in Moss Side. You can get a job in Maccy D's and I'll sell my art."

No.

No.

This isn't what I want. I don't want to end up in a craptacular flat. I like electricity and running water.

6.34 p.m.

Told Dimple. She says I have to finish it. I do.

THURSDAY 28TH OCTOBER

5.45 p.m.

Horrific craptacular day.

I finished with Nicky.

NICKY: Hi, Shorty. Missed ya.

ME: Nicky - it's not…

NICKY: I totally know what you are going to say. I know I shouldn't have tagged a police car. It was a stupid dare thing.

ME: I think we should sort of finish because I sort of need to concentrate on my school and stuff. And Princess - my gran's dog - has got emotional issues and needs my help. She bit the Dog Whisperer. I'm the only one left who can brush her without getting savaged to actual death. ← WHY DID I SAY THAT?

NICKY: Princess is about the size of a cat. Don't make crap excuses, Hattie. Whatever. I get it. First sign of trouble and you're gone. Like everybody else in my life!

ME: No - it's just that I'm … I've got—

NICKY: Bye, Shorty. I know what this is really about. You have totally USED me! Don't think I don't know. I've seen the way you look at HIM. I've seen the way you look at his girlfriend! I've heard the way you talk about him! IT'S OBVIOUS YOU LIKE HIM, HATTIE. You've treated me like CRAP. You're a USER! ← Then he started to cry a bit. A really nasty USING … USER!

> AND by the way, you look REALLY
> stupid when you smoke. AND you
> can't kiss properly.

Then he just stormed off.

Crying.

Why are men so nasty?

7.25 p.m.
Jen says men can't handle rejection. Apparently Nicky has let his inner woman die.

7.45 p.m.
Dimple says Nicky is a pig and it's got nothing to do with his inner woman. Just his outer TOTAL idiot.

FRIDAY 29TH OCTOBER

7.38 a.m.
Just told Gran. She said, "I'm sad for you, Hattie. He's got a lot of growing up to do."

Gran ALWAYS says this about everyone who disagrees with her or does something wrong. She said her friend Ron had to "mature" after he decided to stop watching *Emmerdale*. Ron is 78. How much more mature can you be?

Gran had to go. She was somewhere near Belgium and her croissant was going limp. "I can't speak to you and eat a pastry, Hattie. It could flake in my phone and I'd lose my high score on Candy Crush."

Cakes and apps. More important than my actual heart in pieces. Even though I'm the one who did it.

I hope Nicky is OK.

I really do. I shouldn't have done ... what I did.

I don't mean dump him. I mean ... what he said.

5.46 p.m.

Saw Goose tonight and said, "Could you ACTUALLY keep out of my business?"

When he went to say something I just shouted, "Leave it, OK! And by the way MEGAN IS HORRIBLE TO PEOPLE WITH ZITS. So if I were you I wouldn't eat any chocolate or have hormones!"

Goose didn't say anything.

There are now no boys I get on with. In my ENTIRE life.

Well done, Hattie.

Saturday 30th October

12.38 p.m.

OMG! Florence Morse – ULTIMATE REBEL AND COOLEST GIRL IN SCHOOL EVER – has invited me to her house for Halloween. We are going to watch the film *Friday the 13th*. I'm not nervous about it – even though it's my full first 18 film. It can't be that bad.

4.37 p.m.

I am worried – what if it is that bad?

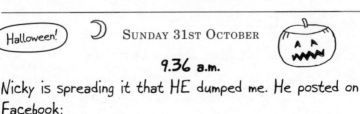

Halloween! SUNDAY 31ST OCTOBER

9.36 a.m.

Nicky is spreading it that HE dumped me. He posted on Facebook:

> If my shorty gives me trouble I say BYE. If she can't kiss properly I say BYE BYE.

Whatever, Nicky. WHATEVER.

Seeing a scary film tonight. At least that will take my mind off my totally scary life.

11.23 p.m.

OMG – it was SCARY bad. Basically there's a man called Jason. He wears a mask and murders people. I can tell why it was an 18. It's really ... I didn't like it. I don't think I like horror. I think I like Disney.

MONDAY 1ST NOVEMBER

5.32 a.m.

Didn't sleep much last night.

4.13 p.m.

Dimple told me something UNBELIEVABLE today. Apparently Florence Morse invited me round to watch the film because:

---

1. She is good friends with Nicky and they all agreed I needed to be taught a lesson. It was a horror-film revenge attack.

2. I am now known as a "user". I suppose I deserve it.

3. I'm a well-known total nerd wimp and everyone in HER gang wanted a laugh. Apparently there's a video of me screaming doing the rounds.

4.46 p.m.

And a video of me covering my eyes with the remote control.

4.56 p.m.

And a video of me biting a cushion in terror.

TUESDAY 2ND NOVEMBER

7.32 p.m.

I fell asleep on the sofa today after school – it's safer to sleep in the day. I know that Jason doesn't exist but that's not the point.

WEDNESDAY 3RD NOVEMBER

6.24 a.m.

Went to bed last night with Mum's vegetable peeler under the pillow. I didn't want to take a knife because that's too dangerous – I could stab myself in the actual face.

Thursday 4th November

7.34 a.m.

These are the times when I really miss Nicky. He could handle a psycho.

7.50 a.m.

No, he couldn't. He'd probably just try to tag him.

ANYWAY he caused all this! Nicky the revenge craptacular attacker has made me scared of the one place I actually loved — my own bedroom.

Friday 5th November

9.14 p.m.

I'm so jumpy that the FIREWORKS are making me feel TOTALLY LIKE I'M CRAZY this year. Went to Gran's. Princess was holding a sparkler. I felt like hiding under the table and whimpering. That is what the dog is meant to do.

Saturday 6th November

3.56 p.m.

Saw Ruby today. Her spots have cleared up so she's happy about everything in the world. I told her about Halloween and how I hadn't slept properly in days. She said I have to fill my head with lovely things every time I think about being butchered. It's how she got through having terrible zits. This is going to be hard but I am going to try.

---

* Chickens.
* Flowers.
* Zebras.
* Biscuits.
* Jason riding a zebra eating a big biscuit ... holding a big knife.

He is still in my head!

Ruby also said she is going to have a go at Florence Morse but then she said, "But you did mess Nicky about, Hattie. You don't play with man fire and not expect to get BADLY BURNED."

7.12 p.m.
Told Mum I need counselling. She said, "Don't talk nonsense, Hattie — try thinking about a nice Disney film instead. Like *Bambi*." GOOD IDEA, MUM.

SUNDAY 7TH NOVEMBER

2.18 p.m.
OMG – Bambi's mum dies! TRAUMA.

MONDAY 8TH NOVEMBER

6.32 p.m.
Any chance all these people could stop letting fireworks off?

TUESDAY 9TH NOVEMBER

4.26 p.m.

Rob says I should have known after last year when I got worked up about murderers "that I do not handle violent crime well — even if it is just a film". Then Rob said, "I think you need a little bit of help, lady. A perk-up."

PLEASE. ROB - DO NOT MAKE ME A REGGAE REGGAE SAUCE SANDWICH.

6.12 p.m.

OMG – GOOSE HAS JUST SENT ME A TEXT!

> Just seen the video of you
> biting a cushion. Do u wanna
> come round? XX

I have replied:

> Are you being sarcastic?

6.23 p.m.

Goose has replied:

> No. Come round XX

2 KISSES!!!

But he's still going out with Megan Fenton...

10.34 p.m.

Goose was great.

He said, "I'm sorry to hear about what's been going on."

I told him I was terrified of going to sleep. He said, "Why don't you have a sleep here and me and Freak will protect you. I can do some homework."

So I did. Then I woke up and came home.

It was weird. But nice.

Z
Z
Z

WEDNESDAY 10TH NOVEMBER

5.35 p.m.

Barry and Gran have split. She told me, "There's only so much you can say about motorways. We had nothing in common, Hattie. It's difficult to deal with a man who wears a Texaco padded jacket to bed and pretends to honk his lorry hooter every time he wants you to move. I prefer an 'Excuse me'. Plus, once I'd told people, some of the mystery had gone."

I told her I was sleeping at Goose's house. She went MAD until I said, "No — actual sleeping — like SNORING, Gran." She said that was fine.

Of course it is. My family would love for me to sleep for 100 years and get no man action ever again.

THURSDAY 11TH NOVEMBER

8.37 p.m.

OMG — fell asleep on Goose's bed whilst he was cleaning out Freak. Woke up to find he'd made me a cup of coffee and some toast but THEN Megan Fenton came round and

---

went MAD!!! LIKE YOU'VE NEVER SEEN ANYONE GO MAD BEFORE! Then they had this MASSIVE ROW!

Meaning ME! ←

MEGAN: What is THAT doing here?

GOOSE: Er ... Hattie is just having a nap.

MEGAN: Don't LIE. WHAT IS GOING ON?!

GOOSE: Megan, seriously, she is just having a nap. I SWEAR NOTHING has happened!

MEGAN: So just coincidentally DERBY'S BIGGEST USER turns up in your bedroom DAYS after she gets dumped by Nicky Bainton for not being able to kiss properly?

GOOSE: NOTHING HAS GONE ON. Hattie, you'd better go...

So I did but I could hear them arguing for ages through the wall. Eventually Megan stormed out.

I honestly don't want to hurt Goose. I'm just glad we are mates again. That sounds like I don't want to be more than friends. I DO. BUT I KNOW he's going out with Megan. NOTHING HAPPENED!

FRIDAY 12TH NOVEMBER

4.35 p.m.

Told Jen and Dimple about Goose and Megan Fenton. They smiled at each other but they also told me there's now a rumour going round that I'm both a user and a stealer of boyfriends.

User. Fair enough but its not like I've stolen ANYONE'S BOYFRIEND!

10.12 a.m.

Asked Goose if I could sleep round his whilst he cleaned out Freak again. He said Freak didn't need another clean and it was probably best if I tried to sleep round mine.

He's right. I've caused enough trouble.

2.45 p.m.

Been asleep WITH NO NIGHTMARES! I texted Goose to tell him and to ask him if he'd fight Jason for me if I needed him to. He said that he'd probably call the police armed-response unit first.

I think that's a totally good idea.

11.54 a.m.

I went to the boot sale this morning to take my mind off horrible things. I did not go to be with Goose. Honestly. Though I noticed that Megan Fenton did NOT go! I saw a fantastic ornamental sword but Rob wouldn't let me buy it. Even when I said it would make me feel better about defending myself against people in films who wear masks and murder people. Rob said a gun would be better but he wouldn't buy me one of those either. He did however buy me a high-pressure water pistol as that would "at least shock a psycho" and give me time to escape.

4.21 p.m.

Just tried the water pistol on Mum. She couldn't move for about a minute. Then she went crazy. If I did try it on a murdering psycho it would make them even crosser than normal so I'd have to run twice as fast. LOL!

8.56 p.m.

Megan Fenton is giggling again.

They have made up. Great.

No, I'm pleased for him. Goose is lovely and helped me sleep again.

I REALLY do HATE her though.

MONDAY 15TH NOVEMBER

3.59 p.m.

OMG - BIGGEST DAY OF DRAMA EVER!

We were all just standing around at lunch when Nicky came in to officially be excluded. (Why do you have to come in to school to be told to go home again?!) ANYWAY Nicky saw Goose and Goose saw Nicky and THEY TOTALLY STARTED FIGHTING! There were punches flying everywhere. Then Goose totally wrestled Nicky to the ground and they started rolling all over the long-jump sandpit! It was MENTAL. They didn't have an argument or anything! Eventually a teacher pulled them apart and said to Nicky, "Mrs Cob's office, NOW!" But Nicky said, "I'm out of this dump! SEE YA!" and just ran off. Then Goose looked at me and just walked off!

WHAT WAS THAT ALL ABOUT?!!

8.34 p.m.

Dimple said the fight was TOTALLY about me. Nicky thinks that Goose has been "after me" for ages and has "filled my head up" with lies about Nicky and how much crime he is into. Don't they both actually realize that I AM MY OWN WOMAN with MY OWN OPINIONS?! I CANNOT be swayed by what a man thinks.

9.26 p.m.

Is it feminist to be excited by 2 men having a MAJOR scrap over you!

10.08 p.m.

I want to go and see Goose to find out if he's OK but I'm worried it's probably not a good idea right now.

TUESDAY 16TH NOVEMBER

4.12 p.m.

Goose has NOT been suspended as several witnesses confirmed he was acting partially in self-defence. However he has been totally shouted at and told that it will be a different story if he ever gets into a fight again.

He never will. It's so not Goose.

6.24 p.m.

Gran wanted to know ALL the details of the fight. She says it's TOTALLY feminist for a woman to know the "power that she wields". "Look at Boudicca," Gran said. "She didn't mind the whole of Britain going to war over

her, Hattie. If you're driving men nuts you're doing your job!
They like wrestling anyway. That's why they do it on the
telly. I wish I'd seen it!"

Who is Boudicca?

7.04 p.m.

She is an ancient WARRIOR QUEEN! I am SO calling my
daughter Boudicca if I ever have one.

8.12 p.m.

Actually I might stick to something more traditional when
I have children. I understand what an unusual name can
do to a person. I might just call my cat Boudicca or
something.

9.02 p.m.

Not my cat because you have to shout its name at night
and sound like a doughnut. Perhaps just my fish should be
called that.

WEDNESDAY 17TH NOVEMBER

6.24 p.m.

All ANYONE could talk about at school today was
STILL THE FIGHT. Some people are calling it FIGHT-
GATE. Here are some of the rumours I heard:

* It was about ME as Goose ← Well – Nicky does a bit
  and Nicky fancy me.   but Goose doesn't – I was
                               lying on his bed asleep and
                               he did nothing.

---

* It was about Megan Fenton as they both fancy her. ← IF THAT IS TRUE I WILL GO MENTAL!

* It was a lover's tiff as Nicky and Goose are actually gay.

↖ THAT rumour has Dibbo Hannah written all over it.

10.54 p.m.

Asked Mum her advice about the entire Goose/ Nicky/Megan situation tonight. She said, "Hattie, just concentrate on your schoolwork."

THURSDAY 18TH NOVEMBER

10.01 p.m.

I just got home after seeing Gran. Mum is asleep on the sofa AGAIN! Remind me NOT to ever make bacon sandwiches for a living.

10.04 p.m.

Goose and Megan are shouting at each other. I think Goose's mum lets her stay there far too late. She should get tougher!

FRIDAY 19TH NOVEMBER

8.24 p.m.

I did something odd tonight.

I Skyped Dad.

It was really early in the morning his time but I just wanted a chat with someone who wasn't a woman or didn't think anything could be cured with a Reggae Reggae Sauce

---

sandwich. I told him all about Nicky, about Megan and about Goose. I mainly talked about Goose. And the fight. He listened to it all and at the end said, "Well, Hattie – just from an outsider's view 10,500 miles away, I'd say you're madly in love with Goose and you'd like Megan Fenton to drop down a big hole. What you did with Nicky was wrong but love makes you do stupid things – especially when you're young. Look at me! But learn from me too. Don't cause anyone any more pain. Leave Goose alone. If it's meant to be it will happen. And really you owe Nicky an apology."

When I said, "But he set me up for death from social-media embarrassment hell!" Dad said, "You set him up for something worse than that. You broke his heart."

I did.

Oh, COW! COW! COW! Not Megan Fenton! ME!!!

Then Dad said, "I'm thinking of coming over next year again. Trace— sorry – Butterfly and me will stay at a caravan park or something? Think it's a good idea?"

Dad was right about everything.

Everything.

SATURDAY 20TH NOVEMBER

9.56 p.m.

Texted Nicky today and just said:

> Sorry, Nicky. I didn't treat
> you well. Was confused. Sorry.
> Hope you're OK.

I haven't heard anything back but at least I did the right thing. For ONCE!

SUNDAY 21ST NOVEMBER

10.34 p.m.

OMG – just saw Goose going to the boot sale without Megan AGAIN!

No, Hattie. You've caused enough trouble. JUST LEAVE IT.

MONDAY 22ND NOVEMBER

5.19 p.m.

I JUST WANT TO SAY BEFORE I WRITE THE NEXT BIT THAT I HAVE DONE NOTHING NOR HAVE I SAID ANYTHING.

Apparently Goose has finished with Megan Fenton. She "shouted too much" and admitted to him that she "actually hated boot sales and lizards". Goose said, "Some things you have to love to love me."

BUT DON'T GO MAD WITH MAX JOY because we've both been single before and NOTHING happened and I don't like Freak. I don't even think I can grow to love him.

I'm off boys anyway.

TUESDAY 23RD NOVEMBER

4.54 p.m.

Weirdo Jen and Dimple nagged me for hours today about Goose. Because Weirdo Jen has been with Simon FOR EVER she thinks she's a HOTNESS expert. My love life is not a soap opera. I am not going to make a fool of myself over Goose. I need a break. I have to learn lessons from this experience and fully mature — OH, I WANT TO SNOG HIS FACE OFF NOW.

I JUST NEED TO KNOW if he feels the same way and if he's ready.

WEDNESDAY 24TH NOVEMBER

6.38 p.m.

Went round to see Goose after school.

Conversation went like this...

```
GOOSE:  Hi.
ME:     Hi.
GOOSE:  You OK?
ME:     Yeah.
GOOSE:  Hats. I just need to, er…
ME:     Yeah. Yeah. Ermm. I'm thinking you
        need to…
GOOSE:  Yeah.
ME:     I will see. You. Then. Around?
GOOSE:  Yeah.
```

He is clearly NOT ready and it is certainly NOT obvious that he wants to SNOG MY FACE OFF.

Thursday 25th November

4.32 p.m.

Ruby called my mob after school today and made the
following statements:

1. "HATTIE – why aren't you going out with Goose
   yet? It is OBVIOUS that you totally fancy the
   hell out of each other. Have you asked him out?!"
2. "Dad is definitely coming over next year! TELL
   YOUR FAMILY!"

Answers – no, no – AND WORLD, PLEASE LEAVE ME
ALONE!

Friday 26th November

8.34 p.m.

Told Mum about Dad. She was unbelievably relaxed about
it and said, "Let's not tell your Gran till we have to."

THEN OUT OF THE BLUE SHE SAID, "By the way,
Hattie, it's obvious you like Goose and he likes you! I
know you've had your ups and downs but no one argues
with a boy and gets annoyed with him unless they LOVE
them. Goose is lovely and I think you should ... concentrate
on your schoolwork but give him a break!"

Saturday 27th November

4.32 p.m.

Gran has given me a lecture on men too. Basically they
are "not women". Thanks, Gran!

Everyone wants me and Goose to happen except Goose. And Megan Fenton. And Nicky. But mainly Goose.

11.12 a.m.

According to Weirdo Jen Nicky is going out with a girl called Stephanie Rowland. She's a skater. So even Nicky probably doesn't care now either.

His heart was obviously not THAT broken!

3.24 p.m.

Goose has texted me to see if I want to go and see a film at his house. He says his mum will be there but would I like to go and join them?

Got nothing else on. Might as well.

9.29 p.m.

OMG!

We watched *The Notebook* on DVD (my favourite) and then it got all weird. I cried at the end. I always do. Then Goose's mum went out to make me a cup of tea and Goose started talking about how it's worth waiting for the love of your life. I said I wouldn't wait for years! And ... Goose went all quiet at that point. He was just about to say something and his mum came in with a packet of chocolate HobNobs.

That ... I mean ... Nicky NEVER did anything like that. SAID anything like that.

OMG – just remembered I've got the dentist tomorrow. That will stop any love with ANY man DEAD in its brace tracks.

It was tense tonight. Erotic sexy tense. You could feel the hotness. Before the HobNobs. They ruined everything.

MONDAY 29TH NOVEMBER

4.21 p.m.

Just been to see Mr Winkler the dentist. I still have to wear my brace. Probably for ever. I will never be able to go abroad without setting off a beeper and being frisked. AND there's still a massive gap where they took my teeth out. I may sue for emotional damage and snog starvation.

6.29 p.m.

OMG – What have I done?! WHAT HAVE I DONE?!

Just went to see Goose:

```
GOOSE:   How was the dentist?
ME:      Great - I have to wear the braces
         for EVEN longer!
GOOSE:   Well, I think they're cute.
ME:      Well, that's OK then - the biggest
         GEEK in the world who I totally
         LOVE thinks they're cute! World
         sorted!
GOOSE:   What?!
ME:      I said 'the biggest geek in the
         world who I'm in love—'
```

OMG – I SAID IT!!!

I SAID IT!!! WHY?! WHY?! WHY?!

I just ran out. Goose said, "Hattie!" but I kept on running. WHAT HAVE I DONE?!

TUESDAY 30TH NOVEMBER

4.34 p.m.

Just ran home. Avoided Goose all day. Dimple and Jen think it was a good thing to do. The fact that he has NOT been round has convinced me it was a BAD thing to do.

10.32 p.m.

OMG – just had the most AMAZEBALLS NIGHT EVER!

Was watching *EastEnders* when Goose burst in and THIS HAPPENED...

I CAN'T BELIEVE I'M WRITING IT!

ME:	Are you OK, Goose?
GOOSE:	I'm fine.
ME:	Are you though? Because I was worried.
GOOSE:	Why?
ME:	Why ... because ... I shouldn't have said what I said—
GOOSE:	Why?
ME:	Because...
GOOSE:	Yes, you should. Hattie, I bloody love you. I thought you might not be interested.

ME: I thought YOU might not be
         interested. I really like you, too
         Goose. Always have. ALWAYS HA—

AND BEFORE I'D EVEN FINISHED MY ACTUAL SENTENCE WE JUST HAD THIS MASSIVE DESPERATE SNOG THAT WENT ON FOR ABOUT 15 HOURS AND WAS JUST HOT AND MENTAL AND COMPLETELY WONDERFUL AND I AM TOTALLY, TOTALLY IN LOVE WITH GOOSE. GOOSE. GOOSE. GOOSE. GOOSE!!!

And then he said, "Why has it taken us this long to do THAT?"

I DON'T KNOW BUT WE ARE NOW IN SNOG CENTRAL STATION ON THE HOT EXPRESS,GOOSE, AND IT'S THE MOST WONDERFUL THING IN THE WORLD.

I'm holding the wall tonight. Goose is holding his too.

This is FINALLY the REAL, real thing.

11.08 p.m.
Texted Dimple and Weirdo Jen. Jen said:

`Finally! HURRAH!!! Luv u!`

Dimple didn't reply. She'll be asleep.

I can't sleep.

Goose.

11.23 p.m.

Weirdo Jen just texted again to ask if I knew Goose's time of birth, as she needed to do a full astrological relationship chart for us. She had done one for her and Simon and he has an "uncomplimentary Neptune". Apparently she has to make "allowances".

I don't care about Goose's planets. I just care about his HOTNESS SOLAR SYSTEM.

WEDNESDAY 1ST DECEMBER

7.23 a.m.

Dimple just texted to say she was:

`REALLY happy for u.`

I am really happy for us. I'm tired though because I held the wall all night. Actually I held Goose all night. In my head. The wall was just a way of being closer when there's an actual wall between you.

Am I even making sense? I don't care.

4.24 p.m.

I am so LOVED up I am totally making other people want to be sick and I don't care either.

Mum seems to be really happy about it. It's because she thinks Goose is a "lovely, sensible boy". He is, Mum. He is also a TREMENDOUSLY AMAZING SNOG MACHINE.

4.53 p.m.

Nathan just barged into my room and started chanting, "Hattie has a LOVER, Hattie has a LOVER!" I tried to throw my duvet over his head but I just knocked over a chair which made Nathan start singing, "Hattie's arms are weak now from all the huggy loving!" HE IS UTTER EVIL. I told him that YES I DID have a boyfriend and that HE should GET A REAL LIFE, A REAL JOB and a REAL GIRLFRIEND. Then he looked sad and said "Actually Hats – I think you and Goose are ... alright."

Then he left.

Feel bad now.

5.35 p.m.

Just went in to see Nathan to say ... sort of sorry for trying to kill him with bedding and sort of thank you.

He grunted. But it was a grunt with a bit of a smile.

6.17 p.m.

Rob just ran in my bedroom singing this song called "Oh Happy Day". Everyone sings stuff in this house! It's like living in a musical. No wonder Goose loves my family.

Rob is happy because he thinks I am coming to every boot sale with him and Goose on a Sunday.

NO!

7.31 p.m.

Ruby just called my mob and said, "Why didn't you tell me about Goose?!"

I said, "Er ... because you did actually go out with him last year, Ruby."

Then she said, "Hattie – that was HARDLY a real relationship. We didn't even snog."

When I shouted, "That's not what I heard!" Ruby snorted, "Rumours, Hattie, are for fools. Unless they make you look good."

Ruby is still Ruby and slightly MGK ... but I like her.

9.43 p.m.
Goose kisses like ... oh, THE best kisser, and – he even smells like ... really nice soap.

THURSDAY 2ND DECEMBER

8.45 p.m.
I just had some brilliant snogging with Goose. I wish Freak the gecko wouldn't stare at us though. Me and Goose start snogging and Freak just STARES. Perhaps he's jealous! LOL!

8.51 p.m.
I DO NOT kiss with my eyes open. I just peeked for a second.

9.04 p.m.
OMG – perhaps Freak is a gay gecko. It doesn't matter if he is, BTW. I totally believe in gay rights and gay marriage.

I LOVE the way that Mum hasn't gone mental about me and Goose. I think she understands that I am utterly mature and can be trusted.

10.13 p.m.
Unless Mum has fitted Freak with spy equipment and that's why he's staring.

10.34 p.m.
Just texted Goose to ask him to check Freak for mini cameras. He's told me to get some sleep. It's probably a good idea.

5.35 p.m.
Gran just called my mob.

She said, "Hattie – I've got something to tell you."

I thought, OMG! WHAT? SOUNDS SERIOUS.

Then she said, "Hattie. I've bought a onesie and it's changed my life. I'm never taking it off!"

When I got cross and said, "Gran – DON'T do that. I thought something serious had happened!" she said, "It HAS! I've got a onesie!" and put the phone down!

I rang her back to tell her about Goose, and she just said "Finally! Now I've got to go. They are repeating *A Touch of Frost*. Bye!"

SATURDAY 4TH DECEMBER

4.55 p.m.

I've bought Goose a stuffed toy lizard! It's because he loves Freak but he can't really take him to bed without fear of squashing him!

5.12 p.m.

Goose seemed to like his stuffed lizard until Gran gave him a parcel! It's not even his birthday! She said, "WELCOME TO THE FAMILY, GOOSE!" It was an onesie with mini frogs all over it. Goose started jumping up and down with joy.

Everyone has gone onesie mad.

7.12 p.m.

I am a bit angry.

Goose and I have had our first actual big domestic row.

1. Goose is going to the boot sale tomorrow as normal. Rather than snogging me.
2. Mum invited Goose to come round tomorrow afternoon to put the Christmas tree up as he is "part of the family now". He has agreed to this – rather than snogging me.

I have gone from HOTNESS feast to HOTNESS famine.

I am sick of my family taking Goose off me. I know that sounds pathetic but it's TRUE.

7.49 p.m.

Just rang Gran. I moaned that everyone was wanting to talk to Goose, invite Goose to something, take Goose somewhere or buy him a present.

Gran just said, "Listen, LADY. That jealous thing is back again. You better get over that. We love that boy. Lots of people do. Get used to it. And get used to onesies too. They will change the world."

She's not right about onesies. She may be right about Goose.

Gran IS right about Goose.

9.45 p.m.

Just been to see Goose. I told him I was sorry for being a bit ... possessive.

Goose just said, "Hattie, if people love you – I just want to spend time with them." Then we snogged. And snogged. And snogged.

Goose and me ... OH IT JUST GETS BETTER. Hattie, don't mess this up because it's MAJOR LOVE.

SUNDAY 5TH DECEMBER

7.12 p.m.

We just had the best DAY EVER. After the boot sale, Goose came round to help put the tree up. Then me, Mum, Rob, Gran, NATHAN and Goose just all ended up in the lounge eating mince pies and watching *The Sound of*

Music. Then Rob said, "Who wants to play a game?" We ended up playing Twister. Gran said she was the best at it because she HAD done yoga and zumba but Rob was like the incredible bendy man! It was LOL! THEN I just MULLERED Nathan at Monopoly. He may be older than me but he's craptacular at buying and selling property. Then Gran got the casino set out that she bought from QVC when she was drunk and we played roulette! Princess tried to kill the wheel but Gran bribed her to stay in the kitchen with an M&S mini pork pie.

I think my family are actually a bit magnificent...

Got to stop writing now. Goose wants to kiss me. <u>GOOSE WANTS TO KISS ME.</u> THIS is going to be THE most perfect December EVER... NOTHING can spoil it. Not even if Gran gives me a reindeer onesie for Christmas and MAKES me wear it in front of the man I love AND WHO TOTALLY LOVES ME.

OMG – I hope she doesn't...

♡
♥

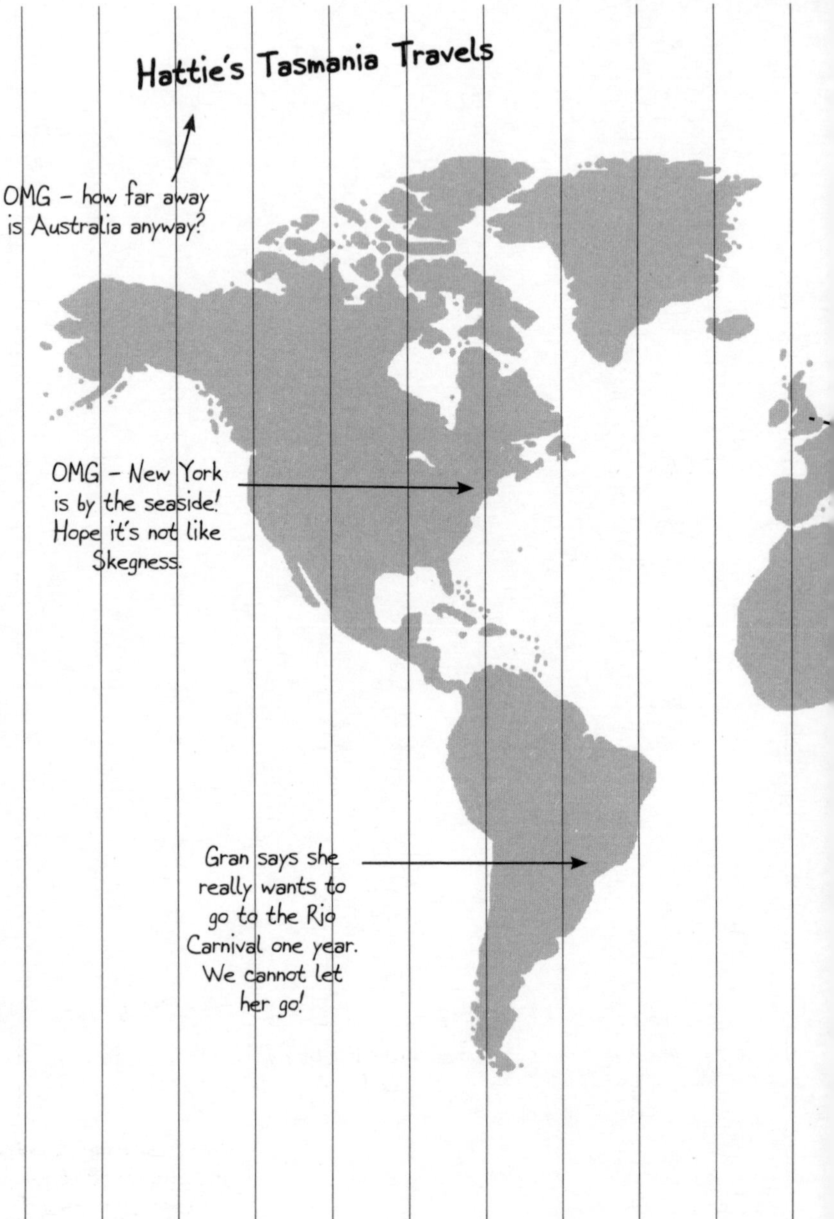
Hattie's Tasmania Travels
OMG – how far away is Australia anyway?
OMG – New York is by the seaside! Hope it's not like Skegness.
Gran says she really wants to go to the Rio Carnival one year. We cannot let her go!

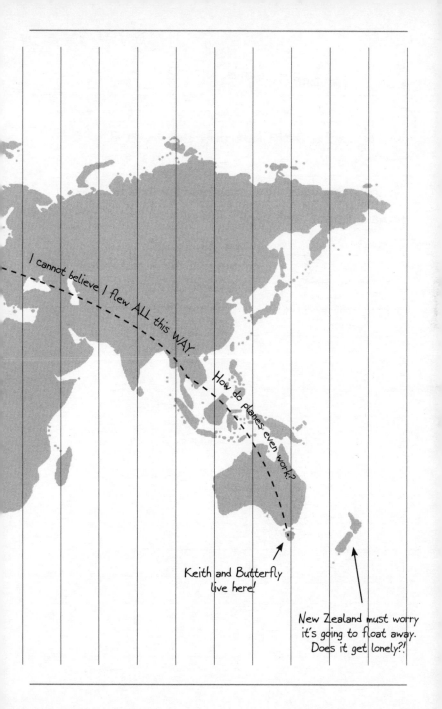

Chocolate Mini Eggs dipped in hot tea may be actually the best thing ever invented.

Actually chocolate Mini Eggs dipped in hot tea may actually be the best thing I invented!

Why are geckos allowed their central heating on ALL the time when humans are just told to put an extra jumper on?

NOTES

Thank You!

Kevin Johnson
For your endless patience and general lifetime excellence.

My mum
For all your magnificent inspiration.

And:

Tom Wagstaff
For having a gecko and Rob Wagstaff for telling me all about him.

NOTES

★ Rae Earl ★

OMG!
is this
ACTUALLY
my Life?

Another UNBELIEVABLE year from Hattie Moore

I'm totally telling you that this year, I'm going to find my real dad! Can you EVEN believe I don't know who he actually is? I won't be stopped by my family or the evil dog that lives 3 doors away. And another thing, with the help of Dimple and Weirdo Jen, I will become a TOTAL hotness goddess and defeat the dark forces of Miss Gorgeous Knickers and her gang. I tell you, this is going to be the most OMG year EVER!

Enjoyed this book? Tweet us your thoughts.